THE CLUB

A NOVEL

SHEILA MURDOCK

ALSO BY SHEILA MURDOCK

DIVESTED
Crystal
THE DIVESTED BWWM SERIES
SHEILA MURDOCK
The Vain Society
SHEILA MURDOCK
Entitled Woman
SHEILA MURDOCK
LAVONNE ON THE JOB
The Hair Salon
SHEILA MURDOCK
This Mess His Stress
A NOVEL
SHEILA MURDOCK
LESSONS Lisa
SHEILA MURDOCK
Billionaire Bliss
SHEILA MURDOCK
THE Club
A NOVEL
SHEILA MURDOCK
STANDALONES and STANDALONE SERIES
MORE to COME!

NIGHT SKY AFFAIR: TABITHA IS COMING SOON IN 2024

I'm Sleeping With Your Husband
A NOVEL
WHEN THE UNEXPECTED BECOMES EVEN MORE UNEXPECTED
SHEILA MURDOCK

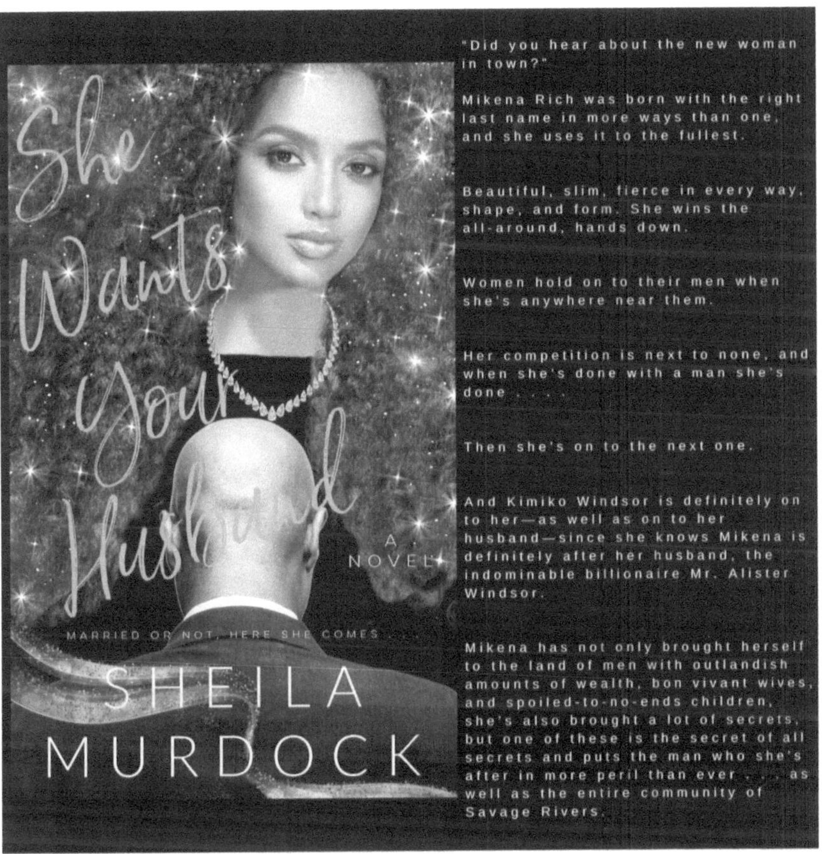

SHE WANTS YOUR HUSBAND - COMING SOON

CHAPTER ONE

Fall 1990

"So, we survived the first month of our senior year which, of course, is our last year in high school. How do you feel about it?" Mary asked, as she drove her and her best friend Deandra to The Club for the establishment's first ever teen night.

Deandra shrugged. "I don't know—how should I feel? I guess I just thought it would be better than how it's been going, that's all. I guess I'm still depressed about Trevor breaking up with me during the summer because he said he wanted to be free for his last year in high school," she replied, as they listened to Janet Jackson's "Come Back To Me" on Mary's brand new installed CD player in her white with a white convertible top Volkswagen Cabriolet.

"Look, I want you to forget about him, Deandra. We're going here tonight so we can blow off some steam from this first month. I have to agree with you. I thought it would be a lot better this year since this is our last year, but we're still very early in the year—*very early*. I mean, this is where the real fun is supposed to begin, and it should also be a new beginning for you since you and Trevor are not together anymore. The two of you don't go to the same school so you know you don't have to worry about seeing him again."

"Yeah, that may be true, Mary, but he knows damn well he still has to see our daughter Ashley; she's two years old and I can tell how smart she's gonna be."

Mary smiled with a nod. "She sure is, Deandra. And you're raising her very well unlike some girls your age. You knew your life changed when you got pregnant, and you took your responsibilities of being a mom very seriously. You need to forget about Trevor as a boyfriend, Deandra, and just focus on him being a father to Ashley because like it or not, the two of you are bonded for life because of her."

"I know we are. I just wish we were still a couple. I was even hoping he would ask me to marry him once I got out of high school and when I turn 18."

Mary rolled her eyes. "Well, maybe you'll meet someone new tonight, and if you do, you need to take it slow with him because you just got out of a relationship with your child's father this past summer. I really wouldn't rush into anything."

Deandra shook her head as she still looked out the window. "I'm not counting on meeting anyone tonight; I just wanna have fun, that's all."

"And that's what we're going here for," Mary said. "This song is too slow and depressing. If you're gonna listen to a song about an ex-boyfriend, listen to this one." She pressed the REWIND button back to Janet Jackson's "Miss You Much."

"Yeah! I love this song just as much!" Deandra said with a big smile. "The whole album, girl!"

"Yes!"

They sang to the song as Mary pulled into The Club nightclub and saw just how many teens had the same thing in mind that they had, as the line was almost a mile out the door.

"Luckily, it's not that cold tonight because it looks like we're gonna be standing in that line for a while. Damn, this many people found out about it?" Deandra asked.

"Looks like it. They were advertising it like crazy on the radio," Mary replied as she tried to find a place to park.

As they sat refreshing their makeup, they watched as people stared at them as they walked up to the club while some looked as if they were just hanging out in their cars.

"Look at all of these people staring at us, Deandra," Mary said, as she powdered her face. "This is the place to be!"

"It sure is! And I hope you don't forget to set your car alarm since you're driving one of the hottest cars and it's clear by the stares that it's definitely been confirmed."

"Yeah, well, it was a birthday gift from my parents last year," Mary said with a smile.

"I wish I lived like you, Mary. You have it all."

"No one has it all, Deandra. Come on now, don't be so naïve; you're smarter than that. You have one of the most precious things a person could have, and that's a baby. So many people can't have kids, and you don't know what my future holds for me—I may not be able to have kids when I'm older and married."

"Don't say that, Mary. Now you know my daughter will be a lot older than your oldest future kid, but they can still be friends. My Ashley can be a big sister to your future children."

"That's what I plan on!"

They got out of the car and began walking up towards the ever-growing line when suddenly, Mary spotted someone she knew.

"There's my brother's friend Paul! I didn't know he was working tonight! PAUL!" Mary yelled and waved at him.

He walked over to her. "Mary, hey! What's going on?"

"Well, we're here to check out the teen night tonight since we can't get in on a regular 21-and-over night," Mary replied.

"You're not missing a damn thing with those nights, Mary. I'm sure Jack told you that as well," Paul said, referring to Mary's older brother Jack.

"Yeah, I know, so we'll just settle for teen night until we're older. Right, Deandra?" Mary asked with a smile.

"Right," Deandra replied with a smile.

"Oh, where the hell are my manners? Paul, this is my best friend, Deandra."

"Hey, Deandra," Paul said with a smile. "Nice to finally meet you."

"Nice to meet you, too," Deandra said as they shook hands.

Mary looked at the line. "You know, Paul? That line is really fucking long," she said, trying to hint at him about letting them in.

Deandra laughed as she nodded in agreement.

Paul laughed as well. "Yeah, it is. But it's not surprising. Management told us it could possibly be like this, but I don't think they were even prepared for *this*. It's already full to capacity in there and it's still several hours until closing time since it is closing early tonight since it is a teen night tonight and the first one at that. Gotta think about the curfews. Damn, it's gonna be a long-ass night!"

Mary and Deandra looked at each other and laughed.

"So, do you mind letting us skip the line?" Mary asked.

Deandra stared at Paul as she smiled as she waited for him to answer.

Paul stared at the line. "Come with me."

They looked at each other and smiled big as Paul led them to the back of the building and to a private entry and exit. He walked in as they were right behind him.

The faint sound of music and voices as well as with the stench of cigarette smoke which fogged the air, confirmed to Mary and Deandra that they were in—but they had to be sure.

"Are we in?" Deandra decided to ask.

"We're in!" Mary said. "Oh, Paul! Thank you!"

"No problem. But I need $5.00 from each of you," he informed them with a grin.

"Are you serious?" Mary asked.

"I got y'all in, didn't I? And that's the cover charge for teen night. I mean, with that line out there, I doubt y'all would've been able to get in tonight because we've only been open for over an hour and it's packed to the max in here already; y'all see when you go into the main room."

Deandra looked at Mary to pay for her since she didn't have $5.00. "Well, I don't get paid for my job until next week."

"Don't worry, Deandra. I got money," Mary said, and handed Paul $10.00.

"Thank you," Paul said with a smile, and escorted them into the main area where teens from all over the city and surrounding ones came to party.

"WOW! It *is* packed in here! It's got it goin' on!" Mary said, as she bobbed her head to MC Hammer's "Turn This Mutha Out" as the wild, partying teens were definitely turning the place out!

"It really does! Thank you so much for paying for me to get in here because I really didn't have any money to get in here, I wasn't just saying that to get out of not paying. Ashley's needs pretty much take up the very little money I have."

"I told you not to worry about it. You have enough to worry about. But now that we're in, this is considered a worry-free zone. We're here to have fun and meet some boys and the last thing we're worried about is school and ex-boyfriends."

"Yeah, you're right. So, let's have some fun!"

"Yes! Let's do that!"

They moved their way through the bottleneck crowd to the dance floor which was packed with people as a couple of boys dressed just like MC Hammer hammered the dance floor with the rapper's signature dance moves.

"Damn it's crowded in here! Makes it look like it's the only thing that's going on in this city tonight for teens!" Mary said, as they danced.

"Yeah! You would think! But this makes me nervous, Mary, I can't lie."

"Why?"

"Because it's too crowded. I just don't trust it when it's like this."

"It's fine, Deandra. We're here to have fun, remember?"

Deandra's eyes wandered around as if she was looking for someone. "Yes, of course. And I wouldn't be in here if it wasn't for Paul as well as you paying my way in."

"So show me some gratitude, girl! We got in all thanks to Paul when we're still supposed to be standing in that long-ass line out there. It was meant to be."

"What was meant to be?"

"Whatever happens tonight."

Deandra nodded with a smile.

After the song was over, most cleared the floor since a less-than-popular song came on.

"Whew! I worked up a sweat out there! I already need a drink!" Mary said.

"They're not serving alcohol here since it's teen night tonight—remember they stressed that on the radio," Deandra said, as they held hands and walked to one of the bars.

"Yeah, that sucks!" Mary said.

"Mary!" Deandra said.

They laughed.

"You want your usual Pepsi if they have it?" Mary asked.

"Of course," Deandra said with a smile.

As Mary stood in line at the bar with Deandra by her side, Deandra checked out the atmosphere and knew almost instantly that this was definitely a place she would want to spend her nights at each time they had a special night like this. She could see that everyone appeared to be having fun, and knew that although everyone had problems, they definitely weren't showing it tonight.

They inched closer to the bar.

Deandra got a tap on her shoulder. She turned around . . .

"Hey."

It was her ex-boyfriend, Trevor!

He smiled down at her as he stood well over six feet tall wearing a jungle print shirt and baggy jeans.

She stepped a few feet away from Mary. "Um . . . hey!" she said, as she tried to sound upbeat. "What are you doing here?"

"Why is everyone else here? Including you?"

"Well, I don't know what everyone else is doing here, but I'm trying to get over you. And now seeing you here, you have made that very difficult. I thought you had a football game tonight?"

"That was last night, Deandra. And I'm surprised you forgot that because we played Saint Maran West—your school. Biggest game of the season. You still know my schedule?"

"I have to know it, Trevor, we have a daughter together."

"That's true. How's Ashley?"

"She's just fine. My mom is watching her since she has the night off of work."

"I know she's in good hands," he said with a smile.

She sighed as her eyes wandered around the club.

"What are you looking at?"

"Why do you care? You broke up with me, remember?"

"And I just wanted to see how you were since we hadn't talked since we broke up. I mean, we should be communicating more than we are, Deandra, and we know we have to because of Ashley."

"Look, I came here to have fun, okay? To forget about you and all of the problems and worries I have if only just for this night."

"Didn't we all?"

"Well, I'm only concerned about me and only me, as well as Mary and Ashley and my family."

"Not me?"

She sighed. "Well, you didn't care about me since you broke up with me, and I don't wanna talk about it anymore, okay?"

"I think we need to talk, Deandra, and I think we need to talk now."

"How come?"

Mary got their drinks and turned around and walked away from the bar . . . but didn't see Deandra in sight.
"Just where the hell did she go?" she mumbled. "EXCUSE ME!" she yelled as she made her way through the crowd. As luck would have it, a small table opened up and she rushed over to it and put the drinks on it. She looked out at the dance floor and noticed Deandra and Trevor slow dancing to Mariah Carey's "Vision of Love."

"Mary."

She turned around and stared her senior year crush right in the eyes. "Hey, Damian. I didn't know you were gonna be here."

"Yeah, I'm here. But the question is, who isn't here?"

"Yeah, you're right about that!" she said with a big smile as she now had a hard time splitting her attention between him, and Deandra dancing with Trevor.

Damian smiled at her. "So, are you here by yourself?"

"No, Deandra is with me," she replied. "She's out there dancing with her ex-boyfriend Trevor. I got us drinks and turned around after getting them and see she's out there on the dance floor with him. I didn't even know he was here."

He nodded with a smile. "That's her child's dad, right?"

"Yeah, it is. But I don't know why she's talking to him much less dancing with him since we wanted to come here to get away from all of the ex-boyfriends and everything and have a worry-free and problem-free night."

"Well, y'all can still have that. I'm here with Montell. Do you think you and Deandra would like to come back to my house after this place closes or maybe even now since it's so crowded? We can go to Taco Bell or McDonald's before then."

"Hell, I'm with it!" Mary said in an excited tone as MC Hammer's "U Can't Touch This" began playing, and once again, everyone crowded out to the dance floor.

"Wanna dance?" he asked.

"Hell yeah!" she said with a big smile. "And you *can* touch all over *this!*"

He laughed. "Sounds good to me!"

They met Deandra and Trevor out on the floor.

"Hey, guys!" Mary said with a huge grin as she was all over Damian already.

"Hey!" Deandra said with a big smile. "Hi, Damian."

"Hi, Deandra," Damian replied with a smile.

"This is my ex-boyfriend, Trevor," Deandra said.

"Ex-boyfriend Trevor, nice to meet you," Damian said as they shook hands.

They all laughed.

"Nice to meet you, too," Trevor replied with a smile. "Great job at the game yesterday, man."

"Thanks, man. But y'all still won!" Damian said with a laugh.

They all laughed once again.

"But you're the best player on your team, man. Y'all weren't easy to beat," Trevor said with a smile.

"That's a great compliment. Thanks, man," Damian said with a smile.

Mary smiled as she continued to be all over Damian. "Hey, Deandra, Damian wants to know if you all wanna go back to his house since it's so crowded here?"

Trevor looked at Deandra as he waited for her to answer.

"I would love to, but I'm gonna have to decline since I have to be home early because of Ashley, otherwise I would go. Plus, I gotta go to work in the late afternoon tomorrow."

Mary gave her a clear disappointed look.

"Hey, cool. You know your priorities, girl. I like that," Damian said with a smile. He looked down at Mary as he still held her close to him. "Still on board?"

Mary looked at Deandra.

"Go on, Mary. Have fun. I can get a ride home with Trevor."

"Okay, fine. Let's go!" Mary said to Damian.

"Bet! Nice meeting you, Trevor," Damian said as he shook his hand one more time.

"Nice meeting you, too," Trevor said with a smile.

Deandra smiled as she watched as Mary and Damian left the floor as they held hands.

"Is that her boyfriend?" Trevor asked.

"No, that's her senior year crush. She's been after him since sophomore year. I just hope she's careful, that's all."

"Yeah, really. Look what happened when we weren't?"

"Well, it happened and we're being responsible about it now."

He nodded. "Yeah, we are. But I still need to seriously talk to you, Deandra."

"Well, I'm right here, so talk."

"Mary?" Damian said, as she laid in his bed completely naked as Bell Biv Devoe's "Do Me!" played on his radio.

"What is it?" she asked.

"Deandra's on the phone," he said, and handed her the phone.

"Hello? Deandra?"

"Hey, Mary. I need for you to come pick me up. I'm still here."

"I thought you were getting a ride home with Trevor?"

"I don't wanna talk about it, okay? Please, just come and pick me up."

Damian continued to stare at her.

Mary sighed. "Okay, I'll be right there."

"Thanks, Mary. I'll be—"

Click.

"Deandra?" she said. She looked at the phone in confusion, and then once again put it up to her ear.

"What's up?" Damian asked.

"The call got disconnected," she replied as she got out of bed. "I gotta go get her. She sounded upset."

"Do you want me to go with you?"

"No, that's okay. I know you don't have a car and I don't know if I'm gonna be able to swing back around here to drop you off since I gotta take Deandra home, too. I, too, have a curfew."

"Okay, makes sense. Just let me know when you get home."

"Of course."

Mary arrived back at The Club. She noticed there were very few cars here compared to when she'd left, and there were very few people standing outside just hanging out. She checked the time. It was closing time. She looked all around for Deandra but didn't see her standing outside waiting for her which was what she knew she was going to tell her she would be doing before the call got disconnected. She got out of her car and walked towards the front entrance.

"Sorry, Miss, we're closed for the night," a bouncer informed her.

"I know. I'm looking for my friend, she told me to come pick her up," Mary informed him.

"Well, you'll have to wait out here for her," he let her know.

She sighed. "Okay." She got back in her car, and waited for Deandra to come out of the front entrance since she knew that was the way everyone had entered and exited. She kept her eyes glued to the entrance.

Several minutes had gone by. Deandra still hadn't come out the front entrance. She knew she could not have been in there talking to people for that long since the only one she knew when she was in there was Trevor, but then again, she wasn't sure.

The lights on The Club's big-and-bright welcome sign turned off.

She got out of her car.

As the remaining cars left the parking lot, she noticed how the bouncer was not at the door waiting for the rest of the club-goers to leave. She rushed into the main entry and looked around as the inside looked completely different than it did when she was in here just a few hours before.

"PAUL!" she yelled.

Paul turned around as it looked like he was leaving for the night. "Mary! What are you still doing in here? I thought you were gone?"

"I did leave with a male friend I go to school with, but I came back here because Deandra decided to stay here with her ex-boyfriend. She told me about a half hour ago that she was still here and that she needed for me to come pick her up, that's the only reason why I came back here. Did you see her?"

"No, I haven't seen her since I got the two of you in here earlier.

It was so crowded in here so that was the only time I saw the two of you."

"Did you see her ex-boyfriend, Trevor?"

"I have no idea what he looks like, Mary."

"Shit!" she said, as her eyes wandered around the near empty room while bartenders cleaned up the bar. The DJ packed up his stuff for the night, and a cleaning crew got to work cleaning up the whirlwind of a mess left by the clubgoing teens. "Look, I just spoke to her, Paul. *Are you sure* you didn't see her?"

"No, not for several hours, Mary. You know I wouldn't lie to you."
"I know." She sighed. "I'm gonna get going then. Thanks for letting me and Deandra in for tonight."

"No problem," he replied with a smile.

"But before I go, can I use the phone?"

"Yeah, go ahead. But you'll have to be quick because no patrons are supposed to be in here since we're closed, only people who work here and the people from the cleaning company."

"Thanks. Where is it?"

He directed her to four payphones around the corner in a quieter area.

She got on the phone and called Deandra's private home number.

No answer.

"Fuck!" she said, as Paul stared at her.

"Not there, huh?"

"No. I just don't know why she would call me about needing a ride home when it's clear to me now that she already got a ride home with Trevor after all and is obviously waiting for me to get home so she can call me to let me know."

"Sounds that way to me, too. Go on home, Mary. It's getting late. I don't want you here all night and especially all by yourself."

She nodded with a forced smile and walked out to her car and left. "Dammit, Deandra! Where the hell are you?!"

"What the?" I said, as I looked at a video about something I'd never heard of before:

<u>THE COLD CASE OF DEANDRA WHITFIELD</u>
17-YEAR-OLD HIGH SCHOOL SENIOR AND TEEN MOM DISAPPEARED WITHOUT A TRACE 33 YEARS AGO. LAST SEEN AT THE ICONIC *THE CLUB* NIGHTCLUB FOR TEEN NIGHT

A reporter stood in front of the newly updated-with-the-times The Club sign at the entryway into the establishment as she got ready to speak.

"Yes, hello, everyone. I'm standing here in front of the iconic The Club nightclub, which has been a legendary club in the city of Saint Maran since 1988, that's 35 years. But in the fall of 1990, a teen mom and high school senior by the name of Deandra Whitfield came here to party with her best friend Mary Landry for this club's first ever teen night. And according to Mary, she left this club with a male friend and left Deandra here with an ex-boyfriend who is the father of her baby. But when she came back here later on to pick her up, she was nowhere to be found. So, this is where—according to Mary—the trail has gone cold for Deandra Whitfield. That's why we need your help out there. If you were at this club that night and had seen Deandra here or have any information of her whereabouts, please contact the cold case authorities as all of their contact information is on the screen. There will definitely be more to come concerning this case as well as others that could have some kind of connection to this establishment, but Deandra's is by far the oldest case dating all the way back to the fall of 1990. This club, as you all can see on the sign, was established in 1988 and is still the most desirable club to attend in this city because of its long history, but now it looks like it has a history of a different kind, and it's a dark one. Back to you."

I was immediately intrigued. I'd lived here my whole life and I'd never heard of the disappearance case of Deandra Whitfield, but everyone knew about The Club. This was definitely a cold case. One that was older than me. And this poor young girl was only 17 years old with a baby and a senior in high school.

Why wasn't this talked about more?

How many more out there went to this particular club, walked in, and was never seen again?

Something wasn't right about any of this, and the sad thing was, someone knew something. Someone always knew something. It'd been 33 years. It was time for Deandra Whitfield to get her long overdue justice.

But where was she?

Was she even possibly still alive?

How many more Deandra Whitfield's were there out there who went to The Club and were never seen or heard from again?

Were *they* even still possibly alive?

Anything was possible, and I was gonna find out.

But first, I contacted the cold case authorities on this case by phone at the phone number given at the end of this video because I wanted to speak directly to someone to see if they already had some vital information even though I was doing my own independent investigation, but they didn't need to know that.

No one ever answered the phone.

CHAPTER TWO

My best friend Porsha bust through the door of my home office as if it was some kind of emergency. "Hey, Mackenzee. I didn't interrupt you doing another video, did I?"

"Is the Live! light on outside of the door?"

She double checked. "No, it's not."

"Okay," I said, as I continued my research on my instant obsession.

She sat in a chair out of view of my cameras. "What are you looking at?"

"Have you ever heard of the Deandra Whitfield case?"

"Deandra Whitfield? No, never heard of her or her case. What happened to her?"

I shook my head. "Wow, this is real."

"What's real?"

"What's real is that this poor young girl was only 17 years old when she went missing from The Club 33 years ago and has not been seen or heard from since."

"Are you serious, Mackenzee? She went missing at the spot everyone goes to and has been to at least once if they're 17 or older and lived in this city since they do have that teen night once a week?"

"And it says here that she attended their very first ever teen night. This was in the fall of 1990."

"Wow, that long ago, huh?"

"Yeah, that long ago. This poor girl was a teen mom and everything. And no one has even talked about this case. I was looking for footage about her story from 1990 and I don't see anything. They had to have talked about it, Porsha. But I can't seem to find anything. I called the phone number to the cold case authorities about it just before you got here to see what they already had, but no one ever answered the phone."

"Doesn't surprise me. And don't be so sure people have talked about this, Mackenzee."

I looked at her. "Why do you say that?"

She sighed. "You know how this city is. It's a small city that thinks it's a big one. I call it the big small city like a lot of people do. It's very corrupt here, that's what my dad told me. Whatever they don't want people to find out or don't want the local news to talk about, they don't talk about, and it's been that way forever."

"Well, I don't think that's right at all. This girl went missing at a place that is now labeled an iconic establishment in this city, and no one has talked about it? This makes me very uneasy, Porsha, especially since the majority of the population in this city is Black and it always has been, and this was a beautiful Black teen girl who had a child who was only 2 years old at the time of her mom's disappearance. Something happened at that club, Porsha, and someone is covering it up and has been for 33 years."

"This is crazy, Mackenzee, but I don't think you should be getting involved in this."

"Why not? I was born and raised in this city. This city is all I know. Its name is Saint Maran but there's nothing saintly about living here, and especially now since I discovered this story. How many other girls and women have gone missing from The Club, huh?"

"Hell, I don't know, Mackenzee. I just don't want you getting in trouble for playing investigative detective over a 33-year-old cold case or any cases that have to do with murder even though there's no proof that Deandra was murdered. Let the cops handle it."

"The cops haven't done shit, that's obvious. I don't even think they've even talked about it. I stumbled upon this video of some other independent news station talking about it—not the news stations in this city—so no, there's no info out there about this at all. Why did it take an independent news station to bring up a 33-year-old story from this city about a missing teen that was last seen at a place that is now marked as iconic?"

"I don't know, Mackenzee. But I still think you should stay out of this."

"Not a chance. I need some new content. I'm tired of my channel being demonetized for the hundredth time it seems just because I speak my mind. But I'm starting a whole new channel dedicated to talking about cases like this because they need to be told. And of all cases, this is a case that happened here. Someone needs to speak for Deandra Whitfield and a hell of a lot of others, and I'm the one who's gonna do it. I stumbled upon that video talking about her case for a reason. No one in this city has done a damn thing about this case. They probably don't even have a file on it at the police station."

"Don't go fucking with the cops, Mackenzee. You're really asking for it if you do that."

"How am I supposed to get to the bottom of this if I don't?"

She sighed. She knew she was *not* talking me out of this, and no one was going to. I was already conditioned for the mission, as the saying went. She continued to stare at me as I did my research. "Well, besides me coming back here to have lunch with you, what did you wanna do this week?"

CHAPTER THREE

"I knew you wanted to come here, Mackenzee, but why for Throwback Thursday: 1990 Night? We have got to be some of the youngest people in here and we're both 28 years old. I see why you have to be 25 and older to get in here on this night. Everyone looks like they're in their 40's, 50's and even older than that. I see more people in here with grey hair than I don't see. I won't be surprised if I see my parents in here."

"Knock it off, Porsha. Your parents are in the Bahamas."

She laughed. "I know. But I do have to admit that the men are really nice looking with their gorgeous dark skin and silver-grey hair."

"They are fine and that's no lie, but they're way too old for me," I said.

"Not if they have a lot of money!"

"True!"

We laughed as we looked at each other as we tried to find a seat as the crowd may have been older, but they knew how to party just like any young crowd as Chubb Rock's "Treat 'Em Right" played throughout this establishment.

This was the first time I'd been to The Club in years, and it was because I was just flat-out tired of coming here. I had serious burnout.

But now I was completely refreshed and in here for a different reason, and I knew that all of these people—with the exception of Porsha and me and very few others in here—were around in 1990 and had probably heard about Deandra Whitfield's disappearance at that time.

Or did they?

But I had to admit this place didn't look or even feel the same to me since I'd stumbled upon Deandra's story. It'd actually creeped me out to know that this was the last place she was ever seen in and hadn't been seen since. I stared out at the dance floor as everyone danced like no one was watching. It took me back to 33 years ago when Deandra could've been right out there on that dance floor, as well as other women like her. But she was definitely right here in this club, and for some reason, I felt her presence here; it was an unexplainable feeling. I just felt she was not the only one who disappeared from here because women go missing all the time and it seemed as if no one cared that they had. Not everyone went missing on purpose just because they had a serious problem with themselves and desperately wanted one of the oldest things in the book—attention.

Disappearances were real, and they were nothing to be played with. They were nothing to be ignored. Every single one needed to be taken seriously and the outcome of it started with how people treated each disappearance. It was if this city treated Deandra's disappearance and so many others like hers like they just didn't care. That was obvious by now. I could not believe already that there were people out there who actually did not care. I couldn't fathom if that happened to me or Porsha or someone else that I knew and loved.

Something must be done.

"Hello, ladies. What can I get you?" the waitress asked us, temporarily snapping me out of my thoughts.

"A Sex on the Beach," I replied with a smile.

"A Canada Dry," Porsha replied as well with a smile.

"Great choices. Coming right up," she said, and left our table.

"So, see any suspects?" Porsha asked.

"Very funny," I replied with a grin. "You know, the person who's responsible could actually be in here, you never know. Look how many men in here look like they could've been at this exact club 33 years ago?"

"And that puts all of them at or over 50 years old," she said.

"Yeah, I know, and I have to start somewhere."

She sighed. "Mackenzee, people are here to party, they're not here to be interrogated."

"Well, I'm here to conduct an independent investigation since no one in this city wanted to do one. Too many years have passed and it's ridiculous that we never heard anything about her disappearance."

"That's because we weren't even born when it happened."

"I know, but still. There are millions of things—literally—that we've heard about that happened when we weren't born yet, Porsha, so stop being naïve, that's why it's called history. Deandra's case is a case from this city therefore it should've been talked about in this city."

"Did you ask your parents about it?"

"Not yet since I haven't spoken to them in a few days, but you know I will."

As I sipped on my drink, a gorgeous man walked up to our table.

"Hello, ladies," he said with a smile.

"Hi," Porsha and I said in our sweet voices we spoke in when a man —or more than one—approached us.

"Would you like to dance?" he asked *me*!

Porsha smiled big as she raised her eyebrows.

"Um . . . sure," I said.

We walked out to the dance floor as MC Hammer's "Have You Seen Her" played, and slowly embraced into a dance.

"I'm District Attorney Richard Elmhurst III," he said as he stared down at me with a smile.

"Mackenzee," I replied as I stared up at him with an even bigger smile.

"Mackenzee . . . what?"

"Lawson," I said, forgetting that fast he'd told me his full name.

"Lawson. It has the first three letters in it of my profession. I like you already; I really like you," he said as he continued to smile at me.

"It's a sheer coincidence, but thank you."

Wow, this man was gorgeous, but he looked more than ten years older than me as he had a little grey in his hair, but his skin was flawless and he was in excellent shape.

"How old are you?" he asked.

It was like he could read my mind.

"I'm 28."

"28? Wow, you look a lot younger than that, then again, you have to be 25 to get into these special nights, some nights you have to be even older. I've never seen you here before."

"I used to come here on the teen nights and the regular 21-and-over nights, but stopped years ago since I got burned out coming here all of the time."

"Understandable. What made you come tonight?"

I gazed around as "Have You Seen Her" by MC Hammer still played. What an unbelievable coincidence that this song could be playing when he asked me to dance as well as him asking me the question he'd just asked me. I wanted to ask him a question that was the exact name of this song.

"I was bored and I'd never been here on this night before." At least half of it was true.

He nodded as he smiled at me. "It's nice to see you here."

"It's nice to be here after a long hiatus." I looked over at Porsha as she smiled at me and then took a sip of her drink. "Have you lived in this city your whole life?"

"My whole life. Went to Saint Maran East and graduated in 1991."

"Oh my god! That's the school *I* went to!"

"Well, hello, Saint Maran East Eagles alumnus!"

"Hello!" I laughed.

He embraced me tighter; I started to feel uncomfortable. "So, you've lived here your whole life, too, huh?"

"My whole life," I informed him as I tried to discreetly slow dance my way out of his tight hold. "So, if you graduated in 1991 then that puts you at—"

"50 years old," he completed my sentence. "Am I too old for a 28-year-old?"

"No, not at all," I said with a smile. "You don't look 50 years old at all. I thought you were a lot younger than that. You're gorgeous."

He blushed. "Thank you, that's a hell of compliment. And so are you."

"Thank you," I replied with a smile and smiled even bigger at Porsha since she was now out on the floor dancing with a man who looked to be more around our age. "Um . . . when was the very first time you came here?"

"The very first time? Wow, that was so long ago—but I remember exactly when it was—it was the very first teen night in the fall of 1990."

I felt I'd struck gold.

"Wow, 33 years ago, huh? That must've been an unforgettable experience."

"Oh, it most definitely was. I was a senior in high school, of course. We'd just played Saint Maran West the day before—always and forever our biggest rivals as you know."

"Yes, I know. I don't think there was a football game I missed all throughout high school since I was a cheerleader for all four years."

"You look like a cheerleader from back then," he said with a smile.

I smirked. "Yeah, back then—*way back then.*"

He laughed. "I didn't mean anything bad by it, Mackenzee, so take it as a compliment."

"If you say so," I replied. But I felt like I was on to something while we danced out here. I wanted this song to go on forever because I didn't want this conversation to end because I felt I was just getting started with my questioning, and I wanted to find out just how much he remembered about that very first teen night, coincidentally, the same and last night Deandra was seen here.

I carried on.

"So, this music was brand new back then, huh?"

"Yeah, it was new for the year, yes. Never thought I would be still very much into it after not hearing it in so long. Brings back a lot of memories."

"Like what?"

"A lot of memories, Mackenzee. Too many to go into," he said with a smile, but also seemed irritated by my questioning.

Too bad.

"Did you have any memories of the very first night you were here?"

"Of course," he said, as he looked around as if he was looking for someone.

Now it was getting very interesting.

"So, what were they?"

He grinned as he still looked around, and then back down at me. "You ask a lot of questions. Are you a detective or something?"

A brand-new, self-proclaimed independent one, I thought. "No."

"Then what's with all the questions? You ask more questions than me, and I'm an attorney."

"Just trying to get to know your history here."

"What for? That's a little odd to be asking me about my history of attending this place, don't you think? I would think we would be getting to know each other on a more personal level because it seems as though that even though we have a pretty big age difference, there seems to be a mutual interest."

"I don't think it's odd at all since we're in here. I think it would be if we were somewhere else."

He nodded with a smile. "What is it you wanna know about my first night ever here on the very first-ever teen night way back in the fall of 1990?"

You asked for it! I thought. "Did you hear about what happened here that night?"

He gave me a confused look. "What exactly happened here that night?"

I returned the look he'd given me but in a more confused state. "You mean you don't know?"

"No, I don't know, Mackenzee. I don't ever remember anything happening that night. If something bad happened then I would've remembered it; everyone would've remembered it and everyone would still be talking about it to this day."

Whoa.

I didn't think for a second he even realized what he'd said.

Something *bad* happening?

I never mentioned if something bad happened or not, but I was just gonna assume that he thought that's what I'd meant since that was usually the case . . . and this was in fact the case.

"A girl came here that night—same night you did—and she was never seen again. It was as if she just disappeared into thin air. They had a short story on an independent news channel about it that I just happened to stumble open. I'm surprised that since I have lived here my whole life that I've never heard of it."

"I don't remember much about that night, Mackenzee, since it was so long ago. All I remember is that it was very crowded in here, much more crowded than it is in here tonight. Remember, it was 1990. Stories didn't get around in minutes and seconds like the way they do now."

"So no one at our alma mater talked about it?"

"Not that I can recall."

"Not that you can recall?" I asked.

"That's what I said, Mackenzee. Thanks for the dance."

I stood in the same spot as he walked away from me and off the dance floor as more people now joyfully came out and crowded the dance floor as they danced all around me to Digital Underground's "The Humpty Dance." I walked off the dance floor as I looked around in a slight embarrassment since it would've appeared to people who were watching us that he'd abruptly stopped dancing with me—but I knew I'd triggered something in him. I had to have done that. I think he knew more about this case than he was telling even though Deandra did not go to our alma mater. I walked back to my seat and sat down and looked at my drink. I decided to order a fresh one. I smiled at Porsha as she still danced out on the floor. Once the song was over, she thanked the man she danced with and came back over to our table.

"Looks like you had fun out there."

"Yeah, it was okay. He's really not my type," she confessed, and took sip of her drink. "He's our age and says he loves 90's music since it was the decade he was born in like us."

"Very true."

She kept staring at me as she sipped her drink. "So, how did it go with the older guy?"

I grinned. "I think I might be on to something."

She gasped! "Mackenzee! You *didn't!*"

"Damn motherfuckin' right I did. I had to know since he is 50 years old, and can you believe he was here that *exact same night* Deandra was?!"

"No!" she said, as intrigue was filled all in her eyes. "What did you find out?"

Suddenly, a very uncomfortable feeling rushed over me. "Um, Porsha?"

"Yes? What did you find out?" she asked me again.

I felt everyone in here was looking at me; everyone over 50. "I need to get out of here. I think I'll come back here on another night."

"What's wrong?"

"Let's go. *Now.*"

CHAPTER FOUR

"*O*kay, Mackenzee, just what the hell is going on about why you wanted to leave so early? I planned on being there all night," Porsha said, as she drove us to Taco Bell. She looked at me. "Well? And why do you keep looking behind you?"

"Just wanna make sure we're not being followed," I honestly replied, and then turned back around and let out a big sigh.

"Being followed? Why the hell would we be followed, Mackenzee? What the hell did you and Richard talk about?"

I continued to stare out the window.

"Oh, no! Mackenzee! You *didn't*! Please tell me you fuckin' didn't!"

"He's 50 years old and has lived in this city his whole life like us, Porsha! He went to the same high school as us!"

"So!"

"He's the DA in this city."

"Uh oh!" Porsha said. "Then you really should *not* have been asking him questions, Mackenzee! You should've shut the fuck up after he told you he was the fuckin' DA!"

"Yeah, well, if I didn't ask him the questions I wanted to then I would've never found out what I found out about—you know, that he was there *the exact same night* Deandra was and was last seen. He's got to know something, Porsha. There is no reason to believe that he doesn't."

"And what do you think he could know?"

"That's what I wanted to find out, but I just got a bad feeling when we were at the table talking after I'd danced with him, and it just seemed as if he wanted to end our dance and conversation so abruptly after I'd asked him about Deandra."

"Yeah, you sounded a little crazy about wanting to leave. What spooked you? You acted as if all of the people in there were grey-haired zombies who kept staring at you because you were asking questions like that."

I laughed. "No, I'm not crazy like that, Porsha. When I get an uneasy feeling, I don't ignore it," I said as I looked at my phone. "I don't know anything about a DA, so I'm looking at what they do, and it says that they have the power to choose which charges should be brought against someone, if any at all. Porsha, we still don't know what happened to Deandra and who the hell knows how many others who could've been at The Club that night and were never seen again. Of course, he wasn't a DA back in the fall of 1990 since he was only a senior in high school just like Deandra, but he is DA now so he has a lot of power in this city."

"All the reasons why you *shouldn't* be questioning him."

"Well, I had no idea who he was when he asked me to dance. He came up to our table, remember? I didn't know who he was or anyone in there. When he told me he was 50, then I knew he was around in 1990 and it was like I felt like I struck gold when he said he was there that same night Deandra was. Porsha, he could've very well have known her and is just lying to me about it."

"It's always a possibility, Mackenzee. You might have stolen the key and opened a door to a past that'd been locked inside a forbidden room for too long—but I don't think you should've been the person to do it."

"If not me then who? No one else has done a damn thing. And that's very unfortunate because as Black people, we should be taking care of each other, not killing each other."

"How do you know Deandra was killed?"

"I don't know that for sure, Porsha, you're right, but this doesn't seem good at all since it's been 33 years since she disappeared. I just know I triggered something in Richard, I know it."

"Now you're probably on his mind for a different reason if you did, Mackenzee. That man seemed very interested in you, you know, like a love interest."

"Well, I'm not looking for love right now, I got a case to solve."

Porsha looked in her rearview mirror. "Who is this fool flying up on us like this?"

I looked back to a car coming up on us very fast as it now blew past us, swerved back into our lane, *and cut us off*!

"FUCKER!" Porsha yelled as she slammed on her breaks!

I screamed as I put my hands on top of my head! "Fuck! What the fuck?!"

The car stopped ahead at the stoplight. Porsha stayed several feet behind it. And it was a very nice car. A black BMW 760i xDrive kind-of-nice car with the darkest tinted windows. Brand new for this year.

"Oh my god! Look at the license plate, Porsha!"

CLUB 88.

"It's someone from The Club, Mackenzee! What the fuck! Is this person following us?!"

"Well, they're ahead of us so it's clear they probably aren't," I said, but I wasn't so sure.

The light turned green.

The car stood at a standstill, refusing to move.

"What the fuck?! GO!" Porsha yelled!

"Don't honk your horn," I suddenly told her.

"Why not? Why aren't they moving? The light is green!"

I looked ahead at the Taco Bell sign since it was only several feet up from this stoplight.

No other cars were on this part of the road right now whether they were going in the same direction or the opposite direction of us. It was dark and dead silent. I could even hear crickets since the music was off because I wanted to talk. And as I stared ahead, I now felt it was very threatening.

"Turn around," I told her.

"Why?"

I looked at the car as it still sat at a green light. The light turned yellow, and then red. It stood in the same spot. "Turn around. *Now,*" I stressed as I still stared at the car. The car hadn't budged.

She looked behind her. She backed up several feet and turned around, and we were headed in the opposite direction.

I continued to look back. I noticed how the car took off when the light changed green once again. I looked back until it was completely out of sight. "Looks like they didn't turn around and follow us."

"So you think that car was really following us?"

"Yeah, I think they were, Porsha."

She stared at me. "You're scaring me, Mackenzee."

"Well, I can't be absolutely sure since they didn't follow us once you turned around."

"They didn't have to, Mackenzee. I think that was a warning to you. It was clear they wanted us to see that fancy BMW and the license plate that clearly stated that it was from The Club."

"It could've been someone who just loves going there."

"Bullshit. It was someone who has some kind of affiliation with it. You danced with this city's DA, and you were asking him questions about a 33-year-old case where a teen girl that was the same age as him at the time was last seen in that exact same club? And he was there that same night she was? You don't know who the hell he knows, Mackenzee, that's the scary part. You've already ruffled some feathers and I don't even think you even realize it."

"He did ask me was I a detective."

"And I think it was a serious question."

"Look, I don't mean to start anything, I just think this case should be properly investigated, and no one has done a damn thing about it. It shouldn't take little ol' me that was born and raised in this city to do other people's jobs for them."

"And I don't want little ol' you to be little no more."

"Don't worry about it, Porsha. I will stay anonymous on my new channel about this."

"*Anonymous?* Mackenzee, *please.* You were already asking questions about the case to the DA. They'll probably know it's you talking about this case."

"They can't prove it."

"Maybe, maybe not, but do you really wanna take this chance for them to find out?"

"Look, I have to do this, Porsha. It hurts to see that no one has done a damn thing for Deandra, and it's been 33 years. I have no idea if her daughter or even mom still live here. I have a lot of work to do. I have barely scratched the surface on this."

She shook her head. "I just don't want you to get hurt."

"I won't get hurt if no one knows it's me who's doing it."

"Richard—this city's DA—will know it's you, Mackenzee. And at this point, I don't think there's really nothing you can say that will convince him that it's not you who will be investigating this. You could've talked about anything while you were dancing with him out on that dance floor, but you brought up Deandra's disappearance. You're already on his radar, and who knows how many other people's radars you're on now since we left from there tonight?"

I looked behind me once again. There was not a car in sight. "Well, it's freedom of speech. I can talk about what I wanna talk about. I think a lot of people no matter where they're from will be interested in Deandra's case, and who knows? I may get people telling me about others. Deandra deserves to have a voice for her as well as other girls, and I feel it's my calling to be that voice."

At a stoplight, she continued to stare at me as if I was downright crazy. Maybe in a lot of ways I was because I didn't know what was gonna happen or what could possibly happen, but it was not gonna stop me from doing what had to be done. It'd been long enough that absolutely nothing was.

CHAPTER FIVE

I turned the LIVE! sign on and began my first video for my
new channel:

"Hello, everyone, and welcome to my very first video on this
channel, *I'm Their Speaker*. On this channel, I will be speaking
about cases that seemed to fly under the radar or were swept
under the rug that no one seemed to have given any thought of
—but I have. I feel like this is my new calling, and it was by
sheer coincidence that I stumbled upon a video from a few
weeks ago that talked about a case in the city of Saint Maran.
Well, I would like to elaborate on this 33-year-old cold case
that happened in the fall of 1990 at a club called simply, The
Club. This club is iconic now, and there's a link below to check
out their website as well as social media pages. But there has
been pretty much no publicity about this case, and I think it's
very unfortunate that in the fall of 1990, a 17-year-old girl
name Deandra Whitfield went there for The Club's first-ever
teen night with her best friend Mary Landry for a night of fun,
and Deandra hasn't been seen or heard from since then. She
had a 2-year-old daughter at the time of her disappearance.

Everyone, it's been 33 years. We need some answers here, that's why I started this channel so I can get some of those answers. So please, if anyone knows anything, please contact the local authorities or even me—I want to hear your stories. Just as I am remaining anonymous on here, you will remain anonymous as well unless you choose to want to go public. I respect everyone's privacy. I just want to find out more about Deandra Whitfield and what could've possibly led up to her disappearance. So let me say this before I go—The Club, Attend at your own risk. Thank you."

I ended the video and turned off the LIVE! sign light. Porsha walked in the room with a bag of McDonald's breakfast for the both of us. "Thanks," I said, and gobbled down my Egg McMuffin with hashbrowns combo.

"You're welcome," she said, and started in on her pancakes. "I heard your show while I was driving back here. How come you didn't mention anything about going to The Club last night?"

"They will know that it's me," I said, and took a sip of my coffee. "I'd thought about mentioning it, but I didn't wanna make it so obvious. I told them in this first video that I'm remaining anonymous and that's exactly what I'm gonna do. No one needs to know that it's me, especially now."

"Do you think people will see this video, Mackenzee? Because this is a whole new channel you clearly don't want associated with your other one, and I can definitely understand that."

"I hope people do see this. I know there are a gazillion videos now out there, so hopefully it will get seen. After what happened last night with that car and everything and me talking to Richard who I found out is this city's DA, I decided to remain anonymous—I wasn't going to at first."

"Well, I'm glad you did because it's better to be safe. I mean, I could barely sleep last night thinking about that car cutting me off and then stopping in front of us at that stoplight and *then* refused to drive off when the light was green, knowing we were right behind it. It reminded me of that scary movie *The Car*."

I grinned. "Or the movie *Christine*."

She laughed! "Yeah, that one, too!"

We laughed as we nodded in agreement.

"But not in any way is this funny. I still believe now that they were following us from The Club," she said.

"Yeah, I definitely can't rule it out, but we can't prove it, either. Look, if I think it's getting too dangerous then I will have to make a serious decision on whether or not I should continue this—but I'm talking about the channel. I will still investigate this on my own, I just won't talk about it online."

"That still doesn't make me comfortable, Mackenzee. I know how you like to go to the extremes."

"I know it doesn't, Porsha. But no one is doing and has done anything for Deandra, that's why I need to do this. I'm sure her family will appreciate that someone has done something since no one else has."

She smiled. "I know they will."

I looked at my phone. "Hello?"

"Hello, is this Mackenzee Lawson?"

"Yes it is. Who is this?"

Porsha stared at me in suspense.

"This is Mrs. Trent calling from District Attorney Richard Elmhurst III's office. Would you have time to see him this afternoon?"

"What the fuck?" I mouthed to Porsha; she returned a look of confusion. "Um, yes, Mrs. Trent, I would have time today. What time?"

"Is 2:00 in the afternoon a good time?"

"Yes, that's a great time."

"Okay, will do. See you then, Miss Lawson."

"Okay, bye."

"Who was that?"

"A woman calling from Richard's office!" I said with surprise since I honestly didn't know what to think of this.

"Richard? The *DA* Richard? The one you met last night, right?"

"Yes! What the fuck? How the hell did he get my number?"

"I thought you gave it to him while you were out on the dance floor with him last night."

"No, I didn't. He didn't ask for it that's why I never gave it him, and he didn't give me his. What the hell, Porsha? Why does he wanna talk to me?"

"I think you know why he wants to talk to you, Mackenzee. It's clear you really asked those types of questions that obviously stuck hard in his mind last night."

"That's gotta be it because I just can't think of another reason. Maybe he found out more about Deandra's case and wants to talk to me about it. Wouldn't that be great?"

"Yeah, that would be awesome, Mackenzee—but I wouldn't count on it."

I sighed. "Well, I know it could not have been about the video because I don't think anyone saw it that fast since this is a brand-new channel completely unrelated to my old one. But since I already said I would be at his office this afternoon then I'm gonna be there."

"And you better be very careful, Mackenzee. You don't know what this man has in mind."

"I know, but I'm gonna find out."

CHAPTER SIX

"Miss Lawson?"

"Yes?" I said, as I got up out of my chair.

"Mr. Elmhurst is ready to see you," Mrs. Trent replied. She held open a door which didn't appear to go directly into his office.

I wasn't sure what I was about to walk into.

"Thank you," I replied with a smile, and entered this room where it looked as if I'd just entered into a maze. I walked down the long hall which made a turn to the right which I walked down the hall some more and then right into his office. I froze when I saw him sitting in his chair behind his desk as he faced the window behind him.

"Come in, Mackenzee. I know you're here," he said. He turned around in his chair as he smirked at me, and it was the type of smirk as if we'd had sex or something that same night we met. He got up out of his seat and walked towards me as I walked towards him. "Nice to see you again."

"Nice to see you, too. I didn't think you ever wanted to see me again after the dance we had at The Club."

We shook hands, and it definitely didn't feel the same as it'd felt the night we met.

"Have a seat," he replied with a grin, and then went back behind his desk and sat down. "What made you think I didn't wanna see you again?"

I sat down in probably one of the nicest chairs my butt had ever sat in. "I just wasn't comfortable about the way we left things that night."

"And why do you say that? It was just a dance," he said as he twiddled his luxury BENU pen in his hands as he sat back in his chair as if I was just some friend in here talking to him.

"I seemed to have asked too many questions."

"You did," he confirmed as he stared me down.

This sent a ripple of chills all through me. I knew there was a reason why he wanted to see me, and I knew it wasn't a good one. I also believed now that he could've seen my very first video about my investigation into The Club because of Deandra's disappearance even though I didn't say it was me and I was serious about remaining anonymous, but if this is what he wanted to see me about, what the hell was his connection to it?

I was about to find out.

"I seemed to have made you uncomfortable when I brought up something that happened at The Club in the past."

He nodded. "Well, anyone would be uncomfortable about something like that, Mackenzee."

Only if they had something to do with it, I thought. "So, you have heard about it?"

"I still don't recall it since it was so long ago, so I decided to look it up to see if anything would refresh my memory."

I continued to stare at him in total suspense. "And? What? What did you find?"

"That there is no record of a Deandra Whitfield disappearance anywhere in this city's history," he informed me.

Bullshit! I thought. But I was in his office, so I had to keep my cool. I didn't wanna lose it already because I just had an instant feeling that he was lying about this. There was no way that news report from that other channel that's not even in this city would've even had a story about it had it not been a true story.

"No record? There has got to be some kind of mistake, Richard. Can I call you Richard since I met you at The Club and we're just casually talking?"

"Of course," he said with a smile.

I sighed. "Richard. I just don't believe that. Someone in this city is hiding something. You're the DA in this city, so it's clear you run things, right?"

"Yes, some things, but not everything," he replied as he continued to smile.

"So, what is up with this? *I know* Deandra existed! She was a 17-year-old girl with a 2-year-old child. She was a senior in high school. She attended Saint Maran West, our rival school. This is all public record in this city and anywhere. Why does it seem as if there is no record about her disappearance from The Club? Someone had to report it! That's where that news channel said she was last seen at."

"Well, this city as no records of her disappearance on file, Mackenzee. Not the police station, not at the courthouse, not here, not anywhere. I just wanted to let you know that since I felt I owed it to you when you were asking me so many questions about her."

"But you were there that night, Richard. You were there that night 33 years ago at The Club, the same night she was. How could a girl go missing and no one knows where she went? There were too many people there so someone had to have seen something."

"Well, I didn't see anything, Mackenzee. I didn't know her and didn't know she was there. Like I said, hundreds of teens were there that night and most didn't get in, but me and my friends were the lucky ones who did. If Deandra was there then she probably went off with some guy or something, but no men have ever come forward to talk to the cops about her; I would have the records if they did. There's nothing more I have to say about it, okay?"

No, it's not fuckin' okay, I thought. I sighed as I shook my head. "Someone really dropped the ball hard on this. This girl is missing. *Missing.* And for *33 years* at that. Have you ever had anyone in your family go missing like this, Richard?"

"No, I haven't. But we're not talking about me."

"That wasn't a nice thing to say," I said as I glared at him.

"Well, what do you want me to say? I told you everything I know about this case. Just because something could've happened at The Club 33 years ago when I was there with my friends doesn't mean I know anything about it. Hundreds of teens were there that night. Are you gonna track them all down and interrogate them with questions?"

"No," I said with my head lowered. *But I already told people to contact me if they know anything*, I thought.

"Well, that's all I have to say about this. I have a meeting with some of my attorneys in less than ten minutes."

"Okay," I said, and got up.

"But, before you leave."

I looked at him as he still sat at his desk as he sized me up. "What is it?"

"Have dinner with me."

"He wants me to have dinner with him! What the fuck?!" I said, as I drove away from his office as I talked to Porsha.

"Are you serious, Mackenzee?"

"Yeah, I am! I'm telling you, I was just as shocked as you! I just knew he didn't wanna see me again. And yes, he did wanna see me about how our night ended after the dance we had at The Club. He also told me that there are absolutely no records of Deandra's disappearance anywhere in the city! Not at the courthouse, not at the police station—*nowhere!*"

"I call bullshit on that, Mackenzee, just as much as I know you do. Someone is definitely hiding something, maybe even more than one person."

"You know that's what I think, too, and I was even thinking that to myself. Now I believe that he could quite possibly be telling me the truth about not knowing anything because there were a lot of people there that night, but I just have a hard time a hundred percent believing it. Richard is a huge figure in this city. With his credentials, he could've gone anywhere after he graduated from high school, but he came right back here to work after college and law school. I looked him up before I officially left to go see him."

"Oh, I just know you did! But Mackenzee, what if he's really seriously interested in you? Why would he want to have dinner with you?"

I sighed. "I just don't know about a serious interest in me, Porsha. This man can't be a hundred percent single."

"Well, he's obviously not married, so he's considered single."

"Yes, that's definitely true. I just think he finds me intriguing just as much as I find this case intriguing. Maybe he does have more to tell me, he just didn't wanna let me know there at his office."

"It's possible, Mackenzee, but if I were you, I would be very careful about men like him. He has a lot of power in this city with him being the DA and all."

"I know, and if I wasn't trying to get it out of him about what's really been going on at The Club for these past 33 years then I will seriously date him."

"So you're just gonna use him, huh?"

"Well, if you wanna know the truth, Porsha?"

"Yeah, what's the truth?"

"The truth is, I feel like he's using me already, too." I stopped at a stoplight and looked to my left . . . .

And there was the black-on-black BMW 760i xDrive!

I started to shake. It was broad daylight. I should not have been this scared to see this car especially with all of these other cars around. But I didn't have the slightest idea what they had in mind.

"Hello? Mackenzee?"

"Um . . . Porsha?"

"Yes?"

"I'm gonna have to call you back."

I hung up and tried to concentrate on the road as I kept my head faced straight ahead, but I had excellent peripheral vision. Since my windows weren't tinted, I didn't want them to think I remembered whoever was in that car from last night, even though I was not in my car.

The light turned green.

They took off ahead of me as I got a glimpse of the license plate . . .

.

CLUB 88.

Same person it was last night.

I continued to drive as I tried my best to concentrate on the road. They slowed down in the left lane and went the same pace I did.

Yes, I was now convinced this person was following me. It clearly was not Richard since I'd just come from seeing him. This was definitely someone who was trying to scare me, but they were not gonna scare me out of finding out the truth about what went on at the establishment that was so proudly displayed on the license plate of their car.

At another stoplight, there was a chime on my phone, indicating to me that I'd received an email:

It's about time someone is investigating this! I need to talk to you ASAP. Call me or email me at this email anytime.

Sincerely,
Mary Landry

CHAPTER SEVEN

"*T*his *can't* be the right neighborhood. I can't even remember this neighborhood looking this bad back in the day," I said, as we were on the street Mary told me she lived on.

"People just don't give a shit these days, Mackenzee. Things aren't the way they used to be when people took pride in home ownership and keeping up properties or whatever. Since we don't live on this side of town, I haven't been over here that much since most people who go to Saint Maran West live in this area of the city, but this particular area looks horrible. I know it could not have looked like this over 30 years ago."

"Yeah, I don't think it did, either. And even if it did, they do have their better parts on this side of town because Mary used to live in it." I looked at my phone, and it showed we were definitely on the right street. I looked at the numbers on the houses, at least the ones I could see. "Oh, here it is!"

Porsha looked at the house. "Are you sure? This house looks like it has *definitely* seen better days; all of these houses on this block look like they have. I thought this Mary Landry lived lavishly back in the day from what she'd told you when you talked to her?"

"Yeah, that's what she told me, Porsha. But as you see, people fall on hard times. Just because someone has lived that way at one point in their lives doesn't mean they're gonna live like that for the rest of their lives. I'll find out what's up when I go in here and talk to her."

"I'll be interested in hearing it. Call me when you're done talking to her."

"I will," I said, and grabbed my purse and got out of the car. I took a deep breath and walked up to this house that I was surprised Mary lived in from what she'd told me about her past life. I looked behind me and saw how Porsha had already drove off. I looked around the area and there was not a person in sight. It seemed so quiet but at the same time the neighborhood seemed so unsafe, and definitely showed significant signs of urban blight. With overgrown lawns, stray dogs and cats wandering around, even some abandoned, unsalvageable homes, I was glad this was a very clear and sunny day because I would be cautious about coming here alone at night. I walked up the dilapidated concrete steps that exposed cracks as I stared at the flimsy silver-colored railing. I was scared to hold on to it while I climbed the steps. I rang the doorbell as I looked around once again as I tried to be aware of my surroundings.

The door opened.

"Hi," a woman said, who had a full head of short grey hair and was a little on the heavy side. She wore a white V-neck tee and blue jeans with house slippers.

"Hi," I replied with a smile. "Are you Mary Landry?"

"I sure am. Are you Mackenzee?"

"Yes I am."

"Great. Come on in," she said. "Excuse all of the boxes, I just moved in three months ago and haven't finished unpacking."

"You moved in three months ago? Where did you live previously?"

"Atlanta," she replied with a smile as she held a cigarette in her hand. She took a puff. "And before that it was Chicago and before that it was Los Angeles. I feel like I've lived everywhere in the past 30 years. Only stayed here 3 years after high school. But it didn't work out in any of those cities so I moved back here, and here is home.

Home sweet home." She led me to her family room where she turned off the TV as the room was filled with smoke. "You want something to drink?"

"No thank you," I said with a smile since I couldn't eat or drink anything in the presence of thick cigarette smoke except for strangely, at clubs.

"Have a seat," she said. She put her cigarette on the ashtray.

"Thank you," I said, and sat down. "I don't wanna take up too much of your time, but when you wrote to me, I knew I had to see you ASAP since that news channel mentioned you in their story, so I wanna hear your story about what happened that night when Deandra went missing."

"I was a complete mess after Deandra went missing. I just knew someday she was gonna turn up—she never did. To make matters worse, I found out that I was pregnant by my senior crush at the time, Damian. It made me sick to think about the fact that I'd gotten pregnant by him the night Deandra disappeared, but the timing was exact."

"Did you have the baby?"

"Yeah, I did, and I kept him despite what my family and friends and what Damian had to say. It was ultimately my decision. I just wanted something from that night to have and cherish forever knowing that was the last time I saw Deandra—but never did I ever think I was gonna get it in the form of a child."

"What did you do about school and everything?"

She sighed, and took another puff off of her cigarette. She flicked the ashes in the ashtray as she shook her head. "I had to leave school and attend one for pregnant teens; my parents forced me to. With Deandra being missing and me being pregnant with Damian's baby . . . damn . . . it was just too much. I just couldn't go back there, but I knew I needed to finish school despite everything that'd been going on. My parents had also just separated at the time as well; they divorced years later. Everything was just too much. I felt the only thing I had to look forward to was my child. But I was warned if I kept it that I would be cut off financially. They meant it. And you can see that by the way I live now. Like I told you when I first talked to you, I didn't live like this in high school. I was one of the most affluent kids at Saint Maran West High School. Had my own brand-new car waiting for me when I turned 16 with an Alpine pullout CD player in it—the hottest car at the time; I wore the hottest fashion trends at the time, carried authentic Gucci handbags, everything. Deandra said I had it all that night we went to The Club; I told her no one had it all. Yeah, and I have proof of that now. I wish she could see me now."

"I'm so sorry to hear about how you've fallen on such hard times since Deandra's disappearance, Mary. I don't think anyone could do well in any way knowing that they saw someone one day and then hours later they didn't see them again. But never in a million years did they think they would never see them again."

"Yeah, you're right, Mackenzee. I never thought for a second in my life back then that what would happen to Deandra would happen— and I still don't know what really happened. My family and friends always thought that I knew, but I honestly did not know what happened to her. I feel like I've told my story a million times to people, but no one has done anything about it."

"Have you gone to the cops?"

"Several times for years, but when I moved from here, of course I stopped going. I even went to the cops the next day when Deandra's mom had called me to ask me had I heard from her because she didn't come home. She knew Deandra was not irresponsible, and considering the fact that she had Ashley, she couldn't be irresponsible. She even turned down going to Damian's house with us that night because she had to be home to take care of Ashley and to go to work the next day. Now I wish she would've gone with us."

"Why?"

"Because if she did then I think she would still be alive today. I wish Trevor never showed up there because he was the reason why she wanted to stay."

"Trevor, her ex-boyfriend at the time—right?"

"Exactly right. I knew she'd never gotten over him. She was even listening to slow love songs that reminded her of their relationship while we were on our way to The Club. He is the father of Ashley."

"Yeah, I saw that on someone's short video about it. Thanks for confirming it. How did Deandra seem the last time you spoke to her?"

"Upset."

"For real?"

"Yes, for real, Mackenzee. It was clear Trevor had left her there so that's why she called me to come pick her up while I was at Damian's house. She actually called him because, remember, no one had cell phones back then. I did ask her what was wrong, but she told me she didn't wanna talk about it and to just come and get her, so I did. I was hoping I could get it out of her when I drove her home, but I never saw her again after that night."

"Damn," I said as I shook my head. "So you think she left with Trevor after all?"

"Yeah, I do. Who else could she have left with?"

"When was the last time you spoke to Trevor?"

"A few days after Deandra disappeared, but that was after numerous attempts at calling him and even going to his house—but no one would answer the door. When I finally did speak to him, he swore on everything he had nothing to do with it—he swears to this day he had nothing to do with it—but I believe he did. I just can't get myself to believe that he's innocent in all of this. She still had feelings for him; it was pretty obvious to me."

"Where is Trevor?"

She blew her smoke up in the air. "Who the hell knows? Especially after 33 years. I heard he left the city and state but didn't tell anyone where he was going. He moved with his mom a week after Deandra disappeared, and that made him the number one suspect. Like I said, I believe he had everything to do with it. That was a pretty quick move he made, and we all know why he did, and his mom was complicit in that shit because she tried to protect him."

"Yeah, it most definitely sounds like it. Wow, I can't believe I'm hearing all of this, especially from a best friend of Deandra. I'm just glad you wanted to talk to me after all of this time since it's been so long."

"It's been too long that nothing has been done about it, Mackenzee. Black girls go missing all of the time from wherever and are never seen or heard from again. I never ever thought it would happen to my best friend."

"So you don't think she's still alive?"

She lowered her head. "I knew I was gonna be asked this question one day. No, I don't think she's alive, Mackenzee. I just believe she would've found some way to contact me or her mom if she was."

"Is her mom still around?"

"Yeah, she's still around; lives in the same house and everything. She refuses to believe Deandra will never come home, and I can't blame her. And she told me she's not going anywhere until Deandra walks through the front door of her home. I feel so sorry for her. The nerve of this city to turn their backs on her when this was her daughter who has a daughter. I haven't spoken to her in a while. We even went to the cops together that day Deandra didn't come home; that's what I almost forgot to tell you. The cops insisted that she was probably with Trevor or other friends and that she would come home. We've been waiting for her to come home now for 33 years."

"This is so unreal, Mary. And it hurts a lot because this goes on all of the time. Have you been back to The Club since?"

"No, not at all. I was actually banned from there because I protested their lack of care about what could've happened to Deandra. I knew after 3 years of being in this city and there was still no sign of Deandra, I had to leave. I was gone for 30 years, and now I'm right back here, and I know I'm right back here now because finally there's someone who wasn't even alive back then who is taking this case seriously, and that is what has been needed from the beginning."

I nodded with a smile. "It has. It's long overdue. So, did you hear about other girls disappearing from The Club years later?"

"Yeah, I heard about them, and I said never rule out that it's the same person who could've had something to do with Deandra's disappearance. I hate to say this because it sounds selfish, but I couldn't concentrate on the other girls, all I could concentrate on was Deandra. I still get nightmares to this day since she's been missing."

"That's perfectly understandable."

"I'm glad you understand." She shook her head. "Damn. It's that clicking sound of the phone on her end that is always stuck in my mind."

"What do you mean?"

She took another puff off of her cigarette, and then took a deep breath. "The last time I spoke to her I was at Damian's, and right in the middle while I was talking to her, the phone just clicked off. Went dead. I never spoke to her again after that. That haunts me to this day."

"Wow, that just gave me chills all over when you said that, Mary. I believe you a hundred percent."

She shook her head. She took another puff off of her cigarette and blew the smoke up in the air. "Mackenzee, I have so many what-ifs about that night it's not even funny."

"Do you mind telling me what they are?"

"Not at all. I think all the time, what if Paul wasn't there that night?"

"Who's Paul?"

"Paul was one of the bouncers that night—security. You know who they are since they're at every club. He was also one of my older brother's best friends."

"Okay. What about him?"

"When we were about to stand in that long-ass line, I all of the sudden saw Paul. I called him over to me and Deandra, and he took us to the back of the club and let us in that way."

"I knew there was a backway to the club, but I didn't and still don't know where it's at."

"Yeah, you're right, there is. There always has to be more than one way in and out of a place. But when Paul got us in, he asked for the cover charge of $5.00 from each of us."

"$5.00? The cover charge back then was only *$5.00?* Wow! Those were the days!"

Mary smiled. "Yeah, they were. But yeah, it was only $5.00 for teen night, and I believe it was $10.00 for a regular 21-and-over night back then even though I never went to one because I just couldn't go back there since I knew that was the last place I'd seen Deandra. I know it's now $25.00 today, so I know it's more for the teen nights as well since I heard they still have them."

"Yeah, it was $30.00 for me and my best friend Porsha to get in for the Throwback Thursdays: 1990 Night since it was a special night."

"I believe it since they always tack on an extra few bucks for a special night. Had it not been for that being the last place I ever saw Deandra at, I would've been there that night. I just can't get myself to ever go back to that place."

"And I can't blame you for that, Mary. No one can. That's why I'm investigating this because no one else will."

"And I greatly appreciate it. But yeah, if it wasn't for me seeing Paul, I think Deandra and I would've both got tired of waiting in that long line to get in and would've eventually left. And I always think what if I didn't have enough to get Deandra in that night?"

"She didn't have enough to get in?"

"Sure didn't. Now I wish *I* was short of cash, but I always had a lot of cash on me back then, at least $50-$100, and that was a lot to carry around back then. If I didn't have an extra $5.00 to get Deandra in, then I really don't know if Paul would've actually let us in since he was doing us a big favor and even risking his own job by sneaking us in the backway to let us in so we wouldn't have to wait in line. But it really all starts with me seeing him outside. I wish I would've never seen him, and I don't mean that in a bad way at all. Like I said, if I didn't see him then Deandra and I would've been forced to stand in line and like I'd mentioned before, we would not have been standing there for that long at all, I knew us well back then, we would've gotten tired of it and left."

"Oh, I know I would've! In fact, me and my best friend Porsha have done that a lot at The Club. We always said what's gonna be so different on this night than all of the other nights that we can come here? And we were right, nothing was different. It was always same shit different night. But I can't believe they have carried on the teen night for this long without any thought about what'd happened at the very first one. And if I knew about what'd happened at the first one then I would've never had my first experience there."

"Yeah, you're right about that. That's why I just don't go to clubs anymore. I tried going to some in the other cities that I'd lived in for these past 30 years, but I would always leave early or decide not to go at all at the last minute. I always felt guilty about having fun since I still had no idea where Deandra was. Every time I would walk into a club no matter what city I was in or what club it was, it always looked the same to me as it did back in 1990, and I would always be reminded of Deandra. Reminded of what could've been with her had we not went for that teen night at all that night."

"Wow, I can't even imagine, Mary. This just sounds so horrifying that I'm sitting here talking to you face-to-face about something it seems like no one has cared about in so long."

"But now someone does care, and that's you, Mackenzee. You could be doing anything right now, but you're here talking to an old woman now about a teen night she and her friend went to and her friend ended up disappearing from it 33 years ago and hasn't been seen since. I can't thank you enough for it."

"No problem at all," I replied with a smile.

"And, you know, there is something I said to Deandra that night that haunts me most of all."

My eyes got wide with interest. "What is it?"

"We got in all thanks to Paul when we're still supposed to be standing in that long-ass line out there. It was meant to be."

"What was meant to be?"

"Whatever happens tonight."

Mary's eyes welled up with tears. "Never did I ever think or even believe that when I said whatever happened that night it was gonna turn into a 33-year-old disappearance of my best friend. What happened to her was *never* meant to be!" She broke down and cried.

"I'm so sorry, Mary," I said, as tears streamed down my eyes. "You're right. It was never meant to be." I wiped the tears away as I sighed. I didn't know I was gonna get this emotional. "Um, are you still in contact with Paul?"

She took a deep breath as she put her hands on her knees. "Paul's dead."

I shrieked! "Oh, no! Oh my god I'm so sorry! What happened to him?"

"He killed himself. He was so distraught over the death of my older brother, Jack. They both died months apart 20 years ago."

"Mary! No! My goodness! I'm so sorry! What happened?"

She took another deep breath. "Drug overdose. He had a bad drug problem. Ever since he was in high school. Paul supplied him the drugs since he sold drugs on the side. So, as you see, he was not only a bouncer at The Club. He was also very upset about Deandra's disappearance which was more than 10 years old at the time. He claims he didn't know what happened to her that night when I'd asked him, but if he knew anything, he took it to his grave."

I was practically speechless. "Wow. I'm so sorry, Mary."

She smiled with a nod. "Thank you, Mackenzee. I know you mean it." She got up. "There's something I want to show you. Follow me."

She led me through her house where there were so many boxes in the way that I tried not to bump into them. I just started to feel more and more sorry for her. I knew she had it so rough in these 33 years since Deandra's disappearance just as much as Deandra's mom did, and there was no way anyone knew what they were going through unless they went through it themselves.

We walked out to her garage which was not attached to her house. She pressed the remote to open it. There were two cars sitting in here.

"As you see, there are two cars sitting in here. Big deal, huh?"

I laughed as I tried to figure out what this was all about.

"Well, the white one with the white top is a big deal, since that was the last time Deandra was in my car."

I gasped! *"For real, Mary?"*

"Yes, for real, Mackenzee. She loved this car and I loved it, too. It's a 1989 Volkswagen Cabriolet. It was exactly what I wanted. Trust me, after 33 years as you can see it has been through hell, but that's why I have another car and have had several in the past 33 years. Some I paid off, some were repossessed, but I always kept this one since it was a sweet 16 birthday gift when I turned 16 back in the fall of 1989, and almost always because it was the last time I took Deandra somewhere in it, and you know where that place is."

"Yes, I know it. It's such a cute and cool little car."

"It was the shit back then, Mackenzee. I have a ton of pictures of it and in it and Deandra's in a lot of the pictures, too. I can email them to you if you want because I have to look for them."

"I'd love to see them," I said with a smile.

She opened the passenger's side door and looked in the glove compartment. She pulled something out and then shut the door. She held up a clear plastic bag. "Here's Deandra's favorite lipstick, Clinique's Cherries in the Snow. She thought she lost this lipstick that's the reason why she bought a new one even though she couldn't afford to, but that was Deandra for you. She always had to look good and be put together like most of us girls back then and of course even more so now. I found it weeks after she disappeared. She wore this a lot, including the last time I saw her. The color was gorgeous on her skin tone."

"Yeah, I believe you. That color is obviously discontinued because I just looked at Clinique's website a few weeks ago at their lipsticks, so this is quite a coincidence. Wow. I can't believe it. The silver tube still looks really good after all of this time."

"It does. You know, what makes me so mad is that the cops didn't ask to search my car for anything of hers, and I would've given total consent and given this lipstick to them for whatever they would've or could've possibly needed it for, but it showed you just how much they cared—but now I'm giving it to you since you do care and is investigating this and I see that you're a hundred percent serious."

"I am, Mary," I reassured her. I took the bag from her. "I think for some reason this could come in use one day, and I hope it's a day very soon. Thank you so much for trusting me with this. It's in good hands."

"I know it is. I think I just had it in my car for this long and had only in recent years put it in a plastic bag because I just feel she's gonna come back and look in the glove compartment and see that I'd found it for her."

"Thank you for trusting me with it."

CHAPTER EIGHT

<u>I'M THEIR SPEAKER</u>
EXCLUSIVE INTERVIEW WITH MARY LANDRY, BEST
FRIEND OF DEANDRA WHITFIELD—THE 17-YEAR-OLD
HIGH-SCHOOL SENIOR AND TEEN MOM WHO DISAP-
PEARED FROM THE CLUB IN THE CITY OF SAINT
MARAN 33 YEARS AGO.

"IT'S BEEN 33 YEARS—I WANT SOME ANSWERS. HER
FAMILY WANTS SOME ANSWERS. WE WAITED LONG
ENOUGH."

*P*orsha and I ate our lunch as we watched the very edited version of this interview, and I knew I had to first and foremost edit out each time she said my name amongst a lot of other things for obvious reasons, and I didn't realize how much she'd said it until I looked over the video. I would not have cared that she said it had I not lived in this city, but the fact of the matter was, I lived here, and also had a man who had a lot of power in this city who had some kind of interest in me, but I had to side-eye what his interest in me truly was for now.

The interview had come to an end.

I turned back on my microphone.

"So, there you all have seen it and heard it. Mary Landry is now a 50-year-old grandmother, and she has not seen or heard from her best friend Deandra Whitfield for 33 years. I want you all to put yourselves in her place for a second and just imagine what she's going through and is still going through. It's not easy to live your life knowing that someone who you were so close to in your life vanished without a trace in a nightclub and no one has ever been able to give you any answers. I don't wanna have to do another one of these interviews with someone else talking about their friend or loved one who went missing when they attended The Club, but unfortunately, I know I'm prob-ably gonna have to. So, please, like and share and subscribe to this channel for more serious content and updates on this case and more of them to come. And remember, The Club—Attend at your own risk. Thank you and have a wonderful rest of the day."

I turned the Live! sign off.

"Well, that was pretty short," Porsha said, and ate some more of her fries.

"The interview said a lot so I didn't have to talk a lot after I played it. Mary didn't hold back. But as you see, I left out her giving me the tube of lipstick, but I had to show the car since that was the last time Deandra had been in it."

"That was such a cute little car from back then. Mary really did fall on hard times. Poor thing."

"Yeah, just her being in that house—and it didn't look much better on the inside than it did on the outside—really showed me just how hard of a time she has had. Her son actually lives with her, but he was at work when I was there. Her granddaughter lives in Atlanta with her mom. She told me her son and her granddaughter's mom never married. And she looked so much older than 50. The pain of what she's been through shows all over her face."

"I noticed that from the older pictures of her and Deandra you showed me and the audience who was watching this. But given what she's been through, I would've been surprised if she would've aged beautifully. I really feel sorry for her."

"So do I," I said, as I shook my head. I looked at the tube of lipstick as it still sat in its plastic bag.

"What are you gonna do with that lipstick?"

"Keep it. I feel like I need it for something, I just don't know what it is."

"Well, when you figure it out, you tell me."

"I will."

"So, Richard hasn't called you to set up your first dinner date?"

"Not yet. He said his secretary hasn't given him his latest schedule yet. That's what he told me before I left when he asked me to have dinner with him, I thought he meant have it with him that night. How the hell is he gonna ask me to have dinner with him and then says he has to get his latest schedule from his secretary to see when it's a good time for him? I'm the one who should've been saying that to him."

She laughed. "True!"

"Um, Mary had me thinking about something," I said, and got up. "Come with me."

"Had you thinking about what, Mackenzee? Where are we going?"

CHAPTER NINE

"Oh, come on, Mackenzee! Can you just give it a rest for today?" Porsha asked, as I slowed down and turned into the entrance of The Club.

"Nope," I said with a huge grin. "Look, if there is something I'm thinking about then I have to act on it." I pulled into the empty lot as there were very few cars here, but I could tell they were getting ready for another fun-filled night tonight.

"What is it that you think you're gonna find? You're not gonna go in there and start asking people questions, are you?"

"No, I'm not gonna do that. I just need to check something out before it gets dark, and people start arriving for the night."

"And what is so important that you need to check out? You still haven't answered my question."

I parked in the middle of the parking lot, similar to where we parked the last time we were here. "If I feel it's relevant to Deandra's case, I will tell you," I said. "Here, switch places with me."

"How come?"

"Just in case I have to run out of here you will be in the driver's seat and we can just take off real fast."

"Mackenzee! If you have to do that then you have no business being here around this time of the day!"

"Part of an investigation is going to places that most won't go—that's how you really get to the nitty-gritty of the story. Since talking to Mary, I'm really into this, Porsha. I feel like I'm really getting started now."

Porsha shook her head as she got out of the car and got in on the driver's side. "Just don't take that long to find whatever you want to find."

"I'll try not to," I replied, and shut the door for her.

I walked towards the back of the club as if I worked here and saw for myself that they did in fact have a backway to get in here that exposed a whole other parking lot. I checked out the luxury cars in the back, and they were most people's dream cars. A Ferrari, a Rolls-Royce Cullinan SUV, and a Lamborghini—all in black. All were brand-new car models. "Damn, I'm in the wrong business," I mumbled, as I snooped around the back.

I stared at the back where there was in fact a back door to get into, just like what Mary had mentioned that Paul had let her and Deandra into that night. It gave me chills looking at it. It looked as if time had stood still. I knew officially that Mary and Deandra were led through that back door to get in here, but Mary told me she went out the front door that night both times—the first time to leave with Damian, and the second time when she came back to pick up Deandra . . . but she left without her.

I searched some more around in the area and noticed that they had some kind of private deck out back here for warmer months, and it looked like it was only for people who worked here and their friends and families, but maybe even for a private outdoor party along with another small building that matched The Club's main building that looked like a place for private small parties when it was cooler out. Mary never mentioned this to me, so I knew she probably didn't know anything about it.

I heard the faint sound of music that was obviously coming from inside, but I started to get a strong whiff of cigarette smoke that I knew was coming somewhere here on the outside.

"WHO THE HELL ARE YOU?" a man yelled to me who seemed to have come out of nowhere while *he had his gun pointed right at me!*

I shrieked as I threw my hands up in the air! "Please! Please! Don't shoot!" I begged, as I now I felt like I was in a big fight for my life to get the hell out of here. I wished Porsha would drive back here so I could jump in the car as planned.

Just what the hell did I actually get myself into?

"You stay right there. Don't fuckin' move," he said, as he slowly walked over to me as he put his gun back in its holster. The moment he approached me, he patted me down as my hands were still in the air. "What the hell are you doing back here? This is private property, you're clearly trespassing." He turned me around to look at him.

Now I was staring someone dead in the eye who had the build that was a cross between an NBA player because of his well over 6-foot-5 height, and more than the weight of an NFL linebacker.

I was about to be destroyed.

I continued to stare up at him.

"Well?" he said, as he crossed his arms in front of him, demanding an answer from me and rightfully so.

I noticed how another man who was practically the same build walked out of The Club with another man with him who had a much smaller build and about the average height for a man. I knew how much trouble I was in now.

"Who is she?" the man with the much smaller build asked.

"She has no ID on her," the man who patted me down informed the smaller-build man.

The smaller-build man looked at me. "Who are you? What are you doing here?"

I looked at him . . . .

And took off!

"HEY!" I heard two of them say!

But before I knew it, I was tackled to the ground . . . *hard*. I kicked and screamed as if they were trying to attack me! "LET ME GO! LET ME GO!" I yelled as they held me.

The cops came from out of nowhere!

They got out of their car as they asked the men what was going on.

"She's trespassing here. She has no ID so we don't know who she is. We saw her on the surveillance wandering around in the back here. She has no business being back here," the smaller-build man informed them.

"What were you doing back here?" one of the cops asked me.

"I thought I lost something from one of the nights I was here," I lied.

"Bullshit. You would not have been back here. This is an entry for employees and others who are authorized to be back here. Where is your lanyard with your authorization?" the man who first confronted me asked.

"Do you all wanna press charges against her for trespassing on this property?" the other cop asked.

"Yes," the man with the smaller build said.

And the cuffs were put on me!

I started screaming and squirming as I tried hard to fight my way out of them which triggered the cops to a point where one took one of my arms and the other one took the other and literally dragged me to the cop car since I felt my legs and feet go out from under me!

Porsha screamed as she ran up to where we all were! "OH MY GOD! WHAT THE FUCK IS GOING ON?!WHY ARE YOU BEING ARRESTED?!"

"She was trespassing on private property. She's going to jail," one of the cops informed her.

The three men who'd caught me gave me one of the scariest looks I'd ever seen. If looks could kill, I would've dropped dead right here, right now.

"WHAT?!" Porsha said.

"Just don't call my parents!" I told her, as they put me in the back of the cop car, all the while trying to figure out how the hell was I gonna get out of a mess that I'd already gotten myself way in too deep with.

CHAPTER TEN

After going through the whole first experience of being arrested—fingerprints, mugshot, locked in a cell; yeah, it was hell—reality set in hard for me when I was led to a cell with only one other very worn-out looking woman in it. The cop opened the cell door and lightly pushed me in. She closed the door, and I heard it lock. That was one of the hardest sounds I'd ever heard. I sat down on a bench completed with profanity-laced graffiti and scratches from real fingernails and classic wear-and-tear as I tried to remind myself that sometimes you're gonna get yourself into trouble for doing something that's right. Not everyone in jail was in here for doing something bad.

Those were facts.

"Hi," the woman said to me with a weary smile.

"Hi," I replied with a smile.

"What did they throw you in here for?"

"Trespassing."

"Wow, really? Damn, Saint Maran is still arresting people for that shit? They need something better to do. Where were you trespassing at?"

"The Club," I replied.

"For real?" she said, as she sat up since she was lying down on another bench right next to mine but up against a wall. "I hate that place. What were you doing there?"

"I thought I lost something on the night I went there."

"What did you lose?"

"One of my earrings," I lied.

She nodded as she continued to smile at me. "Did you find it?"

"No, I didn't have time to," I replied with a smile.

"I've never been there. I've lived in this city my whole life and have never been there."

"Why?"

A cop came to the cell.

"Mackenzee Lawson?"

"Yes?"

"You made bail. Let's go," the cop informed me.

"What?!" I said, because I was truly surprised. I had no idea who bailed me out, but then I believed Porsha called my parents after all since she was so hysterical about what she'd witnessed happen to me. I looked at the woman who was now once again gonna be in here all by herself. "How come you've never been to The Club?"

"Because my older sister went missing from there in 1995. She hasn't been seen or heard from since."

"Let's go, Mackenzee," the cop said again, as if she didn't hear a word this woman had just told me.

I was so stunned I kept staring at her as I was led away from the cell as she waved goodbye to me, and into the processing area where I was getting out of here—and someone who'd just told me something mind blowing was still sitting in there. Now I'd wished someone didn't bail me out just yet, and I still didn't know who actually had.

I walked out of a place that I'd hoped to never walk into again to a man who stared me down.

"Mackenzee?" he said.

"Yes?" I replied, not sure if I should've or not because I had no idea who this man was and how he knew my name.

"Follow me," he said.

"To where?" I asked, as I checked out my surroundings. I looked all around for Porsha or someone I knew, but no one I knew was in sight —so I knew they weren't here—just a strange man who I *still* didn't know how the hell he knew my name.

"Just follow me. You're not in any danger," he tried to assure me.

I stayed put. "How do you know my name?" I finally decided to ask.

"Follow me. Come on," he said, completely ignoring my question.

I walked with caution behind him. He led me over to a black-on-black brand-new Range Rover with deep tinted windows. He opened the passenger's side door for me. I stood back. I had no idea why he wanted me to get in this SUV.

"What are you waiting for? Get in."

"What the hell for?" I said, as I stared at him with my eyes bucked out. I felt at this point this man was leading me into more trouble than I was already in.

"*Get in,*" he said again as he held the door.

I still hadn't seen who was driving or knew where this person was taking me. I knew this sure wasn't an Uber or Lyft or any of those because I never called for one. I took a deep breath and walked over to the SUV and peeked in.

"Hello, Mackenzee."

It was Richard!

"Get in," Richard said.

I looked at the man who was waiting for me when I walked out of jail. He nodded to me as he still stood with his hand on the door, waiting for me to get in.

I finally got in . . . very reluctantly.

"Thanks, man," Richard said.

"You're welcome," he said, and glared at me as he shut the door.

"So, I take it it was you who bailed me out?"

"You're right," he informed me as he concentrated on the road.

"Why?" I asked.

"Because you had no business being in there."

"You're right. But now I officially have a criminal record."

"No you don't."

I stared at him in total shock! "What?!"

"I had the charges dropped," he informed me. He looked at me at a stoplight. "And I hope I'm thanked for it later." He slowly reached his hand over and touched my left thigh.

I slightly curled up away from him. "Thank you. But I shouldn't have to thank you in the way you think I should have to thank you, Richard. If I have to fuck you when I still don't even know you that well to thank you for having charges dropped against me that I didn't know I had dropped until you just told me, then you should've just kept the charges on record."

He cracked a grin. "Fine, I'll have them put back on there . . ."

"NO!"

He chuckled. "Yeah, that's what I thought."

I sighed as I shook my head. This man already knew he had a big hold over me, and I saw for myself just how much power he really had.

"What were you doing at The Club this time of day? You obviously don't work there."

"I lost one of my earrings the last time I was there," I lied, trying to stick to the story I'd told the woman who was in the cell with me.

"And you were in the back of the building looking for it? How do you know it ended up there? Is there something you're not telling me? Because that was the night we met, right?"

"Yeah . . . right."

"And I don't recall us ever being outside together in the back of the building."

"I know we weren't. I wasn't in the back alone or with anyone else that night. I just don't know where it ended up, but I know I lost it there."

He grinned as he concentrated on the road. I knew he didn't believe a word I was saying.

"Where are you taking me?"

"To my house," he informed me. "I thought we could have that dinner date tonight. And you can tell me the real reason why you were at The Club besides making up stuff as you go along."

"Um . . . I'm not hungry. I had a big lunch."

"I know you didn't have it while you were in jail."

"You're right, it was before I went."

"And you were there for hours, so I'm sure you should be a little hungry again by now . . . because I know I am." He eye-fucked me all over while at another stoplight.

I sighed. There was obviously no way I was getting out of this. I stared at the door handle.

Click.

Click.

He unlocked the doors and relocked them. He wanted me to hear that sound.

I felt myself starting to shake. "So . . . is this a date?"

He stared right into my eyes. "One you won't forget."

CHAPTER ELEVEN

He parked his car in a circular driveway of a freakin' mansion.

"Is this your house?" I asked, even though I knew it was because he said he was taking me to his house—but I couldn't even hide how impressed I was.

"Whose would it be besides mine?" he replied with a grin.

You don't have to be a fuckin' arrogant smartass, I thought. "Just asking."

"I know. I was just playing with you, Mackenzee. Relax. You should be happy I had all of the charges dropped against you so once again you have a clean record because you had more than a few stacked against you. Most people wouldn't be able to stop thanking me."

"I thanked you. How many times do I have to?"

He smirked. "Once is enough . . . as long as you don't get yourself into any more trouble. Because if you do, I might not be able to get you out of it."

"I'll keep that in mind."

"You better," he warned me. "Come on, let's get inside."

We walked inside his house, and I could smell the food cooking and I admit I did start to get hungry once again—but I couldn't help noticing the entry of this beautiful home. I thought it was too beautiful for someone with his funky-ass attitude. But then again, he did get me out of jail and had potentially life-changing charges dropped against me—and they weren't charges I thought were a big deal. But this was Saint Maran, so any charges could be a very big deal and would be sure to follow a person anywhere in this world, so it was just like having a record anywhere. And I didn't plan on spending the rest of my life here.

I marveled at the cathedral high ceilings, white marbled floors, and double staircase with that beautiful jaw-dropping black fancy French wrought iron with stairs that matched the floors. This was truly a dream home for me and most people in this world. "Your home is beautiful. Are you the only one who lives here?"

"The only one," he replied with a smile. "Come on into the dining room. I'm sure you can smell that dinner's almost ready."

"My nose is stuffed up," I lied.

"Stop it," he said as he smirked at me. "I didn't see or hear you sniff once in the car."

I sighed. "I'm really not hungry," I honestly said.

"I hope you like steak and lobster," he said, as he walked towards the dining room.

I walked into this too-fancy-for-me dining room. The table was long enough to seat at least 12 people, but only two places were set—one at the head of the table which was obviously his spot, and the other one was to the left of him which was obviously my spot.

"Have a seat," he said, as he sat down in his spot.

"Thank you," I said as I looked around. "This is incredible. This looks like it's out of some fancy movie. You live very well for a DA."

"Yeah, I live better than most," he said, and took a sip of his water.

"You must've won a lot of big cases," I assumed as I still gazed around this beautiful dining room.

"Yeah, I have. But I'm also an investor; have been since I was a teenager."

"Like right around the time Deandra Whitfield went missing?"

He glared at me. "Are we gonna start on that?"

"Just asking," I said, and took a sip of my water, now wondering if he was gonna try and sneak something into my water or any other drink I decided to have. Now I really had to be careful.

A tall, nice-looking man walked in with our food.

"Elron, this is Mackenzee Lawson, my date for tonight. Mackenzee, this is Elron Longfellow, my personal chef and good friend."

"Hello, Miss Lawson," Elron said with a smile.

"Hi, Elron, nice to meet you," I replied with a smile as we shook hands.

"Nice to meet you, too. Enjoy," he said.

"Thank you," I said. I looked down at the savory steak and lobster along with a side of roasted vegetables and had to admit he prepared this as if we were at a 5-star steak and seafood restaurant. "Wow, this does look good. I think I just worked up an appetite."

"That's not the only thing you worked up," Richard said, as he put his napkin in his lap.

I flashed him an offended look. "And what exactly do you mean by that?" I looked around and down the hall and saw Elron staring at me, but he stood in a place where Richard could not see him. It almost freaked me out the way he kept staring at me. He then walked away. I looked up as Richard cut his steak and stuffed his offensive mouth with it. "Well?"

He took a sip of his water. "Well, what?"

"You obviously insinuated that I worked up more than just an appetite."

"Then eat," he replied with a grin, and then dipped his lobster into its cup of hot butter, which I felt like throwing my cup of it in his face!

"You sure have a weird sense of humor," I said, and began to eat the steak, and I had to instantly admit it was one of the best steaks I'd ever had. Perfectly seasoned and very tender and juicy. "This steak is delicious. It doesn't need any steak sauce."

"Elron's the best. We've known each other since high school; he's one of my best friends. He's always been into food."

"He definitely chose the right profession," I replied, as I started in on my lobster.

"He sure did," he said as he scooped up some more of his lobster and dipped it into its cup of butter.

"You know, I met someone very interesting while I was in that jail cell."

He looked up at me. I literally stopped him from eating. "Who?"

"I didn't get her name," I honestly replied. And now I really regret the fact that I didn't.

"You didn't get her name? Well, if she was up in that jail cell with you then she wasn't important to get her name."

"And why would you say something offensive like that?" I asked because I really wanted to know.

He sighed. "Mackenzee. You know perfectly well that people who are up in those jail cells are rarely good people. I bet that wasn't even her first time there. In fact, I know it wasn't. She's probably a repeat offender; practically lives in and out of there. I probably had a few of her cases in the past. If I see her, I'll probably know exactly who she is."

"Well, then it's too bad I didn't get her name, and I'm mad I didn't because she said something very interesting to me," I said, and then ate some of my vegetables, and if Elron made them like this all of the time then I would eat vegetables all of the time.

He rolled his eyes. "Okay, Mackenzee. What was so interesting that she said?"

You asked for it! I thought. "She told me that her sister went missing at The Club back in 1995."

"Oh, goodness! Here we go again!" he said as he shook his head. "I take it she didn't tell you her sister's name just like she didn't tell you her name, right?"

I instantly felt some shame. "No, she didn't," I said with my head slightly lowered. "But I believe her."

"You believe some in-and-out jailbird? Okay, Mackenzee. You know? You're really making me question my involvement with you."

"For what? What did I do? I didn't ask her about her sister. How could I? I didn't know her."

"Then how did the two of you get on the subject?"

"She asked me what I was thrown in there for. I wasn't gonna lie so I told her it was for trespassing at The Club. She told me how stupid it was for me to be arrested for it."

"I agree, that's why I had all of the charges dropped against you."

"Really?" I asked. "But isn't there something you can do about having that trespassing crap dropped?"

"No, because it's the law. It's private property. You had no business being back where you were. You were doing what you were charged with doing. But I took care of it. But I'm warning you once again, Mackenzee, if you do it again then the charges will stick. I'm not getting you out of it."

"I understand."

"I hope you do."

"But do you know anything about any disappearances from there in 1995?"

"Not at all. I wasn't DA back then. I was in my last year in college."

"That's not what I asked."

He put his fork and knife down as he glared at me. "Why are the disappearances of these women so important to you? How is it affecting your life?"

"How can it not affect my life, Richard? And how can it not affect yours? You're the DA of this city—you should know about every unsolved cold case there is. Come on, you must know something about it."

"I don't know a thing about it, Mackenzee—I'm telling you the truth. And even if I did, I couldn't tell you anything about it since I am the DA. There was nothing on Deandra Whitfield and I'm sure there's nothing on this other woman from 1995. When I looked up Deandra's case since you had me curious about it since I was there that night she allegedly went missing, I know I would've also found something on the woman from 1995 as well. I found nothing about any women disappearing from The Club, whether from over 30 years ago to now.

So now, if you don't mind, I would like to finish this wonderful meal Elron specially made for the two of us in peace."

"I understand," I replied. But there were a lot of things I didn't understand, as well as a lot of things I felt he was hiding; stuff he clearly did not want to talk about. Suddenly, I had to use the bathroom. "Um, where's your bathroom?"

"Around the corner to the left. The door should be open since I always like to keep it open when I have guests here because I don't want anyone opening doors in this house that they shouldn't be opening."

I didn't ask all of that, I thought. "Okay, thank you. I'll be right back." I got up as he continued to eat. I looked down the hall and saw Elron looking at his phone. He looked up at me and then continued to look at his phone. I went down another hall and took a left around the corner. There were no doors open. Several doors were in this hall and none of them were open like he said the bathroom would be. As I was about to open one door, another one opened . . . .

To a very young woman. She stood before me with a white tank top and hot pink short shorts on and no shoes on her feet. She was beautiful with long light brown curly hair and matching eyes. She was also very fit.

We stared at each other in some sort of surprise, especially since he'd told me no one was here but Elron who was here since he was his chef.

"Hi," she said with a smile.

"Hi," I replied. "Um, is that the bathroom?"

"Yes. You can go on in. I was just in there looking for something."

"Oh, okay. Thanks."

"You're welcome," she said, and turned around and walked down the hall, then turned another corner and disappeared.

I never got her name, but I figured Richard would tell me. She looked like his daughter even though if I could recall, he told me he had no children. Minutes after being in the bathroom, I walked back to the table and sat down to Richard looking at his phone. He nodded at me and put his phone away.

"Do you wanna take the rest of your food home with you?" he asked.

"Yes, sure. I definitely don't wanna waste it."

"I'll have Elron wrap it up for you," he said, and then took a sip of his water.

"Okay." I wanted to ask him so bad who the young woman was that came out of the bathroom, especially when he told me no one was here. I decided to keep my mouth shut about it for now. "So, are you gonna be at The Club tonight?"

"Why would I go tonight? It's Teen Night."

"It is?!" I said, as if I was a teen again myself.

"You sound excited," he said with a grin. "Do you plan on going?"

"Very funny," I said, and took a sip of my drink . . . but with full caution since he was in this room alone with it.

He looked at his watch. "I have some business to tend to, so let me get you home."

"Okay," I said, relieved that this wasn't gonna last for another hour since I felt our conversation wasn't going anywhere, and neither was a potential relationship. But I had to stay in touch with him because I felt he did know something about these disappearances. He just didn't wanna tell me.

Several minutes later, he was driving me home. "So, who was DA before you?" I asked.

"My dad," he replied as he looked straight ahead.

"What? Really?" I asked.

"Yeah, he was. Why is that so surprising? Everyone knew I was gonna succeed him. It wasn't even a competition. The Elmhurst men have been DAs in this city since my grandfather, Richard Elmhurst I. My dad, Richard Elmhurst II, had been the DA since I was in high school, up until I became it several years ago. No one can do the job that we all have done."

"Sounds like you have some big shoes to fill."

"And I'm filling them just fine, Mackenzee."

I nodded as I stared out the window as I could feel him staring right at me. I looked ahead . . . .

And saw the black BMW coming right towards us in the opposite direction with the Club *88 license plates!*

I looked back at it as it went past us. "Um . . . did you see that car?"

"What car?"

I sighed. "Never mind."

I sat back in my seat. I just didn't wanna get into it with him. There was no way he could not have seen the car that'd just past us, which made me really question what was really going on with him. He was the third generation DA in this city, so that meant these disappearances started happening under his dad's watch, and I didn't even want to think about how many more people I was gonna unexpectedly meet who were gonna tell me about some loved one who'd went to The Club and weren't seen again to this day.

I looked down at my phone. I'd received at text . . . .

I need to talk to you about TC.

TC.

The Club.

The text was from Elron Longfellow.

CHAPTER TWELVE

"*D*amn, girl! Slow down!" I said with a huge grin as Porsha ate the leftovers I brought from Richard's house.

She laughed. "Can't help it! Damn, this is so fuckin' good! Never had a steak and lobster this good before."

"That's exactly what I said."

"What's his name again? Elroy?"

"*Elron*," I corrected her.

"Elron. Sorry. Yeah, he can throw it all the way down in the kitchen. You said he's one of Richard's best friends since high school, not just his personal chef, huh?"

"Yeah, that's what Richard told me. But I really need to find out why Elron texted me since I haven't had a chance to text him back. It's clear he wants to talk to me about something."

"What do you think it is?"

"It could be anything. I really can't be so sure. I didn't wanna text him back in the car because I didn't want Richard asking me who was I texting."

"It's none of his damn business."

"Yeah, you're right, it's not. But you know I have to stay on his good side because he is the one who not only bailed me out, he also had all of the charges dropped against me. If it wasn't for him, I'd still be sitting in jail because there was no way I could bail myself out however much money it was, and I forgot how much it was, actually, since I was so distraught about being arrested and all."

"Just don't get in trouble like that again. You know damn well I didn't have the money to bail you out. But you know he's gonna want something from you because of it."

"Well, he didn't get anything from me tonight but my time and a nice dinner that he didn't even prepare."

She laughed. "Well, you know it's all a matter of time before he wants something more than just treating you to a fancy dinner, especially at his home. Men with that kind of power in this city want something in return for doing something they didn't have to do for you."

"Well, if this city would've investigated Deandra's disappearance as well as now a woman who told me in jail that her sister went missing in 1995 and hasn't been seen since, then I wouldn't have to do all of this, Porsha. When I titled my new channel, *I'm Their Speaker*, I meant it."

She smiled. "I know you did. I just don't want you to get hurt. You see the trouble you got into earlier today, and if you do it again you said Richard will not bail you out."

"If I give him some pussy he will."

"Mackenzee!"

I laughed. "I know, I shouldn't talk like that because I know that's what he wants from me and wanted from me tonight—but he didn't get anything. But I got a very nice meal out of it."

"And I'm finishing this meal since you had a ton of it left over."

"I still wasn't that hungry. Oh! And another thing."

She looked up from eating the lobster. "What?"

"There was a young woman at his house when I went to go use the bathroom."

"Who was she?"

"I have no idea. We never got each other's names. He never told me about having any kids. It was just so weird to see her there, I don't know why. But what I do know is that he lied to me and told me there was no one at his home before we even got there, and I know that because I asked him myself. It was clear to me that young woman is staying with him by her wearing a white tank and pink booty shorts. You know, like loungewear? But we know women wear looks like out of the house all the time."

"And a whole lot less."

"Yeah, you're right about that!"

"But like I said, she didn't tell me her name and I didn't tell her mine. If she was his daughter then I think she would've told me that. Besides, I could've swore he told me he had no children."

"That's what I thought he told you, too. Well, any guesses to who she could be?"

"Not at all, but I will definitely ask Elron when I see him."

"When are you gonna see him?"

I looked at my phone . . . coincidentally, it was another text from Elron.

Hi, Mackenzee. This is Elron. Did you get my first text?

Got it, Elron. I just didn't want to respond to you in the car while I was being driven home.

I perfectly understand.

Glad you do. So, what's up?

I got nervous as I waited for him to respond.

I need to talk to you about Richard.

Okay, what about him? And did you wanna talk in person?

Yes. At The Club.

At The Club? When?

Tonight.

Okay, see you there.

CHAPTER THIRTEEN

I drove into the parking lot at The Club, and it was filling up fast with eager teens from all over the city and surrounding cities who all came here for a night of fun. I definitely remembered these days! But little did I know, there were already allegations of girls going missing from here since 1990, and it all started with Deandra Whitfield, and who knew how many others.

As I watched the eager-to-have-fun teens line up outside as they waited for their chance to get in as I tried to find a place to park, I saw the lights to a black Cadillac Escalade flash twice. I knew this had of been Elron since I'd told him what kind of car I would be in. I drove over to where he was parked which was tucked in a corner where he had a perfect view of everyone going into this iconic establishment. I even couldn't believe how different it looked just several hours ago when I was snooping around here and got arrested for trespassing.

I got out of my car and into Elron's as old school music played on the radio. "Hey," I said with a smile.

"Hi, Mackenzee. Thanks for meeting me here."

"No problem," I glanced around his car. "I love this music."

"Thanks. It's 'Gonna Make You Sweat' by C+C Music Factory. Very popular group back then, and the DJ that night played it on the very first teen night here. It was the shit in the clubs all over the country back then in 1990, a lot of their songs were."

"I just bet they were," I said as I bobbed my head. "You have a nice SUV. It's beautiful."

"Thanks, but it's not mine," he informed me.

"Really? Who's is it?"

"My uncle's. He's a doctor. I didn't wanna drive my own car here."

He already had my interest piqued. "Why not?"

"Because I don't want anyone recognizing my car. It's not an expensive car, but I just didn't wanna drive it here. I don't want anyone who would recognize it thinking I was some predator up here checking out the selection of teen girls."

"Yeah, I don't blame you for that. But why did you wanna meet here of all places?"

"Because it has something to do with Richard."

"What?!"

"Yeah, it does, Mackenzee. And it has to do with the first ever teen night in 1990."

"Holy shit!" I said. "Do you mind if I record this? I won't say it's you because I wanna keep you anonymous."

"And I wanna stay anonymous, Mackenzee. I'm best friends with Richard, and I wanna stay best friends with him and keep my job as his personal chef. He has a lot of power in this city since he's the city's DA, but of course you already know that by now."

"Of course. He bailed me out of jail when I could still be sitting in there because I didn't have whatever amount I needed to get out. He also had all charges dropped against me because he told me I was facing quite a few. But I have to know what's up with him. He seems kind of reserved, but then again he's a fuckin' smartass at times. I'm so confused about his personality."

He grinned and then let out a chuckle. "That's Richard for you. He's always been like that."

"Oh, okay. You should know since you're best friends with him and have been before I was even born. And before I forget, I wanna tell you that was one of the best homecooked meals I've ever had earlier."

He blushed. "Thank you. I love my job, and I like I said, I don't wanna lose it."

"Can't blame you for that. But, okay, let's get to why you wanted to meet me here to talk about Richard. What about him?"

He sighed as he looked out the window. "Like I said, he was here for the first ever teen night back in the fall of 1990."

"Yeah, he told me he was here that night, but he didn't tell me who he was here with; just that he was here with some friends."

"Yeah, and I was one of the friends. He was on the football team; we both were. In fact, all of the guys we hung around back then were on the team."

"Okay, I'm listening."

"Well, I was with Richard and the guys that night right here for the first ever teen night here that night; I don't know why I feel like I have to keep stressing it, I just think it's important because it was the very first night and as you see, nights like these are still going on more than 30 years later. Damn, it was packed just like it is tonight. It's hard for me to believe it's been 33 years since I came here for the very first time, and now I'm watching a whole new generation come here for this night. Damn, times have changed."

"They most definitely have," I said, but I was waiting for him to tell me something important about that night, but I didn't want to rush him.

"Before I go on, you have a channel called *Mackenzee Jacey Speaks*, right?"

"I used to have that channel, but it kept being demonetized so I had to stop using it," I informed him.

"What's your new channel? Is it *I'm Their Speaker*?"

"Please don't tell anyone, especially Richard. It's supposed to be anonymous. I can't have anyone know it's me investigating these disappearances from here. How did you find it?"

"I was looking up the disappearances from here to see if anyone was talking about it since Richard had mentioned that you had asked him about them, and I only saw your channel talking about it. I thought your voice sounded familiar."

"I was the only channel that came up who has talked about this? Because when I was looking at stories about crimes and disappearances of Black women, an independent news station's channel came up talking about this. You didn't see the channel come up?"

"No, I didn't. Just your new channel."

I got out my phone and looked up the channel of the independent news station. "I can't find it," I said in confusion. And I really couldn't. "They took it down. And I don't think it was because they wanted it taken down. They had a lot of subscribers."

He stared at me. "Told you yours was the only one that talked about Deandra's disappearance."

I sighed. "But I wasn't the first one. It was their news channel that made me aware of Deandra's disappearance, and I was instantly intrigued by it because it happened in this city and I'd never heard about it, so I started my own investigation of it—but now it's not up anymore? Elron, *what is going on?*"

"If I knew, Mackenzee, I would tell you."

"Well, if theirs was taken down then it's all a matter of time before mine is as well because this is all I'm talking about."

"There are a lot of channels on that website, so it will probably take them time to find you unless a bunch of people report it. But maybe it wasn't because they talked about Deandra's disappearance. Maybe they had multiple violations of something."

"Yeah, who knows?"

"So that's why I want you to be very careful, Mackenzee, if you still want to investigate this. When I was cooking, Richard was talking to me about this. He said he had to bail his date out of jail, which was obviously you. He said you were arrested for trespassing here. Are you sure you can be on this property?"

"They never said I couldn't, especially Richard."

He grinned. "Okay, just wanted to make sure."

"So, what did you want to tell me about Richard? It sounded

through your text that you were pretty serious about what you have to tell me."

"It is, Mackenzee," he informed me.

"Well, okay, I'm listening."

He sighed and put his head back on the headrest. "Listen, before I tell you what I want to tell you, I need this to stay between us for right now until I say it's okay that you tell others, so that means not even saying anything on your channel about this because he'll know it's me who told you."

I was disappointed by this because I felt my audience should know whatever he was gonna tell me because that was the whole reason why I started the channel. "Okay, but hopefully one day I would be able to tell them, but for right now, it will stay between us. I promise." I extended my hand out for a shake.

He smiled and shook my hand. "Okay, I believe you." He sighed as he stared at the crowd as teens from all over this city walked towards the line and stood in it, and it got very long within minutes. "Okay, as you know, I was here at the very first teen night in the fall of 1990 with Richard and some of our other friends . . . ."

The Club: Teen Night: Fall 1990

"So, we won the game so the bet is on! Who do you want from Saint Maran West, man?" Antonio asked, as C+C Music Factory's "Here We Go, Let's Rock & Roll (featuring Freedom Williams and Zelda Davis)" played.

"Trevor's ex-girl," Richard said with a huge grin, and took a sip of his drink.

They all laughed as they nodded in agreement.

"Trevor's ex-girl is fine as hell, man! She's got to be the finest girl at Saint Maran West!" Antonio said.

"Yeah, she is. Too bad she doesn't go to our school," Elron said, and looked at his watch.

"You really gonna do it, huh?" Antonio said.

"It's a bet, isn't it? Besides, they're not together anymore," Richard said.

"Then why are they out there dancing with each other like they are?" Elron asked.

"Because they have a kid together," Richard said. "That's what Trevor told me."

"Damn, that's fucked up. Who the hell would want a kid when they're only 17 years old?" Antonio said.

"He was 15 when she was born, so that makes her 2 years old," Elron informed them. "Damn! It looks like Deandra's arguing with him! She just left the floor!"

"Shit! I hate to be him!" Antonio said with a huge grin. "But you better make your move, man."

"I am," Richard said, and got up from the table.

"And I hate to miss what goes down because I gotta get home because unlike the two of you, I still have a curfew," Elron informed them.

"I hate to be you!" Antonio said with a laugh.

"Fuck you, man," Elron said with a huge grin. "Call me and tell me what happens if anything does. See y'all later."

I stared at him in wide-eyed suspense. "So? What happened? Did Richard call you? Or Antonio?"

"Yeah, they called me, but not about what happened here. They called me about wanting to go shopping. I thought they were gonna tell me about something happening here while we all went shopping the next day, but they didn't say anything."

"And you didn't ask them?"

"No, because I figured that nothing did happen here. All they wanted to talk about was having fun here and the game we won against West that night before."

"Damn," I said as I shook my head. "You know, Mary told me Deandra called her when she was at a friend name Damian's house that night; a guy she went to school with that she had a crush on at the time. Mary said Deandra was very upset and wanted her to come back here to pick her up. She told her that Trevor and her got into an argument, but she didn't wanna talk about it. But when Mary got here, she said she couldn't find Deandra anywhere because it was closed, and she only knew that because she snuck back inside when the bouncer left the door for the night after she waited outside for several minutes for her since she wasn't allowed back in since it was closed. Now you tell me Richard got up from the table to go talk to Deandra after she stormed off the dance floor after arguing with Trevor?"

"Yeah, but I don't know that for sure, Mackenzee. He got up from the table, but I didn't see if he went to talk to her or not. I saw him walking in her direction, but once again, I didn't see if he actually talked to her or not—I can't stress that enough to you because I think it's very important. I don't wanna lie to you. Remember, I had to leave because unlike Richard and Antonio, I had a curfew. They were still only 17 as well, but they were able to stay out as late as they wanted especially since Richard's dad was DA at the time and Antonio's parents just didn't care since he hung with Richard and me."

"Damn. I feel like everything just fit for those few minutes, now it feels like it fell right back apart. Since you said it was a won bet, it's clear that he obviously did go talk to her that night, right?"

"It's possible, Mackenzee, but once again, I'm not sure. He never brought up Deandra after that night, quite possibly he never had until you asked him about it that night you met him on that Throwback Thursdays: 1990 Night."

"It's possible. And he pretended not to know her at all. He's already lied to me, Elron. Do you realize that?"

"Yeah, I do. But *I* haven't lied to you about anything."

I sighed. "Just when I thought I was getting somewhere."

He looked at me. "What I told you hasn't helped you?"

"Yes, what you've told me has helped me a lot. I realize just how much Richard has lied about all of this, especially about Deandra. Clearly, he knew who she was whether he talked to her that night or not, but I can't shake the fact that he *didn't* talk to her."

"Maybe, maybe not. But he may have not had anything to do with her disappearance, Mackenzee."

"I can't get myself to believe that he didn't, especially not after what you just told me."

"Well, I felt that it was vital information. But I can only tell you what I saw from my perspective."

"I understand. So, did you know about Trevor moving away?"

"Yeah, we all knew. No one threw him a party or anything. He just showed up for his last day of school at East, and we never saw him again after that."

"Really? He never talked about Deandra's disappearance from here?"

"No, he never talked about it. Remember, he was only here for a week after it happened before he moved away from here for good. No one really talked about it because no one really knew about it, especially since she went to Saint Maran West—but I still don't think it should've mattered what school she went to, it needed to be talked about regardless. It seemed as if it was kept so quiet. I asked Richard about it, and he said he was not aware that she hadn't been seen since being here that night—yes, I'm not gonna lie, I thought he was lying because I believed he did have some involvement with her since I saw him headed in her direction that night she stormed off of the dance floor from Trevor."

"Do you still think he did?"

He sighed. "Only he can tell you that, Mackenzee."

"Well, he hasn't told me shit, you know I've tried to get it out of him. Deandra deserves some justice here, and we don't even know if she's even still alive anymore. Do you think she is?"

He shrugged. "There's been no proof that she isn't alive. People go missing all of the time and are found alive after years and even decades. Maybe she got tired of her life here and set this all up. She was only a teen and already had a kid, her boyfriend broke up with her—"

"Wait! How do you know Trevor broke up with her?"

"He told us he did; said he wanted to be free his last year in high school. He told us during football practice when Richard noticed he didn't have Deandra's pictures in his gym locker anymore."

"Oh, okay. Well, do you personally think Trevor moved because of his involvement in Deandra's disappearance?"

"Yeah, I really do. Richard told me the cops were close to questioning him—"

"*Close* to questioning him?" I interrupted him. "He should've been the *first* to be questioned! He was her ex-boyfriend and her child's father! What the fuck is wrong with these cops in this city?!"

"Calm down, Mackenzee. I don't know why the cops didn't question him, okay? But it was like he knew they were moving in, so he moved away. We all think he moved because he had something to do with her disappearance and his mom was complicit in it. We think he did kill her, and if he did, he's gotten away with it for 33 years."

"No one gets away with anything no matter how many years have gone by."

"Yeah, I definitely agree with that, but right now, if he did this, he's doing a damn good job at eluding the cops for over three decades now."

"He hasn't been eluding anyone when they never questioned him or anyone about her disappearance to begin with. Mary told me she and Deandra's mom went to the cops that day she didn't come home, and they haven't done anything they said they were gonna do. It's been 33 years. They just don't give a fuck."

"I agree."

"And I guess you can agree that's why it was kept out of the local news and radio stations here?"

"Yes, I agree with you, Mackenzee. People just went on with their lives as if nothing happened. I even believed that Deandra went missing intentionally because she was probably overwhelmed with her life back then because that's what this city wanted people to obviously believe. Unfortunately, she was simply forgotten."

"But not by me, and especially not by Mary and her mom and I'm sure by her other family members and friends. And especially by her daughter who is definitely now old enough to understand. And they deserve answers. If this happened to someone in Richard's family or other families who have power in this city, then they would've been on this case since day one."

"And I definitely agree with that."

I looked towards the entrance as cars came in by the droves. There was non-stop traffic. This was definitely the place to be and be seen for teens in this city and surrounding areas, and it'd been like this since this establishment opened. I noticed a BMW come into the entrance and headed right towards us.

CLUB 88.

"Oh my god!"

"What?" Elron asked, as I clearly startled him.

"That car!"

"Which one?"

"The new BMW! That was the car that I know had of followed me and Porsha when we left here that night I met Richard!"

"Are you sure?" he asked, as he looked at me and then looked at the car once again.

I noticed how the person in the car pulled up beside Elron on the driver's side. I could hear him getting out of the car!

"Get down!" he ordered. And then rolled down his window.

"Shit!" I said, and dove down on my seat to where he couldn't see me.

"What's up, man?" the man said, and slapped hands with Elron.

"Not much, man. Just checking out the crowd. Brings back a lot of memories."

"Sure does, man. You meeting someone here?"

"Now who would I meet here? This is Teen Night. I don't have an interest in any teens. I honestly don't know what the hell I'm doing here. I was just about to come inside to see how things were."

"Well, come on in, man. You know this place is practically yours as well as mine and the others."

"I know, man. I'll be in there in a few minutes. Y'all watching the football game?"

"It's in the second quarter; I've been listening to it on the radio. Let me get in there, man."

"Okay," Elron said, and slapped hands with him again. He rolled up his window. "Stay down," he told me.

I nodded as I tried to control my breathing. I knew it wasn't Richard since I knew it wasn't his voice and I knew his voice well by now. I watched from being ducked down almost underneath the seat as Elron's eyes seemed to have followed this person.

"Okay, you can get up."

"Damn, I'm glad you told me to get down because I didn't want that person to see me either. In fact, when Richard was driving me home, I saw the same car go past us as if he was on his way to Richard's house. Did anyone come to his house after he left to take me home?"

"No, they didn't," he informed me.

"Okay. Oh! Also, while I was there, there was a very young woman there. She could not be any older than 21 years old. She actually didn't even look older than 18 years old. Who is she?"

He gave me a confused look. "Mackenzee, there was no one at his house when you were there. Just you, Richard, and me."

My mouth dropped in shock! "No, Elron. That's where you're wrong. There was a young woman there. I ran into her when I was looking for the bathroom. She walked out of the bathroom. She was really beautiful. I thought she was Richard's daughter or something."

"Richard has no children."

"That's what I thought so I was wondering who she was."

"Mackenzee, there was no one there. I was there all day preparing the meal I served the two of you."

"STOP!" I screamed.

"Calm down now," he said.

"Then stop fucking with me!"

"I'm not fucking with you. I know it's a big house and I would've known someone else was there. I think we should end this conversation. I need to get inside there since I said I would go in."

"Go into a teen night? What the hell for?"

He laughed. "I'm not going in there to party with teens, I'm going in there to be with my friends who own the place. There's a whole other area in there that's for people who work there and their friends and families." He unlocked the doors. "Thanks for meeting me here."

"No problem at all. You told me a lot tonight," I said. *But not enough,* I thought.

"Glad to have been of some help," he said with a smile.

I got out of the SUV with caution and walked back to my car. I looked around for the BMW; it was clear whoever he was, he drove to the back of this building where I was caught trespassing since I'd seen for myself there was a parking lot back there. I watched as Richard drove off as the SUV went towards the back of the building, turned a corner, and disappeared. I felt there was still so much he hadn't told me; he was just too afraid to do so. I knew just what he'd told me tonight was the beginning of something much bigger than even he wanted to admit, and there was so much I believed he knew but he just wasn't sure if he could trust me with it.

CHAPTER FOURTEEN

"think I already need to take a break on this case," I said, as I laid down on the couch in the family room. "But I can't."

"And why can't you?" Porsha asked, as she brought me a hot cup of tea, and sat it on the table in front of me.

"Because no one else cares about this besides me and Mary. That's enough people to care, of course, because at least some people do. But it's not enough, you know what I mean?"

"Yes, I know what you mean, Mackenzee. Well, I care, and it seems like Elron cares, too, since he wanted to talk in private to you. But is this really worth you getting hurt over? I mean, you got arrested and Richard could've made sure those charges stuck. I think he really has a more-than-friends interest in you, Mackenzee, so you really need to be careful with him."

"But I have more of an interest in these cases than I have in being more than friends with him. Sorry, but I do. I still think he's hiding something about it. Elron told me Richard was gonna talk to Deandra that night because of some bet that was won; I guess it was for them winning the game against West, which we know is the school Deandra went to. Elron said Richard said he wanted 'Trevor's ex-girl' which was Deandra."

"Wow," Porsha said, and sat on the reclining chair adjacent to me. "So, Richard *did know* who she was?"

"Yeah, he did. But I don't think he ever met her previously; Elron never said that he had. They were all sitting at their table and saw Trevor and Deandra arguing and Deandra storming off the dance floor. Elron said Richard then got up and was gonna make his move to go talk to her, but he told me he had to leave because he had a curfew unlike Richard and a guy name Antonio who was also there with them that night."

"So Elron never actually saw Richard approach Deandra and talk to her?"

I sighed. "He told me he never did."

"Do you believe him?"

"Yeah, I actually do," I said, as I still laid down. Suddenly, I jumped up! "Oh, shit!"

"What?"

"Dammit!"

"What is it, Mackenzee?"

I shook my head. "I forgot to ask Elron who that was in the BMW! You know how I told you when I got back here that the person in the BMW with the CLUB 88 license plates came up to The Club and pulled right up to Elron while we were sitting in his uncle's SUV talking? Damn! He told me to get down because he obviously did not want that person to see me, and it was obviously a man he was talking to, but I didn't recognize the voice."

"Damn," she said as she shook her head. She took a sip of her tea. "So, you have no idea who he was, huh?"

"No idea," I said, and took a sip of my tea. "And it's clear to me that Elron didn't want him to see me or for me to see him."

"Yeah, I wonder why that is?"

"Me too," I said, and took another sip of my tea. "But you know I'm gonna find out."

She sighed as she shook her head. "Look, Mackenzee, I think you should seriously consider taking that break you mentioned. I just think all of this is too much too soon. I believe you're getting close to some shit that people don't want you to know about and especially be involved in."

"And that's exactly why I need to keep at this. Oh! And another thing."

"What is it?"

"I asked Elron who the girl was who was at Richard's house when I was there, and he told me there was no girl at the house."

"What?!"

"Yes! That's what he told me! I know I wasn't going crazy. I talked to a girl who was at Richard's house when I went to use the bathroom. She came out of it when I was just about to open another door since all the doors were shut. I know he knows who she is; that house is big but there's no way he didn't know she was there."

"What if he didn't?"

"He's full of shit. He knows who I'm talking about. I just have to find her connection in all of this."

"You think she could have some kind of connection to what's going on?"

"Yeah, I think she could. I mean, after all, she was at Richard's house. She's obviously not his daughter because Elron told me he has no kids."

"Sounds like something is up with her. But I don't think she's his girlfriend or whatever since he had you over there."

"I know, but you never can tell." I looked at my phone. "Oh my god!"

"What?"

"The woman!"

"What woman?"

"The woman who was in the jail cell with me! She just contacted me!"

"What?! How did she know your name?"

"She doesn't! She found my channel talking about Deandra's disappearance! She's the one who told me her sister went missing from The Club in 1995! Oh my god!"

"Well, she's gonna know it's you that she was in the jail cell with her when you talk to her again, Mackenzee! Or are you gonna tell her it's you?"

"I'm gonna have to, but I'm gonna have to tell her not to tell anyone. I don't want my cover blown. Elron said he found my channel, too, after talking to Richard about me and about the fact that I was asking him questions about Deandra's case the first night we met. I need to call her," I said, and dialed the number she gave me through the email. I put it on speaker.

"Hello?"

"Hi, is this Kamiah?" I asked.

"Yes, it is. Who is this?"

"This is . . ." my voice trailed off.

Porsha looked at me in suspense since I still didn't know whether or not I should've told her my name. *"Tell her!"* she mouthed to me.

"Hi, Kamiah. This is Mackenzee. You contacted me through an email and told me to call you since seeing my show *I'm Their Speaker?"*

"Yes! Hi! I didn't think anyone would get back to me this fast!"

She sounded very excited that I had, but I had to tell her that I was the one in the same jail cell as her earlier today. I was actually surprised that she was out as well. "Yes, I do respond pretty quickly when someone writes to me; I think it's rude not to. So, you wanted to tell me about your sister who you said went to The Club in 1995 and hasn't been seen since?"

"Yes, my older sister, Gazelle. I really haven't talked about this that much, but I feel I really need to since it seems like someone is finally giving these cases the attention they deserve because no one in this shitty city has done a damn thing about it. I really wanna talk in person."

I looked at Porsha; she nodded back as a way of telling me that I should because this was too important not to. "Okay, that's fine. When and where?"

"At my house tomorrow. Are you gonna put me on your show?"

"If you don't mind because like Mary Landry for her best friend Deandra Whitfield, I think people need to hear about it."

"There's nothing I would love more."

CHAPTER FIFTEEN

I walked up to one of the many bottom-floor apartments in this older complex. It was a very lively complex with kids running everywhere and people just hanging out. I'd never been here before but had been passed it numerous times going to or from wherever, and it'd been here for as long as I could remember. I rang the doorbell as I took in the surroundings as I'd hoped to have some more information about Gazelle like what Mary gave me about Deandra.

The door opened to the woman I was in the jail cell with.

"Mackenzee?" she asked. It was as if she couldn't believe I was standing here in front of her.

"Yes, I'm Mackenzee," I said with a smile.

"Oh my god! You were the woman I was in the cell with—am I right?"

Yep, she remembered!

"Yes, that's me. I'm sorry I didn't tell you my name in there."

"It's perfectly okay. Come on in."

"Thank you," I said.

She held open the door for me and then stepped outside and looked around. She came back in and shut the door and locked it.

"You can have a seat on that couch. I tried to clean it up as much as I could since I knew you would be over here."

"It's fine, thank you," I said, and sat down.

"Can I get you anything to drink?"

"No thank you, I'm good."

"Okay," she said with a smile, and sat on the couch with me. She turned off the TV, and then grabbed a pack of Newport's and took a cigarette out of it. "Do you mind?" she asked before she lit up.

"No, I don't mind," I lied. I really didn't want to tell someone what they could do in their own home even though she'd asked, so I tolerated it like how I did at Mary's.

She lit up and took a puff. She shook her head. "It's amazing that fate would have it that I decided to steal something at the store that day—essentials since I hadn't gotten paid yet from my former job, so yeah, I was fired—that I would end up in a cell with a woman who has a show about investigating these disappearances. A friend of mine told me about it when I got out of jail, so I decided to check it out."

"I'm glad you did and that your friend found it. I just started the channel because I wanted to give Deandra Whitfield a voice as well as your sister and others who were last seen at The Club and have not been seen since. It's a damn shame that this city has ignored this for so many years."

"Yeah, too many years," she said, and took another puff off of her cigarette. She shook her head once again. "I meant it when I told you I hate that place, Mackenzee. Just having to go past that ugly brick black building whenever I have to go somewhere in this city just makes me sick knowing that was the last time Gazelle was seen was there. And she hasn't been seen or heard from since 1995."

The Club: Spring 1995

"I can't believe we're finally 21 now! No more fake fuckin' IDs trying to get in here or other places!" Gazelle said with a big smile as she walked in with her friend Vonda for a typical 21-and-over night at The Club.

"Yeah, it wasn't as long as a wait as we thought it would be when they found out that our ID's were fake just a year ago, but now that we're officially in here legally, I really don't see the big deal, do you?"

"Actually, I do. Everyone is older and we can drink legally!"

"Okay, yeah, I *definitely* agree with that!"

They laughed as they headed to the bar as the place was packed as Craig Mack's "Flava In Ya Ear" played.

"It's actually a pretty busy night since this is on a weeknight," Vonda said.

"It is. I'm glad I have the week off of work, so I don't have to worry about what time I have to get home tonight and waking my mom and everyone else up in the house."

"Well, you know you can stay with me if we get out of here really late tonight," Vonda said with a smile.

"It's a deal," Gazelle said.

The bartender approached them.

"Excuse me, ladies," he said.

"Yes?" they replied with big smiles.

"The man over there with the black shirt on wants to buy the two of you a drink," the bartender informed them.

They looked at each other and smiled even bigger!

"Um, since I'm driving, he can buy me a Pepsi," Vonda said.

"Well, I'm not, so he can buy me a Zima," Gazelle said.

"Coming right up," he said with a smile.

Minutes later, the bartender gave them their drinks. They lifted them up to the man in the black shirt; he smiled as he returned the gesture.

"He looks familiar," Vonda said, and took a sip of her Pepsi.

"Really? From where? Because you know we didn't go to any of the Saint Maran public schools."

"Of course not. I didn't live in this city at the time. We probably would've never met each other if we didn't go to a private school for all four years of high school."

"And that's rare that I did because everyone in this city usually went to Saint Maran East or West high schools."

"Yeah, but you didn't!"

"I know, so that's why I really don't know too many people my age in this city."

Vonda nodded. Her eyes got big. "Oh my god, Gazelle!"

"What?"

"He's coming over here!"

"Who?"

"The guy in the black shirt who bought us the drinks!" she reminded her.

"Oh, shit! I need to refresh my makeup!" Gazelle laughed.

But before they knew it, he was standing right behind them.

"Hello, ladies," he said with a smile.

"Hi," Gazelle and Vonda replied with even bigger smiles.

"Thanks for the drinks," Vonda said.

"Yes, thanks," Gazelle said.

"You're both welcome," he said, as Adina Howard's "Freak Like Me" began playing.

Everyone cheered and crowded the dance floor.

"Wanna dance?" he asked Gazelle.

"Sure!" Gazelle said with excitement.

Vonda smiled and then took a sip of her drink as a man approached her seconds later and asked her the same thing, and all of them headed out to the dance floor. During the song, she watched as this man kept bending down to Gazelle as if he was asking her questions. She noticed how Gazelle nodded, and before the song was over with, she saw her leave the dance floor with him. "GAZELLE!"

"What are you yelling for?" the man asked her with a grin.

"Thanks for the dance," she replied, and quickly left the floor.

She tried her best to muddle through the bottleneck of this crowd as she tried to keep her sights on Gazelle and the man who bought them drinks, but she lost sight of them as they turned a corner and disappeared.

"And she was never seen or heard from again," Kamiah said as her head was lowered. She lifted it and took another puff off her cigarette and blew the smoke up in the air. She shook her head. "That's really all I know about that night. That's really all Vonda could tell us."

"Where is Vonda today?"

"Who knows?" she replied, and put out her cigarette in the ashtray and immediately lit up another one. "My family gave her hell about Gazelle's disappearance. I believe every word she said about what happened that night. I don't think any of this was her fault. Gazelle loved attention from men. She was very attractive. And she really loved the fact that this guy gave all of his attention to her after he bought her and Vonda drinks. Vonda told us she knew he bought them drinks because he wanted to talk to Gazelle, but was being nice and bought her one as well since she was with her."

"Who was this guy?"

"He was a pro-football player, I guess. This is his hometown and he went to one of the Saint Maran high schools. I guess he was the first player ever to make it to the pros from this city so they apparently made a big deal out of him so I believe Vonda when she said she can see why Gazelle was so excited to talk to him, but she didn't even know who he was until he'd told her."

"What's his name?" I asked, as she had my curiosity piqued.

"Vonda told us his name was Damian Wesson."

I gasped! "*Damian Wesson*?! You're kidding, Kamiah!"

"No, I'm not. That's what Vonda said his name was."

"Do you know he's Mary Landry's baby daddy? The best friend of Deandra Whitfield? The girl who went missing 5 years before from The Club in 1990?"

"I saw the video of your interview with her, but I don't remember her mentioning him. If she did, she obviously only mentioned his first name, not his last. Damian is a popular boy's name."

"Yeah, it is. I'm just shocked about this, that's all. He went to Saint Maran West, by the way."

"Oh, okay," Kamiah said with a nod.

"Damn! This is getting more and more interesting. Now I gotta find Damian because he may hold the key to Gazelle's disappearance."

"Hold the key? *I know* he's the direct cause of her disappearance, and there's nothing he can do or say that will convince me that he isn't. He obviously thinks just because he was an professional athlete back then that he could and still thinks he can get away with what he did, and yeah, he's right. He's gotten away with it for 28 years."

"So you really think he had something to do with her disappearance?"

"The way Vonda told it to me and my family, I think he is the one-and-only suspect. And we found out from Vonda that the police never questioned him, either, just like how no one questioned anyone about Deandra Whitfield's disappearance."

"This is getting crazy," I said. "But I know Damian didn't have anything to do with Deandra's disappearance from The Club since he was at home with her best friend Mary when it happened."

"Well, Vonda said Gazelle was with Damian when they turned that corner and she never saw her again. It's like out of some horror movie or something, Mackenzee. I thought Vonda was making all of this up when she first told us, but then I saw how real it was when the days, weeks, months—and now years and years and almost three decades—have gone by, and Gazelle never came home or called us to let us know she was okay."

"You think she went off with Damian?"

"Yeah, I think she did. I think that fucker is hiding so much, and he's gotten away with it for 28 years."

"Well, you know I'm gonna do all I can to contact him since I have Mary as a direct connection to him. Everything just seems so connected now."

Kamiah nodded. "It does. Thank you so much for investigating this."

"You're welcome. Like I say on my show, I'm definitely their speaker."

"And it's been a long time since we've needed one. These disappearances have been unsolved for way too long."

"And I won't stop until I solve every one of them."

"I know you won't. But I got another question for you?"

I smiled. "What is it?"

"Were you really looking for your earring at The Club when they caught you trespassing?"

My smile broke out into a laugh. "No, I wasn't. I was looking around the place to see if there was a back entry since Mary had told me that her and Deandra were led back there by a bouncer name Paul —a good friend of Mary's older brother, Jack—at the time since the line was too long. They got in that way. I saw that she wasn't lying about it, but I never thought she was. I just had to check it out for myself. I also saw that it definitely was a nice area with another parking lot and spacious deck for the warmer months and another building that was smaller in size that was probably for private parties I'm assuming for the colder months. Looks like a nice place on the outside just like how it is on the inside."

She smiled. "That's what I thought. Well, I really wish you luck in your investigation on this. I can't wait to tell my family that someone is finally investigating this like how they should be, but I won't show them what you look like since you said you want to remain anonymous, and I respect that and can't blame you for it. If I remember more, I'll let you know."

"And I appreciate that."

CHAPTER SIXTEEN

"So, you think Damian has something to do with the disappearance of Gazelle in 1995, huh?" Mary asked, as she sat down across from me at her kitchen table.

"Well, that's what Kamiah told me. I really believe she thinks so, and I can't blame her for thinking it because she was only told what she was told by Gazelle's best friend Vonda at the time."

"So I take it you haven't been able to get in touch with Vonda?"

"No, I haven't," I informed her. "I did ask Kamiah did she know where she was today and she said she didn't know, especially since Vonda wasn't originally from this city. Her and Gazelle also didn't go to any of the Saint Maran public schools; just the private religious ones."

"Yeah, I figured that because I would've definitely remembered them since Deandra and I would've been in the same grade or a grade above them, something like that. But yeah, it doesn't surprise me that Gazelle got involved with Damian, I just wish he was involved with his first son, my son, Demetrius."

"I'm so sorry to hear that, Mary. It's sounds like you've really had it rough."

"Yeah, I have, Mackenzee, more than anyone would ever know.

Damian doesn't even know he's a grandfather now and wanted nothing to do with Demetrius when he was born. Remember, I left this city three years after Deandra's disappearance because I was so disgusted with the fact that they never did anything about it, so I wasn't here when Damian came back here, obviously, and he probably came back here during the time when he had some time off because he left college early to go to the pros; I heard he only had a year left of school."

"Wow. Well, do you know where he's at today? Because I really need to talk to him since it was confirmed that he was probably the last one to see Gazelle from what Kamiah told me what Vonda had told her."

"He doesn't live here anymore; I know that for a fact."

"I didn't think so. But do you know where he is?"

She lit up a cigarette and took a puff. "He lives in Saint Thomas, yes, the island. Funny how he could go from living here in a city called Saint Maran to living on the beautiful Caribbean Island of Saint Thomas—and there's nothing saint about him. He ran away from his responsibilities of being a father to Demetrius to pursue his dreams of being a professional athlete—and he did it. Now he's 50 years old living on an island with his wife of over 20 years with their teenage kids. She probably doesn't even know he had a kid while he was a senior in high school—*our* kid together. A kid he has never seen and hasn't given me any child support for, and he made millions in his career as an athlete but didn't give me shit for Demetrius."

"I'm so sorry to hear this, Mary. I know you've had it rough with never being able to find out what happened to Deandra and everything else. Do you think Damian will talk to me? Because I really need to find out from him what happened that night and see if it matches to what Kamiah told me about Gazelle."

"I don't see why not. I know for a fact he would talk to you before he'd talk to me. I'll give you his contact info."

"That would be great," I said with a smile.

Suddenly, I heard the front door open. I looked at Mary.

"They're home! Just in time!" she said with excitement as she got out of her chair.

"Grandma!" a cute little girl said as she came up to her and hugged her.

"Hey, baby!" Mary said with a big smile and lifted her on to her hips. I noticed how there was a man standing with her as he smiled at me. "Mackenzee, this is my son, Demetrius and my beautiful granddaughter, Syriana."

Wow, this was real, I thought.

"Nice to meet the two of you," I said with a smile as I shook Demetrius's hand, and I knew Mary didn't want to hear this, but he looked just like his dad from the pictures I'd seen of Damian.

"Nice to meet you, too, Mackenzee," he replied with a smile. "My mom really appreciates what you're doing for her best friend from high school."

I smiled at Mary as she smiled back at me. "Thank you."

"You're welcome, Mackenzee. No one has cared as much as you have, and I don't think anyone ever will."

"Like I told Kamiah, I will do everything I can to make sure the disappearances of your loved ones will be solved."

"And I can't wait until they are," Mary said.

"Me too," Demetrius said with a smile.

Several minutes later, I waved to them as I left the house. I walked down the stairs and almost completely stopped cold.

There sat the BMW with the CLUB 88 license plates!

And I knew they weren't in a neighborhood like this by accident.

I tried to keep my cool as I walked to Porsha's car and got in.

"So, how did it go?"

"Go," I ordered.

"What? What's wrong?" she asked, as she slowly pulled off.

"It's them. The person or people in the BMW."

"What?!"

"What the hell do you mean *what*, Porsha?! You didn't see them sitting right behind you?"

"No, Mackenzee, I didn't! I was looking at my phone!"

"I told you to never let your guard down in this area or anywhere, you're too grown not to know that by now."

"I know, I'm sorry. But I saw a car drive up in the driveway of Mary's home. Who was that?"

"Demetrius with his daughter Syriana. She's staying with them for a few weeks, that's what they told me. Oh my god, Porsha, that man looks *just like his dad!*"

"Oh, I believe it! It's too bad Damian never wanted anything to do with him."

"Well, that's his loss. He's a very nice man and has a beautiful and sweet daughter who should know her grandfather. But he's not gonna have a choice but to have something to do with me talking to him about this investigation into Gazelle's disappearance because right now, I feel I'm only one person away from solving this one, that's if he tells me the truth."

"If he has nothing to hide then he should tell you the truth."

I looked behind me. "Looks like the BMW didn't follow me."

"Do you think they were sitting there waiting for you?"

"Yeah, I think they were. But I have a feeling they were also checking out Mary's home as well and actually followed her son and granddaughter home."

"You really think so?"

"Yeah, I do. I'll find out from her because they were not sitting there when I came there to talk to her because I know I would've seen them. I think this has more to do with her than it has to do with me. The Club definitely knows something is up with someone investigating these disappearances, and they saw Mary on my show, more than likely."

"And they also saw you coming out of her home, Mackenzee!"

"They have no proof I was there talking about the disappearances, now do they?"

"Yeah, that's true—but still."

"But still as long as they don't follow me all around this city and try and hurt me, I'm still gonna continue with this investigation, and Damian is next on the list to contact."

CHAPTER SEVENTEEN

<u>I'M THEIR SPEAKER</u>
EXCLUSIVE INTERVIEW WITH FORMER PRO-FOOT-
BALL STAR AND SAINT MARAN NATIVE DAMIAN
WESSON
WHAT HE KNOWS ABOUT THE 1995 DISAPPEARANCE
OF GAZELLE RAGLAND AT THE CLUB; HIS CONNEC-
TION TO THE CLUB 1990 DISAPPEARANCE OF
DEANDRA WHITFIELD, AND THE FIRSTBORN SON HE'S
NEVER FORGOTTEN ABOUT

"Wow, you sure are a long way from home. Your home and the background are beautiful," I said, as I stared in complete admiration at the screen of Mary's one-and-only baby daddy, the former pro-football star Damian Wesson. And even though Mary didn't want to hear this from me, but he was quite handsome as well, with medium dark skin, bald head, and a close-shaven, full-greyish-white beard. His logo Gucci T-shirt exposed both of his arms that were full of beautiful, colorful tattoos of various things that meant a lot to him. He'd also appeared to be in great physical shape and had aged just as well as he lived.

"Thank you. I'm a long way from Saint Maran, that's very true. But Saint Thomas has been my home for almost 20 years. I was actually wondering when someone was gonna contact me about this story. It's been so long since I'd heard anything about it."

"Yes, it has been 33 years for Deandra and 28 years for Gazelle. These women both went missing after being at The Club. No one has seen or heard from them since. I'm thinking since it was said that you met Gazelle there that night she went missing—"

"I've met a lot of women," he interrupted me. "Millions over these years and that's no exaggeration. It's just the profession and lifestyle I was in; and I'm still in the lifestyle all due to great investments and not spending all the money I was blessed to make. But it only took one woman for me to wanna be with for the rest of my life."

"That's nice, Damian. So, how long have you and your wife been married?"

"For 25 years," he said with a big smile, and then took a sip of his energy drink in a tall and lean black can. "She was and still is the only woman for me."

"I see. So, let's go back to 1990."

"Way back to when MC Hammer ruled hip hop, huh?" he said with a huge grin. "Damn, those were the days!"

I nodded with a smile. "So, you were at The Club, too, with your friends on the first ever teen night that night, right?"

"Exactly right."

"Who were you there with?"

"Just Montell," he replied, and took another sip of his drink. "It was crowded as hell in there; could barely move. I just remember seeing Mary first and saw how Deandra was dancing with her ex-boyfriend, Trevor. Mary wanted to dance since a popular song came on, so we danced next to Deandra and Trevor, and I'd asked Mary and Deandra did they wanna come back to my house with Montell since it was so crowded in there. Mary was down with it, but Deandra wanted to stay since she said she had to be home early to take care of her daughter Ashley who was only 2 years old at the time. I said how good that was of her that she knew her priorities and all, and Mary and I left The Club to go have some private fun."

"You left your friend Montell there?"

"Yeah, he wanted to stay there; saw some other guys from the football team and wanted to see if he would get a girl and get lucky. We got whooped bad by East just that day before."

I stayed quiet about that being my alma mater since I had to remain anonymous. "So, when did Mary get that phone call from Deandra?"

"About two hours after we left."

~

Damian's House: Fall 1990

"Hello?"

"Hi, Damian?" Deandra said.

"Yes, it's me. What's up, Deandra?" he said, as he closed the refrigerator door.

"I need to speak to Mary. Is she still there? Because I tried her on her private line at home and she didn't answer."

"Yeah, she's still here," he said, as he walked back towards his bedroom. "Something wrong? You sound upset."

"I just need to speak to Mary."

He walked back in his bedroom as Mary laid butt-naked in the bed. He told her it was Deandra and that she'd sounded upset. Minutes later, he watched as she got dressed immediately and then left out the door. Not too long after she'd left, his phone rang once again.

"Hello?"

"Hey, Damian man," Montell said.

"Hey, man. What's up? Are you still at The Club?"

"Yeah, I'm still here, man. I'm just about to leave."

"Okay, what's going on? Just to let you know, Mary's on her way back there."

"For what?"

"To pick up Deandra."

"To pick up Deandra? I just saw Deandra go off with some dude several minutes ago."

"For real, man? With who?"

"I have no idea, man. Look, I'm about to get out of here; just wanted to ask you if you wanted me to stop and get you something to eat before I come by."

"Sure, man. My mom didn't go grocery shopping once again, so whatever you wanna get is fine with me."

"So Montell had absolutely no idea who she went off with that night? Because Mary told me that it seemed as if Deandra got disconnected from her while they were talking on your phone."

"Yeah, that was true. That disconnection had her really concerned so she quickly got dressed and was in a big hurry. I even asked did she want me to go with her and she said she probably wouldn't have time to drop me back off at my home since she had to drop off Deandra and had a curfew as well. I'm lucky I did stay at home because I got that call from Montell minutes later telling me that he saw Deandra go off with some dude minutes before. Remember, this was 1990. There were no cell phones back then and my family didn't have the caller ID, either, like most didn't."

"So Montell didn't know who this guy was? Are you serious?"

"Yeah, unfortunately I am. There were a lot of people there that night."

"So he knew for sure it *wasn't* Trevor, her ex-boyfriend?"

"I don't know that for sure. He didn't say it wasn't him, he just told me he didn't recognize the guy so I'm assuming he either didn't know it was him because Trevor didn't go to our school, or it was a whole different guy he didn't know at all. I vaguely recognized Trevor myself and even asked Mary to confirm it with her was Trevor in fact Deandra's ex-boyfriend since they were out on the floor dancing when I walked up to her, and she told me that he was."

"Damn. Just when I feel like I'm getting so close it just all falls apart once again. So, how can I get in touch with Montell?"

"What do you need to get in touch with him for? He doesn't know anything. Besides, I lost contact with him over ten years ago. Who knows where he is now."

"Did the cops ever question him about Deandra's disappearance?"

"No, they didn't. They didn't question any of us because none of us had anything to do with it. She disappeared from a night-club, not at school. There were too many people there that night to sort through everyone. There are no surveillance videos."

"And how do you know that?"

"Because it was 1990. No one was recording any and everything on their cell phones for the world to constantly see 24/7 as well as all that livestreaming and FaceTime stuff, or there being live cameras of different angles on the inside and outside of the place for the whole world to watch on YouTube. It wasn't like how it is today."

I sighed. I couldn't hide how disappointing this was. "Yeah, you're right. So, Mary found out she was pregnant with your child not too long after Deandra's disappearance, right?"

"Yeah, that's right," he said, as I seemed to have taken his upbeat mood and brought it down.

"You look a little down now. Are you sure you wanna talk about it?"

"Now is finally the time."

"Okay, so tell me how it went."

"Well, as you know, Mary was dealing with Deandra's disappearance, and at that time it'd been a week since she'd been missing when she told me she was late and that she might be pregnant. I told her I didn't want any kids at that time and that I would help her pay for an abortion. She told me she didn't want one and was having the baby because it was her right. I told her it just wasn't a good time to have a child with the stress of her best friend missing and everything. But if she went on and had it that I would help her take of it."

"You did?! Because she told me you wanted nothing to do with it."

"That's a lie. When it was found out by everyone that she was pregnant, she took off to one of those schools for pregnant teens. She told me she had her rich family to help her and that she didn't need anything from me and that I would always be broke and miserable and jobless and a loser and will always be living in Saint Maran. Man, she went the hell off on me. I know she was stressed about Deandra, so I just let everything she said about me go. But even though I was broke at the time, I did get a job after football season was over with to help support the baby I knew was mine, but she didn't wanna talk to me; her parents didn't want to talk to me and didn't want me around and refused to let me see my own child. I said fine and went on with my life. I became everything she thought I never could or would be."

I nodded. "Do you know you're a grandfather now?"

"Yes, I know. But I can't consider myself to be one because I haven't even met my son who was born while I was in high school. It's amazing how someone could keep a person who is a part of you away from you for so long and blame you for it just because I wouldn't marry her after high school like she wanted me to do. I didn't love her back then and really don't have any love for her now."

"I'm sorry to hear that, Damian."

"I'm sorry I ever slept with her that night. The same night Deandra went missing. Wow. Now I always wonder had we both stayed at The Club that night if Deandra would still be here."

"It's something I'm sure everyone wonders about, Damian, but we can only still try to find out what happened to Deandra that night. But now, let's forward to five years later to 1995."

"Okay," he said, and seemingly took a nervous sip of his drink.

"As you already know, a 21-year-old woman by the name of Gazelle Ragland was last seen at The Club in the spring of 1995, coincidentally, one of the only times that year you actually went there."

"I think I was there some other time, so are you sure I was there that night Gazelle disappeared?"

"Yes, I'm sure, Damian."

"How so?"

"Because Gazelle's sister, Kamiah, told me that Vonda—Gazelle's best friend at the time who was with her that night—had told her. She said Vonda said that you bought them drinks and then came up to Gazelle and talked to her. Then, the two of you went out to the dance floor for a dance."

"Now you've refreshed my memory."

~

The Club: Spring 1995

"So, you must've gone to Saint Maran East because I know I would've definitely remembered someone as fine as you throughout my high-school years," Damian said as him and Gazelle danced to "Freak Like Me" by Adina Howard.

"Actually, I went to Saint Cecilia High School for all four years. The all-girls school that's right outside of this city. That's why no one really knew who I was or Vonda. That's where we met."

"Okay, that makes sense then," he said with a smile as he stared down at her. "So, what are you getting into tonight after this place closes?"

"I'm not sure. I had nothing planned, well, Vonda and I had nothing planned," Gazelle said, as she stared at Vonda for a second while she also danced on the floor with a man she'd just met.

"Wanna go someplace quiet? It's pretty loud in here and I can barely hear our conversation."

"Sure, that's fine," she said.

They left the floor.

"GAZELLE!" Vonda yelled.

But due to the loud music, her call for her went unheard.

"Where are we going?" Gazelle asked.

"Someplace quiet," Damian said once again, as he led her by her hand through the bottleneck of the crowd where they turned a corner and went into an area less crowded and a lot quieter as cigarette smoke still filled the air.

"Ooh! I know that guy! I just wanna say hi to him. Excuse me for a minute," Gazelle said, and let go of his hand.

Damian flashed a smirk as he watched her run up to a man who was right down the hall from where they were. She caught up to this man as they walked around another corner.

"And that's when I said forget this shit, got another girl, and left the establishment," Damian informed me.

"Seriously?!" I said. I couldn't believe what he'd told me. "So, you didn't even see who it was that she wanted to say hi to?"

"No, I didn't see him from the front, and I didn't care. I thought nothing of it. I assumed that she knew the man because she told me she did, so I decided to wait for her to get done talking to him. But it's like they walked some more down the hall and turned a corner—and they were gone. The hall was dark and dimly lit and filled with cigarette smoke. I wasn't chasing any girl down; didn't have to. She thought that man was more important to say hi to than to have some fun with me that night, so it is what it is. Never saw her again."

I thought this was awfully rude at the way he said this. Maybe it was just the way he worded it, but I didn't like it. "Well, she hasn't been seen or heard from in 28 years. Not from anyone. So, you said you just got another girl from The Club that night and left with her?"

"That's right."

"Did you see Vonda after you decided that you weren't gonna wait for Gazelle to get done talking to the man she said she knew?"

"Not at all. In fact, I just left after Gazelle went and chased that man down the hall. I met another girl as I was leaving and took her home with me."

"I see. So, had you ever been in that area of The Club before?"

"A few times. They usually have security back there, and they did that night as well. But they obviously let Gazelle walk right past them when she saw that man she said she knew and wanted to say hi to."

"Damn, I wish I knew who he was. Now the trail just went cold once again since you didn't follow her when she went to go talk to that man."

"I wasn't gonna follow her. Like I said, I don't chase down women like that. I knew I could have another woman there that night, and within minutes, I did. I was gonna wait for as long as I was gonna wait for her, and I decided to wait for no more than two minutes tops. I hate to say it like this, but once I got with the other woman and left with her, I forgot all about Gazelle. I didn't hear anything more about her until years later when her family had said she was missing since 1995, but I had nothing to do with it."

"*D*o you believe him?" Porsha asked me, as she handed me a hot cup of tea after my interview with Damian.

"Yeah, I actually do. He just didn't look or sound like he was lying, you know? Especially since back then he had a very lucrative career as a pro-football player and was making a lot of money, so he had a lot to lose—*a lot* to lose. It's just too bad he didn't recognize the man Gazelle was talking to because if he did, he could quite possibly hold the key to her disappearance. This is just getting crazier and crazier. Just when I think I took a huge step forward it just pushes me several steps back. This is gonna be harder than I thought to solve. It's like someone is always one person away from the person Deandra and Gazelle were last seen talking to and they don't know who they were, you know?"

"Yeah, I know. But what this all has in common is that both of their last moments were at The Club, so that's been pretty consistent with what you've been told."

"Yeah, you're right, it is. I just wish I knew where Vonda was."

"Well, I think you'll find her if you're really persistent, and I know you are, especially now since it's not that hard to find anyone these days."

"And it's the only way I'm gonna be until these are solved." I took one of the cookies that tastefully complemented this hot tea and took a bite out of it. "Shit!"

"What? What's wrong?"

"Shit!" I said again, and held the right side of my mouth.

"What is it, Mackenzee?" Porsha asked, as she stared at me.

"I think I just broke one of my bottom teeth!" I said, and spit out the cookie . . . along with half of one of my bottom teeth. "FUCK!"

"Oh my god, Mackenzee! *You just broke your tooth* on a cookie?"

"Yep, here it is," I said, as I held out the palm of my hand while the broken tooth sat in a mist of a half chewed up cookie.

"Goodness. Do you still have dental insurance?"

"Yeah, I do. Let me see if Elron's busy. He said his uncle is a doctor, but I don't know what kind. And if he isn't a dentist I can see if he can recommend me to someone." I waited for him to answer the phone.

"Hi, Mackenzee. What's up?"

"Hey, Elron. I don't mean to bother you, but I just broke half of my tooth on a cookie and was wondering if your uncle was a dentist since you told me he was a doctor?"

He chuckled. "Sorry to hear that, Mackenzee. Unfortunately, my uncle is not a dentist, but he has a connection to one of the best in this city."

"Oh! Okay, who is it?"

"It's Dr. Norman Capers. I'll give you his information. My uncle was his mentor so I know he would love it that I recommended you to him. He is accepting new patients."

"Great! Thank you so much, Elron."

"No problem."

There was a half second of silence.

"Um, Elron?"

"Yes?"

"Since I have you on the phone, have you heard any new info from Richard about the cases?"

He sighed. I knew he didn't wanna talk about this.

Tough shit.

"Mackenzee, Richard hasn't mentioned anything to me about the cases. But I'm not gonna lie to you, I did see your interview with Damian Wesson on the cases and his connection to both of them. He was a great football player back in the day back in high school, and even though he went to West, we all knew he was gonna make it to the pros."

"I don't care about any fuckin' football, Elron. Excuse my language, but I just broke half of my tooth and don't wanna look like a junkie and I don't know how I'm gonna pay for it because even though I have dental insurance, I don't know how much I'm gonna have to pay if things get all screwed up."

"Dr. Capers will take care of you, Mackenzee. Have a nice rest of the day."

I sighed. "Thanks for the recommendation." I got off the phone and texted Dr. Capers office directly for an appointment. They got back to me and told me they could get me in first thing tomorrow.

CHAPTER EIGHTEEN

"Mackenzee Lawson?" the dental hygienist said.

"Yes, right here," I replied, and then quickly flashed a closed smile. Even though the tooth that broke was towards the back of my mouth, it didn't make me any less cautious.

I was seated in a room and I always didn't know what it was, but being in a dental chair always brought on some instant anxiety. The tools looked shiny but scary, and I'd thought this way since I was a child. Just the thought of the sounds when some of them turned on made me want to leap out of the chair and fly out the door. But I knew I needed to get this done, and didn't wanna make Elron look bad by cancelling my appointment since I'd told them on the online forms I'd filled out that he'd recommended me. I tried to calm myself down as I watched a small TV they had in this room about all of the dental procedures they performed, and I had to admit that the moment I'd stepped into this office overall that it was definitely a beautiful state-of-the-art one.

Minutes later, the dental hygienist did what they do which was too complicated for me to figure out, so I sat back and felt a little more at ease while I thought about the cases I was investigating. I just wanted more leads and felt like I'd talk to enough people by now to get some-where, but all the while I still felt like I wasn't getting anywhere.

After the dental hygienist was done, no more than a few minutes later, the doctor walked in . . . and it definitely wasn't a man. "Um . . . I thought I was seeing Dr. Norman Capers," I said to the very young attractive woman.

"You were. He had an emergency dental procedure to perform. I'm his wife, Dr. Ashley Whitfield-Capers."

I sat stunned!

I could not believe this at all!

"Wha . . . what? *You're* Ashley Whitfield?! Oh my god!"

She gave me a confused look with a slight grin. "Yes, I'm Ashley Whitfield. You sound like you're surprised to know who I am and I know it can't be because I'm a dentist. Can I ask why?"

I didn't know where to start as I stared stunned at the woman whose mom had been missing for 33 years, and she seemed genuinely surprised that I was surprised . . . and I was. There was a reason why my tooth broke when it had. There was a reason why I was scheduled to see her instead of her husband at the last minute. I was now convinced of it. "*You're Deandra Whitfield's daughter?* The teen girl—"

"Who went missing at The Club 33 years ago. Yes, I'm her daugh-ter," she confirmed with a smile.

"Are you okay that I brought it up?"

She smiled. "Yes, I'm okay with it. I guess I am surprised that you had because no one has asked me about it. I think they all know about it, they're just too afraid to say anything to me about it. I guess it's also because I was only 2 years old when my mom went missing. My grandmother believes she was abducted from there."

"The Club?"

"Yes, The Club," she replied uncomfortably. She looked at my chart that was displayed on a small TV screen in front of me. "I see you're only 28 years old, so you weren't even around yet when this happened."

"No, I wasn't, but I'm very much into what happened to your mom and to Gazelle Ragland and others who probably will never get mentioned. It just seems like everything is leading back to The Club."

"Yeah, it seems like it," she replied with a smile. "I guess I am so shocked that you're the first patient to ask me about this. Are you investigating it?"

Here was my chance to shine.

"Yes, I am. I don't know if you know, but I am investigating it and speaking under complete anonymity on my *I'm Their Speaker* channel."

She nodded with a smile. "I'm glad someone finally is. Wow. This couldn't be more luck that I get you as a patient. This definitely happened for a reason."

"It sure did," I said with a smile. "So, is your grandmother still around?"

"She sure is. She pretty much talks about my mom every time I see her. My husband and I have a 17-year-old daughter. Had her when I was only 18 years old; just three years older than what my mom had me at, and coincidentally, my daughter is the exact same age now my mom was when she went missing. My husband and I got married when I found out I was pregnant—but that's a story for another day."

"And you know I wouldn't mind hearing it."

"And I'm glad you wouldn't because I'm actually having dinner at my grandmother's house tonight—she still lives in the same house she's lived in since my mom went missing. It's just gonna be me and her since my husband is having a night with friends while they watch a basketball game, and my daughter is also gonna be with friends. I'd love it if you joined us."

I thought I was dreaming. This could not have happened at a better time. "I would love to. I wouldn't miss it for the world."

"Great! I'll let her know we're having a guest and brief her on who you are. Now, let's get to why you're here."

I laughed. "Yes, let's do that!"

I smiled as she went over my x-rays and everything while I couldn't stop looking at her. I could see her mom all in her even though she was much older than what her mom was when she was her age. I also couldn't stop thinking about the night I was gonna have tonight, and I already knew it was gonna be a night to remember.

CHAPTER NINETEEN

I arrived ten minutes early at Ashley's grandmother's home. I could smell the Cornish game hens, wild rice, potatoes, and green beans cooking. This was coincidentally one of my favorite dishes because I rarely got it, and Ashley claimed her grandmother made the best around so I couldn't wait to try it.

I looked around the neighborhood as it was completely dark, but it didn't look like the one Mary lived in, as the street of small, white modest one-story homes that looked just like each other sat in a row, and from what I'd seen, all of them looked occupied with at least one car in the driveway. People seemed to have still taken pride in home ownership since every house had manicured lawns and the sidewalks weren't riddled with overgrown weeds, unnecessary junk, and children's toys everywhere. It appeared to me that people respected each other and their property.

As I waited for the door to open, I heard footsteps. I looked around with extra caution as I moved closer to the front door and had my back towards it. Suddenly, Ashley appeared out from the back!

"Hi, Mackenzee," she said with a smile.

"Hi," I said with relief.

"Did I scare you?"

"No," I lied.

She grinned. "Glad you could make it. Come on in the back. I was just out here getting something out of my car and my grandma is in the bathroom. She doesn't have any of those apps like Ring or the others, just typical old-school home security. She thinks this neighborhood is as safe as it was when she first moved in, and in a lot of ways, it is."

"It looks and feels safe to me," I said, as I followed her to the back of the house. I watched as she closed the garage door as it had an older model car that I recognized as a Ford Escort possibly from the 80's or early 90's, and a new model Mercedes SUV which was obviously Ashley's.

Ashley opened a side door, and I walked in after her. We were practically right in the small kitchen as the strong odor of the food made my stomach growl. I was glad no one could hear it since Al Jarreau's "I Will Be Here for You (Nitakungodea Milele)" played loudly throughout this kitchen as an elderly woman stood at the sink as she stared out the window at the garage.

Ashley turned the music down. "Grandma?" The woman turned around who looked like a much older version of Deandra. I would've known this was her mom if I'd seen her out somewhere in this city. She smiled at me. "This is Mackenzee Lawson, the young woman I'd told you about from earlier today. She's more than my patient now. Mackenzee, this is my grandmother, Cloris Whitfield."

"Nice to meet you, Mrs. Whitfield," I said as we shook hands.

"Nice to meet you, too, Mackenzee. And you can call me Cloris," she said with a weary smile.

"Thank you," I said with a smile. I could see all of the decades of stress she had from Deandra's disappearance. I'd hoped to never feel what she'd been feeling. Now I really felt what I was doing was worth it and I was not gonna stop until I found out what'd happened to her daughter and Ashley's mom, and all of the others who disappeared from The Club.

"Dinner is ready," Cloris said with a smile.

"It smells delicious," I honestly said. I helped them bring the food into the dining room where the table was beautifully set.

"I wanted to have dinner in here since this is a special day," Cloris informed me with a smile.

"Very special indeed," Ashley said with a smile.

"Thank you," I replied, as I tried not to let tears well up in my eyes. They already appreciated what I was doing so much, and it'd showed me even more how much no one ever did anything for them when it came to Deandra and, of course, Gazelle and who knew how many others.

Shame on this city.

We held hands and blessed the food, and then sat down while Duke Ellington's "What Am I Here for?" played at a comfortable volume throughout the room. I thought this was the perfect song because I knew what I was here for, and I was hoping to get more out of what I was here for besides the food and getting to know them.

I sat to the right of Cloris as Ashley sat on the other side of the table from me to the left of her. After gobbling down a great portion of this delicious food, I was ready to talk for the entire night. "So, have you lived here your whole life, Cloris?"

"No, I haven't. I'm from Kansas, but moved here in the 1950's with my parents. They're both gone and have been for decades. My mom passed when Deandra was a freshman in high school, my dad passed two years after she disappeared without ever knowing what'd happened to his beloved granddaughter since Deandra was my only child."

"I'm sorry to hear that," I said as I lowered my head. I glanced up at Ashley as she smiled at me.

"Thank you, Mackenzee. Yes, it's been a very rough 33 years. I am very mad at this city for not doing anything to help me find her, as it is my right to know what'd happened to her and why and most of all, who's responsible for it. I was hoping we would've found Deandra before Ashley got old enough to understand what'd happened to her, and that Deandra and I would just explain to her when she was older what went on. But as the days, weeks, months, and years went on, I just lost hope that we would ever find her. But now I have a new sense of hope because of you, Miss Mackenzee."

"Me too," Ashley said with a smile, and took a sip of her soda.

"And I can't tell the two of you enough that I'm gonna do everything I can to find out what happened to her because the two of you are owed so many answers. So many people dropped the ball on this to the cops to even potential witnesses and I know there had to have been some, but it seems as if everyone that I've talked to always seemed to be one person away from seeing the person Deandra went off with. I always believe in the fact that someone saw something."

"I've always believed that, too," Ashley said.

"And me as well. And I just don't know why they're so afraid to tell what they know. I think after 33 years that they've been holding it in for so long, what do they think they're going to get in trouble for? You know? It's like no one cares that I've been suffering for so long because I haven't had my baby in my life for 33 years and have no idea where she is. And I feel that people just gave up on her disappearance before they even went to go look for her."

"What? You mean there was no search efforts to find her?"

"Just the ones I put together with friends and other family members. No one cares about Black girls in this city, Mackenzee. They've proven that."

"Shame on them," I said, and ate some more of my green beans. "Everyone back then needed to be fired, from the cops to the DA, and even the mayor, in my opinion."

"I definitely agree with that," Ashley said. "In fact, I did try to contact all the legal authorities about my mom's case when I was old enough to understand what was going on, and no one ever got back to me. I always felt like I was fighting a losing battle. Grandma told me I would have a tough fight on my hands, and she was right."

"But I wanted her to get her education and go off to college and then to dental school since she said she wanted to be a dentist. I didn't want her to give up on her dreams just because she had a baby. I never wanted Deandra to do it when she had her, and I told her that millions of times. But she never got the chance to do anything after high school."

"What high school did you go to, Mackenzee?" Ashley asked.

"Saint Maran East. And you?"

"Saint Cecilia, it's an all-girls high school."

"Oh, wow! That's where Gazelle Ragland—the other girl who went missing from The Club in 1995—went. You never heard about her?"

"No, I've never heard about her, Mackenzee, while I was in high school. It's like no one really knew who she was or that she'd gone missing from The Club. I was even talking to some of the girls I'd graduated with, and they'd told me they'd never heard of her until they saw your show."

"This is crazy. Wow, this city really didn't care."

"No, they don't," Cloris said, and took a sip of her wine.

"And what's more crazy is . . . ," Ashley said. She looked at her grandma. "Is it okay that she knows?"

"Yes, I think it might help her investigation," Cloris said.

"Is it okay if I know what?" I asked, and then ate some more of my wild rice.

Ashley took a deep breath. "Someone—and we don't know who it is—paid for my high-school tuition all four years while I was at Saint Cecilia."

"What?!" I said in shock. "Are you serious, Ashley?"

"Yes, she's serious," Cloris said.

"I am," Ashley confirmed. "And it didn't stop there."

"You're kidding!" I said. I couldn't believe I was getting this information for some reason, but I felt it was definitely important to my investigation.

"Someone also paid for all of my years in college as well as when I was at dental school," Ashley confirmed.

"What?!" I said. It was like for some reason I couldn't believe she was telling me this.

Cloris nodded with a smile. "Yes, she's not lying, Mackenzee. I didn't have to pay a dime for any of it. It was like a secret grant was given to her. Someone has been following her schooling since she's been in high school and has paid for everything. I didn't have to use the little money I had saved up for Deandra's college fund at the time, either, since that's what I was gonna use for Ashley. Well, to this day, someone has been very generous in wanting to see Ashley succeed."

"Do you have any idea who it is?" I asked.

"No, I have no idea who it is. They also paid for my husband and I to have a state-of-the-art dental office which is always nice."

"Yeah, I noticed when I walked in y'alls office that it's the best-looking dental office I've ever been in. It's beautiful. I just knew your husband was probably fixing everyone's teeth in this city!"

They laughed.

"Far from it! Too many mouths!" Ashley said with a laugh. "But yes, someone is definitely behind this, and my husband even said he didn't know who it was, either, but feels it has everything to do with me and nothing to do with him. Our daughter also goes to Saint Cecilia—she's a senior—since we didn't want her to have to deal with people harassing her like the way Grandma didn't want them to harass me had someone brought up my mom's disappearance."

"And they never did, or did they?" Cloris asked.

"No, Grandma, they didn't. It was a great move to have sent me there instead of to my mom's high school."

"I think it was, too," I said with a smile. "So, you both think this person who has paid for your schooling, Ashley, has some connection to your mom's disappearance?"

"Yes, I think it's a possibility," Ashley said.

"I think it's definitely possible," Cloris said, and ate some more of her food. "At first, I wasn't accepting of it, but it was already paid for and I felt that was less stress—a lot less stress—that I had to deal with when it came to having to have her get financial aid and or having to pay for it myself because I wanted her to go to college and pursue her dreams since her mom was never able to. I didn't want anyone or anything stopping her."

"And I did get scholarships, but it was nothing compared to having all four years of my tuition paid and beyond that. I still can't believe it and I still can't believe I have no idea who it is."

"I honestly think the two of you will find out someday," I said with a smile.

"But it just all seems fishy to me as to why they did it," Cloris said.

"How so?"

"I just think they don't want us to bring up Deandra's disappearance anymore. That's why I feel that knowing this is very important for your investigation, Miss Mackenzee," Cloris said.

I nodded as I looked at Ashley. "Do you think this could be this case, Ashley?"

"Yes, I think it's a possibility," she repeated as she had said minutes before. "I've never ruled it out and I'm never going to."

"And I don't blame you. I'll see what I can find out," I assured them. "Do the two of you know that Mary moved back here?"

Ashley looked at Cloris.

"You mean Mary Landry? Deandra's best friend back then?" Cloris asked.

"Yes," I replied with a smile.

"She did, huh? Interesting. Very interesting," Cloris said.

Now what she said was very interesting to me. "So, what's going on with her?" I asked.

"I honestly don't know what's going on with her now, considering the fact that she left this city three years after my baby went missing and didn't tell me. I honestly don't think she even cared anymore. And I also think something else."

My interest was piqued. "What is it?"

"That she knows more about Deandra's disappearance than what she told me," Cloris informed me.

"Really?" I asked. I couldn't even hide how I'd said it. I looked at Ashley. "Have you ever met Mary?"

"No, I haven't. Grandma told me how much she was over here when I was a baby, of course, but I have no recollection of her since I was so young at the time."

"Yeah, she loved playing with you and going to the mall with your mom and you on the weekends most of the time, but everything seemed to have changed with her when Deandra disappeared, and she was with her that night."

"Well, from what she'd told me, she went there with Deandra, but left The Club with Damian Wesson, a man who I interviewed for my latest video and who's the father of her child. I just don't think either one of them were lying about what they'd told me. Did you watch the interviews?"

"Not Mary's. I watched Damian's because Ashley told me about it."

I looked at Ashley as she nodded at me with a smile. "Do you think Mary left something out? Or Damian?"

"Only they can tell you that," Cloris said. "I hope they didn't because I will be very mad at the two of them if they had. They have lived this long and were able to have children of their own and at least with Damian, he was also able to get married. All I have is my Ashley who gave me a beautiful great-granddaughter, but I always felt something was missing—and that's my Deandra. Wow, she has missed so much in these past 33 years."

"She has," Ashley said with her head lowered as she pushed her food around.

"Well, you know I will ask Mary and Damian if there's more they need to tell me about that night," I informed them. "Um, I also want to ask, do either of you know who Richard Elmhurst is?"

"The son or the dad?" Cloris asked.

I don't know why I looked so surprised. "Well, the son since he's the DA. I met him when I went to The Club for a throwback night featuring the year 1990."

"Coincidentally the year my Deandra went missing," Cloris said, and took another sip of her wine. "Richard's dad was DA at the time Deandra disappeared. Mary and I went to go see him; he never had the time to see us, and neither did the cops. I honestly think he was always there in his office and was slipping out the back door when he found out that we were there. Now his son has taken over his pathetic position."

"I'm sorry to hear that, Cloris. Wow, this is so real. I was just asking because Richard seems really standoffish when I'd asked him about it while dancing with him since he asked me to dance. I had no idea who he was. I'd made up my mind before I went there that night that I was gonna investigate this. He bailed me out of jail when I was caught trespassing at The Club during the day and had the charges dropped against me. I had dinner with him that night and he still didn't wanna talk about Deandra or about any other girls who went missing there."

"Did he say why?" Cloris asked, as Ashley stared with suspense at me.

"Yeah, he'd said when I was actually invited to his office after meeting him—this was before I went to jail and went to his house for dinner that same night—that there were no records of Deandra's disappearance anywhere. Not with the police department or at the courthouse or wherever. It was as if her case didn't even exist."

"That's a complete lie, Mackenzee, and I think you know that by now. Mary and I went everywhere from the police to trying to talk to the DA to even the mayor's office and no one ever had time to talk to us. I think these people are very much connected, and whoever did this has a connection to probably everyone in this city or they're just very good at not getting caught."

"They'll be caught eventually because I have a feeling they're still around and even have a feeling they're still in this city because people are very arrogant. Whoever is responsible for Deandra's disappearance knows they've gotten away with it for this long so they don't think they'll ever be caught, and I think they know I'm investigating this, they just don't know who I am."

"But Richard does," Ashley said.

Cloris looked at me. "Does he?"

I sighed. "Yeah, I think he does know it's me even though I'm trying to stay under complete anonymity on my show, but I have to admit it's hard. Without Richard having any proof that it's me, there's nothing he can do."

"As if him and his dad had ever done anything to begin with. I just don't think he's gonna prosecute the case when you find out who's responsible for it, Mackenzee," Cloris said.

"Well, I'm gonna do everything I can to make sure that he does because he was also there that night Deandra disappeared."

"What?!" Cloris and Ashley said at the same time.

"Yeah, his personal chef told me this when I met with him to talk about Richard after having dinner at his home. Richard took me straight to his house after picking me up from jail. But I knew he had something to tell me about him and I knew it was probably about that night."

"What did he tell you?" Cloris asked.

"He just told me that he was with Richard that night and that Richard did have an interest in Deandra."

"I believe it," Cloris said. "My Deandra was beautiful. I knew how much attention she got from the boys. So, Richard Elmhurst III was interested in my daughter on that night she went missing. Wow. What else did he tell you?"

"That he did see Richard get up from the table to go and talk to Deandra, but he had to be home himself because he had a curfew, so he didn't actually see Richard talking to her."

"Damn," Ashley said.

"Yeah, you're telling me, baby," Cloris said. She shook her head. "I think I believe this man. What is his name?"

"Elron Longfellow," I told them, since I felt they had the right to know. "But please, don't tell anyone I told you about what he said because he said he wants to remain completely anonymous."

"Why?" Cloris asked.

Ashley looked at me as she waited for me to answer.

"That's what I wanted to know as well. He gave me some vital information, but it's like the trail went cold when he told me that he had to leave so he didn't see if Richard actually approached Deandra. He said Richard called him to go to the mall the next day and didn't bring Deandra up at all. He said he thought he was gonna tell him about him meeting her. He assumed that nothing happened between the two of them and Richard was probably embarrassed about being rejected by Deandra and just said forget about her. Richard never brought her up again."

"Wow," Cloris said, as she shook her head once again. "Just when I was sitting up here thinking about going to his office and cussing him out."

"Don't do that, Grandma," Ashley said with a smile. "I think we're getting close to finding out a lot more than what we have found out over these years, all thanks to Mackenzee."

"All praises to Mackenzee, yes indeed," Cloris said with a smile.

"Yes indeed," Ashley repeated with a smile.

"Thank you," I replied with an even bigger smile. I knew the work I was doing was definitely more fulfilling now more than ever. As I'd always said from the beginning, I knew I'd stumbled upon that video that day for a reason, and just sitting here with Cloris and Ashley, as well as talking to Mary and Kamiah gave me every reason to keep going at this, and to keep prodding someone like Elron to keep giving me info about Richard and anything else he knew because I had a feeling there was so much more he wanted to tell me. "Um, I wanted to know if you both have seen a brand-new black BMW around the city with the license plates CLUB 88?"

"Yes," they both replied without hesitation.

Wow, I thought. *This guy is everywhere!* "Do you know who he is by any chance?"

"Not at all," Cloris informed me.

"I don't know who he is, either. I even asked my husband who he was, and he told me he doesn't have any idea as well. I guess since it has something to do with The Club, we both really don't wanna know, to tell you the truth."

"And I can't blame you for that," I said. "Have you ever been there?"

"No, I haven't. Grandma never let me go there and I never wanted to go there since that's the last place my mom was seen at," Ashley informed me.

"Yes, I told I never wanted her to go there no matter how much pressure she got from her friends about wanting to go there for those teen nights. I told her if they ever asked—"

"And they did," Ashley interrupted.

"And what did you tell them?" I asked.

"Exactly what Grandma said—that I can't go there due to my mom being last seen there in 1990. They said they understood but went without me. I felt like I wasn't missing anything—well, maybe a little since I wanted to see some boys since I went to Saint Cecilia and I knew I would see them at The Club for sure—but I always had to keep in the back of my mind that that place was the reason why I never grew up with my mom."

"It was. I'm convinced that if Deandra and Mary didn't go there that night that she would still be here," Cloris said.

"Excuse me," Ashley said, and got up from the table.

I watched her as she left the table and walked around a corner.

"I've upset her," Cloris informed me with a somber smile. "I'm gonna go talk to her. You can finish your food."

I nodded with a smile. I felt that there were some things I needed to stay out of no matter how much I wanted to know about them because it was very private, and I was seeing that firsthand. I was gonna sit here as long as I had to and wait for them to return to this table. I also saw firsthand the decades of pain a beautiful woman had gone through without ever knowing what'd happened to her mom, only where she disappeared from. I'd hoped to never feel what her and Cloris were feeling.

CHAPTER TWENTY

"**I** want you to see something. Follow me," Cloris said.

"Okay," I replied with a smile. I looked back at Ashley as she was in the kitchen doing the dishes with her AirPods in her ears. I looked around and stared Cloris right into her eyes as she stopped in front of a door.

She opened the door. "This is Deandra's bedroom. It's in the exact condition it was when she left that night with Mary to go to The Club. Have a look around."

Before I even walked in, I felt as if I'd stepped back in time. As I slowly stepped in, this bedroom felt like what it was—left in the past. But I felt Deandra's presence all in here. Cloris was exactly right. Evidence showed all around it that it was left in the same condition as if time had stood still for 33 years, and in this bedroom, it had, to the MC Hammer, Janet Jackson, Salt-N-Pepa, and Milli Vanilli posters plastered all over her light pink walls. A small TV sat on an elevated shelf with a VHS tape player right next to it.

I glanced into her open closet which had one sliding brown wooden door where she had her clothes on one side and Ashley's baby clothes on the other. I looked over at her twin-sized bed in the corner with a brass headboard along with white floral disheveled covers which made it appear as if she'd just gotten out of bed this morning. I looked at a small brass vanity set that had Revlon and Loreal makeup all over it which looked like she was doing just what she'd done—getting ready to go to The Club that night. I glanced at the Diet Pepsi can as it sat on here as well and could see how real this was because the logo on the cans looked completely different now. There were also pictures of her and Ashley when Ashley was just a few months old, to one that looked as if it was just taken before she disappeared. I stared down at a chair in another corner that had a black poet's style shirt with long mesh see-through sleeves along with a red mini skirt neatly laid out on it.

"Those were her work clothes. She always liked to lay out what she was going to wear for work the day before, much like she did for her outfits for school. She loved that outfit. Saved her work money to buy it since where she worked at most girls who came in there were those spoiled suburban girls who drove expensive cars to high school and never had to have a job in high school."

"Like Mary?"

"Yeah, like Mary," Cloris confirmed, as she shook her head. "I didn't wanna say this at dinner because I don't ever wanna upset Ashley because as you saw, I upset her enough. But I think Mary knows more than she's told you about what happened."

I looked up from looking at some of the high school textbooks that laid on a chest of drawers. "You think so?"

"Yeah, I think she's hiding something. What? I have no idea. I felt like she just didn't care after a while when she left three years after Deandra disappeared. I know she has her own child now and was going through a lot with her family at the time, but it's like I felt she left because she just didn't wanna deal with me or what'd happened to Deandra anymore."

"Did you see my interview with her?"

"Yes, I saw it. Ashley actually told me about it. Like I said before, I just think she knows so much more than she's telling. She comes back after 30 years away from this city, and she doesn't even tell me?"

"She didn't?"

"No, she didn't. I had to find out from a woman I work with. Yes, at my age, I'm still working because I have to keep busy, plus, I've always loved to work; that's where Deandra and Ashley got their work ethic from. I'm just glad someone is showing an interest in my baby's case because it's been cold for way too long."

"It has, and I'm gonna do everything I can to solve it." I walked over to her nightstand next to her bed which had a pink vintage 50's-style radio sitting on it along with a few cassette tapes. I looked at Cloris as she stared back at me. The pain in her eyes was so hard to describe. "Can I look in these drawers?"

"Certainly," she replied with a smile.

I opened the first drawer . . . and didn't feel I had to look any further. I found something that I never thought I would ever find especially since I didn't expect to actually be in Deandra's house, much less her bedroom.

I found her diary.

"Her diary," I said, as I lifted it up so her mom could see it.

"That's her diary," she confirmed with a sad smile.

"Can I—"

"Yes, you can take it with you and look over it—but I would like it returned. I just feel something is definitely different about you, Mackenzee. I feel that you really do care about my baby. Even Ashley said when she saw you as a patient earlier today that she knew you were for real in wanting to solve her mom's disappearance as well as the other girls because we believe there are others who went missing as well that just haven't gotten the attention that they should've gotten just like my baby. I guess they weren't the right color to get the attention those other girls would've gotten had they gone missing."

"Well, that's why I started my independent investigation, and I hope this diary helps me a lot. Have you looked in it since she disappeared?"

"No, I haven't. Everything was just too much for me and it still is even 33 years later. I felt like I've aged over 50 years since Deandra's disappearance. I'm not ruling anyone out. No one. I just wish I knew where that Trevor was because I believe he also knows more than he wants me to know. I just don't like to talk about it around Ashley."

"I understand why you don't, and you're just being a very respectful grandmother to your granddaughter."

"Yeah, I am, but I slipped up at dinner. Ashley always leaves the table when something upsets her, and it's usually something that I said that really triggered her about her mom. It's just so hard for me to say the right things, yet still I always want her to know about her. I'm doing a little better since I have been going to therapy for it—sometimes alone and sometimes with Ashley—but it's still hard. It'll always be hard to deal with."

"I can't even imagine your pain, Cloris, or Ashley's because I feel she was cheated out of a lifetime she could've had with her mom, and now her daughter will probably never know her grandmother."

"Very true, Mackenzee. Because I definitely didn't want to say this at the table, but I just don't think Deandra is alive, but I just can't have her legally declared dead yet even though it's been 33 years since I've seen or heard from her. I have to have proof that she is. But then there's this small part of me that's saying and praying that she could still be alive out there somewhere, but I just don't want to get Ashley's hopes up."

"I understand."

She nodded. "I've had that same Ford Escort since 1988. Bought it brand new back then when Deandra was entering her second semester of her freshman year in high school in January 1988. I remember the last time Deandra drove it. It was when she went to work because I had the week off. That same week—just a few days later—she went to The Club for the very first time. Haven't seen or heard from her since."

"I'm so sorry, Cloris."

She nodded once again. "And the Al Jarreau song you heard when you walked in the house? That song came out when Deandra was only 10 years old. I would sing that song to her all of the time, but especially when she was upset about something. Never did I know that seven years later I was not gonna be there for her for whatever happened to her that night. I started singing the song to Ashley while she grew up because I felt I needed to extend my promise to her to be there for her since I couldn't be there to protect her mom. That's why I'm in Nayana's life as much as I'm in Ashley's. I just never know about anything anymore. That's my great-granddaughter's name," she said with a smile.

I nodded back with a smile as tears welled up in my eyes. I looked down at the pink floral diary as I held it in my hands. "Well, I'm gonna try to find out as much as I can from this diary if anything in here could quite possibly have some connection to Deandra's disappearance."

"Well, I know something in that diary definitely has some connection to her disappearance, and like I told you, I have never read her diary."

"And what is that?"

She shook her head. "I just can't get myself to read it since I have no idea what happened to her. But I know she wrote about Trevor and all of the things that were going on with the two of them. They didn't have the perfect relationship, I know that much, so I still think he had a lot to do with her disappearance."

I looked down at the diary once again. "If I find something in it that connects him to it, I'll be sure to copy it and send it to you so you can see it for yourself."

"And I would greatly appreciate that."

I couldn't wait to read this diary knowing that it could definitely hold the key to Deandra's disappearance, and Deandra was gonna be the one to tell me in her own words.

CHAPTER TWENTY-ONE

There was a knock on my bedroom door.

"Come in!" I said.

"Damn, Mackenzee! You're *still* reading her diary?! It's 3:00 in the morning!" Porsha said. "Must be pretty interesting."

"Yeah, it is, especially since it's from 33 years ago and she did start writing in it at the beginning of the year, so it starts in January 1990 which was her second semester of her junior year in high school. She just talks a lot about Ashley and her and Trevor which is confirmed in here that they were together at the beginning of that year. I haven't gotten to the part when they broke up, but I know she wrote about it in here somewhere."

"But isn't it kind of freaking you out to be reading it, though? Because even her mom doesn't think she's still alive. Do you?"

I sighed. "Well, I don't wanna say she is or isn't because I really don't know. I hope she is because it's very possible although there is a very slim chance of it. I'm still holding out hope that she is just like Cloris and Ashley."

"That's good," she said with a smile.

I flipped through some of the pages of her diary. "Well, she sure loved to write a lot. Remember, there was no social media or cell phones back then so people didn't have the things to do back then that they have now even though, yes, I know some people write in diaries today but we call them journals more now than we do diaries."

"I know I do," Porsha said. "But I write in my journal on my computer."

I nodded with a smile as I still looked through her diary. I yawned. "Yeah, I'm getting a little tired since I didn't take a nap yesterday since I was so excited to have dinner with Ashley and Cloris. I just took some NyQuil over an hour ago so I think it's starting to take effect now."

She laughed. "Yeah, that's what I kind of thought." She came over to me and tried to take the diary from me.

"No!" I laughed. "Mine!"

She laughed as she shook her head. "I just want you to get some rest, Mackenzee. I think you're wearing yourself out over all of this. You need to rest. The diary will be safe with me."

"The diary stays with me. Get out of my room and go to bed yourself. Don't you have to work tomorrow?"

"No, I don't, that's why I'm still up. Oh! And there's another reason."

I took my nose out of this diary and looked up at her. "What is it?"

"There's a Date Night at The Club this weekend."

"Really?"

"Yeah, really. I thought you would like to know just in case you want to go do some investigating."

"Well, I really haven't found out anything yet to lead me back there, but I might go there anyway to check everything out. So, you have to have a date since they say it's a date night, huh?"

"Yeah, having a date is required, they even said it on their social media pages and the text I received from them. I decided to sign up to receive their texts since you're investigating them for these disappearances."

"Well, thanks for telling me. Maybe I'll see if Richard asks me."

"Do you think he will?"

"I hope so. He seems to still be interested in me even though I haven't heard from him in a while, so in reality, I really don't know where I stand with him."

"I thought you said you weren't interested in him like the way he seems to be in you?"

"I'm not," I reconfirmed to her. "But I have to stay close to him because I feel he knows a hell of a lot more than he's claiming he does about Deandra's disappearance, especially since Elron told me he was there that night she disappeared. There are just so many suspects, you know? But Trevor is definitely one of the number one suspects and I just can't seem to find where he is since he moved away 33 years ago and it doesn't seem like he's been back since because I think if he had then Cloris would've told me since he is Ashley's dad, and I think Ashley would've told me she's seen him in these past 33 years but it's clear she hasn't."

"Yeah, that's very unfortunate. It just seems like everyone is so connected in this city."

"That's because almost everyone is. This is a big small city, as they say. Everyone is connected in some way or another." I yawned, and then closed Deandra's diary. "I'm gonna get some sleep. Hopefully, I'll find out more from this diary tomorrow. Goodnight, Porsha."

"Goodnight," Porsha said with a smile, and shut my door behind her.

I smiled as I put Deandra's diary on my nightstand. I stared at it as I stared at my latest iPhone and saw just how old her diary looked compared to my phone. I shook my head as it showed me just how much she'd missed out on for over three decades, stuff that she should be enjoying like everyone else in today's world. It just wasn't fair at all.

CHAPTER TWENTY-TWO

I woke up to the loud ringing of my phone. I picked it up off my nightstand as Deandra's diary still sat on it. I looked at the number as I didn't recognize it . . . but I answered it anyway. "Hello?"

"Hello? Is this Mackenzee Lawson?"

"Yes, it is. Who is this?"

Silence loomed in the air for a few seconds.

"Hello? Are you still there?"

"Yes, I'm still here. Do I know you?"

"No, you don't know me, Mackenzee, but someone told me about you."

"Someone told you about *me*? Who are you? How did you get my number?"

"That's not important."

"The hell it's not!"

I started to get mad because this person had yet to tell me who they were. A number came up on my phone that I didn't recognize at all, but this person obviously knew it was me. "Look, if you're a bill collector, I don't have any damn money right now so I would appreciate it if you leave me alone until I can figure out how I can pay off what I owe, okay? I've told you all that before."

"I'm not a bill collector, Mackenzee."

"Then who are you?"

"I'm . . . I'm Trevor McPherson, Deandra Whitfield's ex-boyfriend from 1990."

"WHAT?!" I screamed as I jumped up out of bed!

"Did I frighten you by telling you who I am?"

"Yes! I mean, no! You just surprised me, that's all!"

He chuckled. "Sorry about that, Mackenzee. It's just that my mom came across your show talking about the disappearances from The Club—she was even shocked that someone brought it up after 33 years—so she saw your contact information after one of your shows and gave it to me. I was able to get your phone number through one of those sites where you can find people and get their numbers and info about them for a price. I wanted to talk to you directly, not go through any texts or emails. I hope you don't mind."

"Not in this case," I admitted as I walked around my room. I stared back down at Deandra's diary. I didn't know whether or not I wanted to tell him I was reading it, and that she'd mentioned him in it like a million times from what I'd read, or that I'd met her mom and his daughter and had dinner with them. I decided to stay quiet about it for now. "So, you're Trevor, Deandra's ex-boyfriend. Wow, I have so many questions to ask you."

"And I know one will be the obvious about having something to do with her disappearance from The Club in 1990, and my answer is no, Mackenzee. I have nothing to do with it."

"Will you be willing to go on my show to let everyone know that?"

"Absolutely. I have nothing to hide. I have a lot to say about Deandra, my daughter Ashley, and about that last night we saw each other. I just feel I have to talk about this, and I've held so much in for so long."

"Well, you won't believe how happy I am to hear from you, Trevor. I know a lot of people have been wanting to hear from you since it's been so long since they had. But the first thing I wanna know is do you live here in Saint Maran again?"

"No, not since my mom and I moved away from there in 1990. I moved a week after Deandra had disappeared, but I didn't move because she disappeared. That's a lie I want to have cleared up with everyone because I know a lot of people think that and still think that, right?"

"Yeah, I think a lot of people do. Well, where do you live now?"

"I'd rather not say for my safety. I have been getting threats over the decades since Deandra went missing since I am her ex-boyfriend from back then and the father of Ashley. Look, I can't talk for much longer because I need to get to work, but I would love to set up a show interview with you."

"Whatever time you have available is absolutely fine with me."

I'M THEIR SPEAKER
EXCLUSIVE INTERVIEW WITH TREVOR MCPHERSON,
DEANDRA WHITFIELD'S EX-BOYFRIEND FROM 1990
WHAT HE KNOWS ABOUT THAT LAST NIGHT
DEANDRA WAS SEEN AT THE CLUB, HIS DAUGHTER
ASHLEY, AND WHERE HE HAS BEEN FOR 33 YEARS

"Hello, everyone, and welcome to *I'm Their Speaker*. For those of you who are still following the cold-case stories I've been investigating about the disappearances of young women from The Club, I thank you for it and for all of your support during my continuous investigation of a story that has meant a lot to me since hearing about it myself. Today, I have a very special guest who I was hoping I would have on my show since I feel he is very vital to this particular case. Please welcome, Trevor McPherson."

Trevor nodded to the audience as if this was some talk show from the 1990s. "Thanks for having me."

I breathed a sigh of relief to myself because I'd told him that before I went on the air with him for this interview that I was on this channel in complete anonymity because I didn't want anything to ruin my investigation. "So, Trevor, you were Deandra Whitfield's boyfriend back in 1990. When did the two of you get together and when did you break up?"

"We got together after meeting each other at the mall when we were sophomores at the beginning of the school year in 1988. We hit it off very well even though we went to rival schools—her going to Saint Maran West and me going to East."

"So, the two of you were together non-stop? There were no breakups and then getting back together, were they?"

"No, not at all. We almost broke up when she told me she was pregnant—and we were only with each other for a few months —but I told her I would support what she wanted to do, and she obviously decided to have the baby and keep her."

"I see. So, the two of you didn't have any kind of history of violence or anything?"

"Not at all. I think since she had Ashley we just started growing apart. It happens. Our relationship just wasn't the same and we both knew it. A baby changes everything, and we were so young back then we didn't realize just how hard it was gonna be on us and how much it was gonna change us. I tried to live a normal life, but it was damn near impossible. I just didn't know if I could do it anymore, and I admitted my feelings started to change for Deandra once I was about to enter my senior year in high school."

"How so?"

"I just didn't want a girlfriend—not at my school and not at any school. Deandra swore up and down that I was secretly seeing someone else, but I swear I wasn't, and I even told her that. I just wanted to be free of any serious relationships even though I knew I would always have to have a relationship with her because of our daughter, but Deandra thought I was gonna marry her after high school. I have no idea in the world where she got that from."

I read about that in her diary, I thought. I knew I couldn't say that I had her diary—not even to Trevor during this interview—because I knew my cover would be completely blown. "Okay, so getting to the last night you saw Deandra which was at The Club, did you know she was gonna be there?"

"No, not at all. But I knew there was a chance she would be there since it was their first ever teen night. Damn, that place was so packed with teens. I thought every teen in the city including surrounding ones was there. I was surprised I was able to get in."

"You went by yourself?"

"No, I went with one of my friends—Bronson. He was one of my best friends in high school at the time. We were on the football team and everything."

I nodded. "So, when did you see Deandra and what did the two of you talk about?"

He sighed. "I saw her when she was standing in line with Mary waiting for drinks. I led her away from her so we could talk. We just talked about Ashley, and she was telling me that she needed help because she couldn't do everything by herself with her working and going to school, and she was wondering why I quit my job recently. Well, I told her there was a reason for it and I had something very important to tell her."

~

The Club: Teen Night: Fall 1990

Deandra walked off the dance floor with Trevor by her side as she watched Mary and Damian go towards the front entrance and exit.

"Are you sure you didn't wanna go with them?" Trevor asked.

She sighed. "Yeah, I'm sure. I have to be home early plus I have to work tomorrow. I have to make sure Ashley is also settled in for the night. I think I spent too much time here already."

"Already? How long have you been here?"

"Not even for a half hour yet."

"Damn, Deandra. You should not have come here at all if you wanna leave already. It's jammin' up in here as we all knew it would be. What other place would any teen have wanted to be tonight? At work or school?"

She sighed once again. "Look, I have more responsibilities in here than most, and it's both of our faults that I do. I just wanna set a good example for our daughter. She's very, very smart already. She will start catching on if I'm out all of the time if I'm not at work or school."

"You need time for yourself just like I need it, Deandra." He sighed as they approached their table. "But speaking about work and school."

She looked at him as she sat down as Chuckii Booker's "Turned Away" began playing. "What about it?"

"I quit my job," he informed her.

"What?! Just why would you do that, Trevor? You have a child to support!" she angrily reminded him.

"I quit because I'm not gonna be here to work there anymore," he informed her.

"Wait, *what*? I'm confused. Just what are you getting at?"

He sighed once again. "Deandra. I didn't know how to tell you this so I'm just gonna have to come right out and say it because it wouldn't be right not to say anything at all."

"Say what, Trevor?"

"I not only broke up with you because I wanted to be free my senior year in high school, I also broke up with you because my mom and I are moving away."

"WHAT?!" she yelled, practically being heard over the deafening loud music. "What the hell do you mean *you're moving away*, Trevor? You have a life here in this city! We have a daughter together! You *can't* move away!"

"My mom doesn't like it here, Deandra. And she hasn't liked it for years. You know that because I told you that. You also know that just like you, I haven't seen my dad in over 10 years. We have no idea where he's at but know he doesn't live in this city anymore. She said she needs a change of scenery, a change of life, and so do I. She thought about doing this for years and just needed to save up enough money to do it and now she has."

"Does she even care about her granddaughter? *Our daughter?* I can't believe this, Trevor! Can't you just stay here with your best friend or a relative?"

"I have no other family here, Deandra. They all moved away from here years ago and live their lives far away from here throughout this country. Look, I told my mom I really didn't wanna be uprooted my senior year in high school to some unknown place, but she didn't wanna wait anymore. I'm sorry."

Deandra stormed away from the table.

"HEY!" Trevor said, and went after her. He grabbed her arm.

"LET GO OF ME!" she yelled, and jerked her arm away from him and headed to the back of the club.

"I'm sorry, Deandra! There was nothing I could do about this! I didn't want this! I didn't wanna hurt you or Ashley! You know that!" he said as he still followed her.

"The hell you didn't!" she said.

"Where are you going?" he asked.

"Why do you care?"

"Just stop and talk to me, okay? *Stop*," he said, and softly grabbed her arm.

She turned and looked at him as tears welled up in her eyes as "Something In My Heart" by Michel'le began playing throughout the establishment. "Your mom is selfish, just wanna let you know that. She doesn't give a shit about her grand-daughter."

"Her granddaughter is not her responsibility, Deandra, it's ours."

"Yeah, well, you're going with her so it's clear Ashley is now gonna be just my responsibility."

He lowered his head. "Don't you wanna know when I'm moving?"

She continued to stare at him with her arms crossed.

He shook his head and sighed. "I'm moving in a week. I've known for months. I just didn't know when it would be the right time to tell you."

She let out a sarcastic laugh. "Yeah, okay! Telling me a week before you move out of my life and our daughter's was the perfect time to tell me, Trevor!"

"I'm sorry, Deandra, but you know how hard this was for me to tell you. I knew it would have this effect on you. I know this would hurt you and hurt Ashley. I will try to come back here and visit when I can, but I am still a minor and my mom has full custody of me. Next year I will be 18 and able to do what I want."

"And you didn't mention anything about moving back here."

He sighed once again. "Look, can I buy you dinner or something so we can talk about this some more? We can go to my house since my mom is out with her friends. Come on, I feel like I gotta do something."

"I'm not going anywhere with you, Trevor. Get the fuck away from me!"

"How are you gonna get home since Mary left with Damian?"

"None of your fuckin' business! Get the fuck away from me!!"

"Bye, Deandra," he said, and slowly walked away. He turned back around just as she was about to turn another corner. "DEANDRA!"

She turned around and looked at him.

"I'll give you my contact info once I'm settled in, okay?"

She gave him the middle finger and disappeared around the corner.

Trevor shook his head, looked up, and saw Richard headed his way. "What's up, man?"

"What's up, man," Richard said as they slapped hands. "You all right, man?"

"Yeah, man. I'm just gonna get up on out of here if I can find Bronson."

"Haven't seen him around, man. But have a nice night," Richard said.

"Thanks, man, you too."

~

"And that was the last time I'd seen or heard from her," Trevor said.

"Wow," I said, and shook my head. "Did you see where your teammate was going?"

"I assumed he was going to the bathroom since he was by himself. I didn't know he was there until I saw him there."

"I see. So, when did you find out that Deandra didn't come home that night?"

"From Mary and Cloris. They actually came over my house while my mom and I were still packing our stuff. That was the very next day after I'd talked to Deandra at The Club."

"Did they question the two of you about your moving?"

"Yeah, they did. They asked me did Deandra know, and I told them that I'd told her last night when I saw her at The Club, and yes, that she was understandably very upset about it. They started cussing me and my mom out about how we didn't give a shit about Ashley and now they couldn't find Deandra and thought I had something to do with it and that was the real reason why we were leaving in such a hurry. It was purely a coincidence that we were moving in a week and Deandra came up missing. You couldn't even make it up."

"Yeah, you really can't. The timing was obviously bad for when you moved, and Deandra came up missing from The Club just that night before. But you can understand why they thought you could've had something to do with her disappearance, right?"

"Yeah, I understand, but I stand a hundred percent by the fact that I had absolutely a hundred percent nothing to do with any of it."

"Do you have anyone in mind that could've had something to do with it?"

"Not at all. I mean, since we weren't together anymore, I didn't know if she'd been secretly seeing someone at her school or at another school, but she didn't tell me she was so I'm gonna assume to this day she never was, even though I'll just never know. I just don't like the fact that everyone thought I had something to do with her disappearance because I left the city a week after she disappeared. It was just plain old-fashioned bad timing."

"So, have you seen Ashley since Deandra's disappearance?"

"Not at all. The last time I saw Deandra was at The Club, the last time I saw her grandmother, Cloris, and Mary, Deandra's best friend back then—well, it was all on a bad note. None of them ever reached out to me after my mom and I had left the city, and I admit that I never reached out to them because I myself was trying to get settled into my new life. And knowing that I'd left my old one behind as well as not knowing the status of Deandra, well, it was harder than anyone thought it would be to handle. Throughout all of these decades, I have never forgot about her or Ashley. I just knew Deandra would be found later that next day or something, but she never was. I'm at a loss just like everyone else about what could've happened to her. I just wished I would've pushed her more to come home with me that night so we could talk more. That's my biggest regret that haunts me to this day."

"I'm sure it does, Trevor. So, do you think someone who was at The Club that night had something to do with her disap-pearance?"

"I don't see any doubt about it. There were hundreds of teens there. That was the last place she was. I left that night without her, but I never thought in a million years that I would never see her again."

"Yeah, it's definitely something that no one ever thinks of because what are the odds of it happening? But in this case it did happen and I'm doing all I can to solve it. Well, I know everyone watching or listening to this wants to know where you have been for the past 33 years?"

"Someplace warm and far away from Saint Maran," he replied.

"Thanks for doing that interview with me, Trevor. I know how hard it was for you," I said, as we continued to talk after my show was over since he insisted that he still wanted to.

"You're welcome, Mackenzee. I didn't realize just how hard that interview with you was gonna be for me until I started talking about Deandra. I haven't talked to anyone about her much less on camera. Everything just started coming back to me. I will never forget the look on her face when I told her I was moving away. I actually was gonna go home and ask my mom could I stay with a friend or someone to at least finish out my senior year at East, but I knew she wouldn't let me so I wasn't even gonna ask."

"Yeah, that's too bad. I just wish Deandra would've gone with you that night instead of storming off from you when you told her you were moving with your mom. I think the outcome would've been a lot different if she had. I think she would still be here. Even Mary said the same thing that if she would've gone with her and Damian that night that she would still be here. I just wish now she would've gone with either one of you."

"But I believe she left The Club with someone that night, I just don't know who."

"How well did you know Richard?"

"Richard? Richard Elmhurst III? My former high-school football teammate?"

"Yes, that's him," I confirmed.

"I didn't know him that well. We were teammates, not friends. He had his own group of friends that were exclusive to him—Antonio, Elron, and some others. He was a really popular guy at school; had been all the years I was there up until I moved. I think it had a lot to do with his dad being the DA at the time."

"Yeah, sounds like it. Do you know he's the current DA in this city?"

"Yeah, I know. Found out some years ago."

"So you really haven't spoken to anyone about Deandra's disappearance since you left here?"

"No, I really haven't. I still have a hard time believing that it's been so long since it's happened and that no one did do anything about it. I was shocked that the police never questioned me; even my mom said it. I told her I would've fully cooperated with them if they had, but we had a big move coming up and we were busy packing, and I was trying to get so much done that I was trying not to think about the reality that Deandra could've been missing. I just thought she could've been out with other friends from work or something and that she would come home. I was always waiting for that call from Mary or Cloris about the fact that she'd come home—I never got the call."

I shook my head. "Damn. I can't even imagine. So, you think that they think you still had something to do with her disappearance?"

"I know they do. Everyone still thinks I moved because I had something to do with it; I know that's what people think, but I told the truth in that interview with you about exactly what happened that night between me and Deandra. I have never changed my story."

"And I believe you, Trevor. You just don't sound like you're lying or trying to hide something about it. It is fucked up that people thought since you moved a week after she disappeared that it was strictly due to you having something to do with her disappearance since you were one of the last ones to see her."

"A lot of people were the last ones to see her at The Club, it seems.

But of course I'm gonna be singled out because I was her ex-boyfriend back then and the father of her child."

"Do you know Ashley is a dentist now who's married to a dentist and that they have a 17-year-old daughter name Nayana?"

He shook his head. "Damn. I've missed so much in these past 33 years, and I'm still here."

I tried not to look shocked at the last part he said. "How do you know Deandra is dead?"

"I don't," he replied. "I didn't mean to make it sound the way like I'm sure it sounded to you, Mackenzee, not at all. It's just that after 33 years, I'll be very surprised if she is. I mean, since Cloris had not had her declared legally dead because I know she would've called me if she had, I believe a part of her believes that she could still be alive out there somewhere as well. But I honestly don't think Deandra would've ever left Ashley intentionally."

"I don't, either. Ashley is a very nice young woman. She's done very well for herself. I ended up being a patient of hers when her husband had an emergency dental appointment to tend to since I was originally scheduled to see him due a referral I got for him. I couldn't believe it when she told me who she was, and then when I continued to look at her, she does look like her mom."

"There's nothing I would like more than to see her and meet my son-in-law and granddaughter. Wow, I'm a grandfather and I had to find out through the young woman who's investigating my ex-girl-friend's disappearance from 33 years ago, a woman who wasn't even alive herself when Deandra disappeared. You can't make this up."

"You can't. But I could put you in touch with her if she says it's okay."

"And I definitely understand you having to ask."

CHAPTER TWENTY-THREE

"Do you know who this *I'm Their Speaker* woman is?" Richard Elmhurst II asked.

"I think I have some idea, although I can't be a hundred percent sure," Richard replied to his dad as he sat at his home. They had just got done watching the latest show.

"What do you mean you have *some idea*, Rich?" his dad said, since this is what he called him for short.

Richard sighed. "It's just what I said, Dad. I can't prove that it's her, but I think it is and I want to know that it is before I do anything about it."

"Well, who is it?"

He sighed once again. "I think it's a woman I actually had a genuine interest in. A young woman I met at The Club on Throwback Thursday: 1990 Night."

His dad sat up in his seat since he was sitting behind his desk in his home office. "And who might that be?" he asked in a raspy voice, and then cleared his throat.

"A woman name Mackenzee Lawson."

"Mackenzee Lawson," he repeated, as he gave a somewhat confused look. "Do I know her or her family?"

"I don't think so, Dad. She's only 28 years old."

"You have an interest in a woman that young? What's wrong with a woman your age?"

"Nothing's wrong, Dad. I actually prefer a woman my age. But you know how it is. A lot of them have too much baggage and is probably on their third or fifth marriage, and don't get me started on the kids they have and even a ton more grandkids and some even have great grandkids. I don't need any of that crap. I know I waited too long to find someone, but my work in running this city is more important."

"It was to me as well, son. But the mayor runs this city, not you. You just help out in it."

Richard glared at him. "So I pretty much have this job as the city's DA for nothing?"

His dad grinned and sat back in his seat. "No, I'm not saying that at all, son. You do run this city in a lot of ways, but there are some things you need to stay out of."

"I know, Dad. But if you're talking about the show we just watched, I told Mackenzee I couldn't find anything about the first girl who went missing in 1990 or any of the other ones."

"So Mackenzee is *I'm Their Speaker*, huh?"

Richard sighed once again. "I can't confirm it, Dad. I had dinner with her after bailing her out of jail."

"You should've let her sit in there and had a friend or family member of hers bail her out. You spoiled her, son. Now she thinks she can talk about a case she has no business talking about since I do think it's her. She wasn't even alive when this supposed first disappearance happened."

"I know she wasn't and she's aware of that, too, Dad. But did Mary and Cloris come to your office wanting to talk to you about Deandra's disappearance? Because they said they did."

"If they did then I don't remember. That was a long time ago, son. I had a lot of responsibilities being the DA of this city and unfortunately, I couldn't hear every case much less decide to want to prosecute them, and quite frankly, I couldn't and didn't wanna be bothered with them."

"Well, I told Mackenzee what I'd told her about what I knew about it since I was there that night it happened."

"I remember you were because you asked me to go there and not your mom."

"I know, Dad, I clearly remember."

His dad stared him down. "Are you sure you didn't have anything to do with that girl's disappearance, son? Or any of your friends? Because as you heard from your ex-teammate Trevor, the ex-boyfriend of Deandra, he said you and your friends were there that night. Was he talking about you as being the one who he passed in the hall when he was leaving after his failed attempt to talk to Deandra?"

"I don't know who he was talking about, Dad. He could've been talking about Antonio or Elron—I honestly don't know and don't remember. Like you said, it was a long time ago."

His dad continued to stare at him, not knowing whether or not he wanted to believe him. "You got home pretty late that night, much later than you normally did when you were out—*that* I do remember clearly. If you didn't get back to the house in about ten minutes, I remember telling your mom that I was gonna go out to look for you. So could you please refresh my memory about that night about why you were so late coming home?"

"Maybe later, Dad. I have to get home to get ready for tonight since it's Date Night tonight at The Club."

"I know it is. Your mom and I are going. Remember?"

He sighed. "Yeah, I remember." He got up.

"Sit down!" he barked.

Richard sat down fast as if he was 5 years old and not 50. "Dad, I have to get home so I can get ready," he pleaded.

"Tell me why you were so late coming home that night, Richard. *Now.*"

The Club: Teen Night: Fall 1990

After walking past Trevor, Richard continued his pursuit to talk to Deandra. He had no intentions on losing the bet he had with his friends. "Damn, where did she go? I know she walked down this hall," he mumbled to himself. He looked back to see if Trevor decided to follow him; he hadn't. He turned the corner and saw Deandra talking on one of the four payphones as she had her back turned towards him. *She's still obviously very upset,* he thought, as he got on one of the other two payphones and pretended as if he was calling somebody. He continued to pretend as if he was talking on the phone until he was able to get her attention.

Finally, she turned around and stared him right into his eyes.

The phone slipped out of her hand and dropped on the phonebook!

Richard smiled . . . and got the phone and hung it up.

"I wasn't done talking," Deandra let him know.

"I'm sorry about that; I thought you were. You seem upset."

"I am," she replied, as she wiped her tearstained eyes.

"Wanna talk about it?"

"I have to get home. I gotta wait for my best friend to get back here to come pick me up. That was her I was just talking to."

"You can talk to me while you're waiting for her. I'm Richard, by the way."

"I'm Deandra," she replied with a slight smile.

They shook hands as Samuelle's "So You Like What You See" played throughout the club.

"Um, let's go this way," Richard suggested.

"Why?" she asked.

"Because it's quieter," he replied with a smile.

Richard's dad continued to stare at him. "Well? What happened? *I just know* it didn't end there."

"It didn't, Dad. But I have to get ready for tonight and confirm that my date is not gonna cancel this date. If you wanna know more, I'll let you know at The Club." His dad glared at him as he got up and walked towards the office door.

"Son?"

Richard turned around. "What is it, Dad?"

"You know I'll do anything to protect you. I'll *still* do anything to protect you. But you have to be honest with me, and it's clear that you haven't been a hundred percent honest; it's pretty obvious. I'm looking forward to tonight."

Richard nodded. "See you there."

CHAPTER TWENTY-FOUR

I watched Porsha as she got ready for her date. "Wow, Porsha. He sounds like a great guy. Where are the two of you going? I forgot to ask."

She stared at me, and then continued applying her makeup.

"Well?" I asked.

She sighed. "I didn't want you to know, but you're gonna find out anyway."

"Yeah, you know I was gonna ask!" I laughed.

"The Club."

"Oh, yeah?"

"Yeah, Mackenzee. And remember what I told you before, you have to have a date to go; they haven't changed that for tonight. They're not letting in people who wanna come with friends or just go solo. Having a date is required to get in tonight. I guess it's also 25 and older, they said. Genesis wanted to go there, but don't worry, he doesn't know that you're the one hosting your show."

"I gotta go with you guys!"

"Mackenzee! You *can't* get in tonight without a date! I just told you that!"

"Well, I'll call Richard since I was waiting for him to call me about tonight and he never did," I said, and got on my phone.

"Do you think he'll go with you since it's such short noticed?"

"He likes me, remember? I know he will," I said with straight-up confidence. I waited for him to answer the phone. He never did.

Porsha looked at me as if she'd caught secondhand embarrassment. "Not there?"

"No, he's not there. I feel like I haven't spoken to him in some time so what do I expect? Look, I *have* to go with the two of you there. If there's a will there's a way. I got to get in."

"Mackenzee, Genesis is picking me up, I'm not picking him up. I don't want my date ruined with your investigation. I know how important your investigation is to you and you've proven that, but I'm going out on a date—"

"To a club that Deandra, Gazelle, and who the hell knows how many others went to one night to have fun and were never seen or heard from again."

"I know, Mackenzee. I just wanna have a nice night with Genesis. I really like him."

I smiled. "He is a nice guy, and I don't wanna do anything to ruin your date with him."

"Thank you."

"So, I'm gonna go solo."

"Mackenzee!"

I arrived solo at The Club, and yes, it was packed. Just as what was expected, all I saw were couples going in, some hand-in-hand, some with their arms around each other. It looked as if some were on double dates and even triple dates. Somehow, I felt so left out over all of this. I was able to get a great parking space—right here right up front—and if there was a chance I was able to get in for tonight, I wanted to be completely incognito, so I opted for a wig in a long black-brown straight slightly wavy look, fake eyelashes, and heavy makeup.

I looked to my right and saw a van parked in the handicapped parking space. I noticed how it was a business van for a dry-cleaning company. I watched as the man got out of the van as he had a sparkling looking garment in a clear plastic bag with the business logo on it.

"EXCUSE ME!" I said, as I walked over to him. I didn't even realize just how fast I got out of my car.

"Yes?" he asked, as he sized me up.

"Is that a uniform in there?"

"Yes, it is."

"It's mine," I lied. "I've been waiting all day for it."

"Well, I'm glad the wait is over. Here you go."

He handed the uniform over to me!

"Have a nice night," he said with a smile.

"You too," I replied with a big smile.

He got back into the van and left.

Wow.

I got back into my car which now had tinted windows as I couldn't believe it! I even had to breathe a sigh of relief that I couldn't believe the odds of something like this happening! I lifted the plastic up and noticed how it was a sparkly, black multicolored skimpy uniform which was obviously a waitress uniform since I noticed the women wearing these the time I was here when I met Richard. I looked at the size.

She wore the same size as me!

It was meant to be.

Couldn't even make this up.

I looked at the name that was pinned to it: Keeshana Renault.

I took it off and put it in my purse. I was Keeshana Renault for tonight, as I'd hoped and prayed that she didn't show up tonight which there was a strong possibility that she could, especially since she had a nice, clean uniform. I felt more confident in getting in there since I had something that the waitresses wore. I thought I would just walk in there with this obvious waitress uniform on, and they would automatically assume that I worked here.

But I decided to walk in with the garment bag all nice and neat with the sparkling waitress's uniform underneath. I took a very deep breath and got out of my car and walked towards the back entrance. I started to get some crazy anxiety since the last time I was here I was caught trespassing and was arrested, and I was back at it again, except this time in total disguise with one of the waitresses just cleaned uniform in my hand.

Just what the hell was I really doing?

I was serious about my investigation and was going through any extreme means to find out what happened to the women who came here for a night of fun and was never seen or heard from again.

I walked up to the back entrance as not surprisingly, a big-and-burly man stared right into my eyes wearing an all-black outfit with The Club logo on his tee shirt. I approached him as if I was Keeshana Renault. "Hi, good evening."

"Good evening," he replied with a smile. He looked at my garment bag in my hand and opened the door!

"Thank you," I replied with a big smile.

He let me in!

I knew it was because of this garment bag with the uniform in it. He obviously recognized it and clearly thought I was one of the waitresses.

This was my night. I could feel it.

CHAPTER TWENTY-FIVE

As I was still stuck in a streak of great luck, a waitress appeared right in front of me while I tried to find the dressing room where the waitresses got ready and probably took their well-deserved breaks. I knew they had one here since after all, I was carrying Keeshana's uniform.

I followed her . . .

Right into the dressing room!

And it was a dressing room, all right. Almost even looked like a stripper's dressing room, but this was not that type of club.

Or was it?

I walked in to a woman sitting in front of a mirror while she talked on her phone.

"Keeshana," she said.

I froze and looked right into her eyes.

"You're lucky you're not working tonight," the woman continued. "I don't wanna be here, either, serving drinks all night to people who are pretending to be so much into each other. They need to call this *Fake* Date Night. People are so fake it's unreal."

I turned around and tried to find a clean space to put my things as I breathed a quiet sigh of relief that the woman was talking to the woman whose uniform I had right in my hands. Since I'd never been a waitress before and had never worked as a stripper, I didn't know what their routines were before work. But I heard all I needed to hear. Keeshana was off for the night. You couldn't make any of this up.

"Has your uniform come back from the cleaners yet? No, not that I know of. But I'll let you know when it does," the woman said, as she still stared at me. I think she knew that I'd never been here before.

I took the uniform out of the garment bag and fumbled around with it, trying to find out how to put it on. It also looked pretty expensive now that I got a good closeup of it.

"Hi."

I turned around to the woman who was just on the phone with Keeshana. "Hi," I replied with a smile.

"Are you new?"

"Yes, I'm new," I lied as I still kept my smile.

"That's what I thought since I've never seen you here before until now. Welcome."

"Thank you."

"I'm Ajaria."

"Lanisa," I said, as I made up the name on the spot.

We shook hands.

"I hope you like working here," she said with a smile.

"Me too," I replied, but for different reasons. "How long have you worked here?"

"Five years," she replied, as she applied the finishing touches of her makeup.

"Five years?" I repeated.

"Yes," she reconfirmed.

"Um, have you heard about what supposedly happened here?"

I felt like I had to say *supposedly* since there was no proof that anything actually had, even though I felt that something did and more than once at that.

She laughed! "Damn! Where do I start?"

"Well, I mean something more drastic and serious than fights or whatever. I'm talking about disappearances."

"*Disappearances?!*" she asked, as if I'd piqued her interest. And it seemed that in a lot of ways I had.

"Yes, disappearances. It was said that a few girls came here one night and they were never seen or heard from since. Most notably, one from 1990 and the other from 1995."

She stopped applying her makeup as she stared at me through the mirror in front of her. "Are you serious, Lanisa?"

"Yes, I'm very serious."

"Where did you hear about these disappearances from?"

I paused for a second. There was no way I could tell her who I really was unless she had some vital information about these cases, but it appeared to me that she knew nothing about them.

Or was she just pretending that she didn't?

She looked young—younger than me—so I would've automatically assumed that she didn't know a thing because she seemed genuinely surprised that I'd mentioned these disappearances to her, and they'd happened five years apart right in here where she worked.

I took a deep breath. "I saw it on a video of an independent news station that was doing a story on a cold case, and they said it happened here in 1990. I think I was so intrigued by it because it happened right here in Saint Maran when I wasn't even born yet and I'd never heard of it, and then I looked it up some more and found out this wasn't the only case."

"Wow, that's something. Have you lived here your whole life?"

"Yes, I have. And you?"

"Yeah, I have. But I don't plan on staying here. Well, since we both have then we both know how corrupt it is and how they are about hiding things. I'm not doubting what you've told me, but I wouldn't really talk to anyone here about it. We have a lot of big names in this city who attend here on a regular basis, and they're not the type of men who liked to be asked a lot of questions."

Yeah, don't I know? I thought.

A chime went off on her phone. "Well, we better get out there to get our trays and notepads from Jamari and get to work since it's filling up fast from what you can see on the live monitor."

I looked up at the mounted screen TV at everyone arriving, and as usual, it looked like the only thing that was going on in this city tonight. "Who's Jamari?"

She gave me a confused look. "The bar manager. He manages all of us waitresses as well. You must've been interviewed by Cedric."

"Um, yeah, I was," I lied.

"Cedric never tells any new hires what they need to do. He just looks at a woman and decides whether or not he wants to hire her but doesn't tell her everything she needs to know. Some hiring manager, huh?"

"A lot are like that," I replied with a smile.

She put her makeup brush down. "Well, I'm off. Gotta find out what tables I'm assigned to tonight since we switch it up often. See you out there."

"Okay," I replied with a smile. But suddenly, I went into a panic. I knew there was more than one bar out there and didn't have the slightest idea who Jamari was.

While I was still getting ready, a young woman stormed into the dressing room, slammed her tray down on the dressing table, and stomped around the corner. I believe she didn't even see me since I was behind a rack of clothes. I hurried to put my shoes on, grabbed the tray, and ran out the door. As I found my way into the main area, I had no idea what this night had in store.

CHAPTER TWENTY-SIX

"WAITRESS! My date and I want a drink!" a man practically shouted at me as I walked by him while his date hung all over him.

"Go to the bar and get one! I'm busy!" I lied in an aggressive response as I kept walking and walked right into the bottleneck of the crowd.

It was definitely crowded in here—personally to me it was quite overcrowded already—so I didn't know for the life of me why they would let any more people in here. The night was still very young, and it appeared to already be full to capacity with everyone coupled up like the way everyone was supposed to come here for this particular night. I tried my hardest to see if I knew anyone here. I knew Porsha was gonna be here with Genesis, but I had yet to see them, and with how crowded it was already, I would've been very surprised if they would've gotten in.

Suddenly, I spotted them!

I rushed over to the table that Genesis obviously had reserved for them as the hostess gave them menus and then left the table, but I got slowed down because I got caught in another bottleneck. I tried my best to keep my eyes on their table since there were so many people here, and saw Genesis tell Porsha something. She nodded and he got up from the table. I started to push my way through the crowd as my tray was practically above my head. "EXCUSE ME! I HAVE TO GET TO ONE OF MY TABLES!" I yelled, as I made my way over to Porsha's table. I finally reached her table as she looked at her phone.

"Hey, Porsha."

She looked up from her phone. "Hi. Do I know you?"

Wow.

My own best friend didn't recognize me. I did more than a great job disguising myself tonight!

"Porsha, it's me."

She sized me up and then stared me right into my eyes. "*Mackenzee?!*"

"Yes, it's me," I confirmed to her.

"Mackenzee?! Oh my god! What the *hell*?! Where the hell did you get that waitress uniform from?!"

"You wouldn't believe me if I told you, but I can't explain it right now since I have to keep busy in here and see if I can get into places in here that only employees are allowed to go."

"Have you lost your damn mind, girl?! Whose uniform is that you're wearing?!"

"It's not important to my investigation, all I know is that I found out she has the night off tonight—can you believe it?!"

She sighed as she shook her head. "Mackenzee. You know damn well you're *not* supposed to be in here for this night tonight much less wearing a waitress uniform that belongs to a woman who has the night off tonight."

"That's why I'm here in disguise and undercover. Look, I'll tell you all about it when we're at home." I took a quick look around. "Where's Genesis?"

"He had to go to the bathroom, and from what I saw, that line was out the door so I hope he didn't have to go that bad."

"Okay, just don't tell him it's me, okay?"

"I wasn't going to," she informed me.

Out from nowhere, *Ajaria appeared*! "Hey, Lanisa! Did you get your correct table assignments for tonight?"

Porsha looked at me as she raised her eyebrows with a slight grin.

"Yeah, I have," I lied.

"Okay, because I thought there was a mix up or something because this is one of the tables I'm assigned to tonight."

Porsha shook her head as I could tell she thought it was a bad idea that I was disguising myself as a waitress, and now I didn't know if this was even a good idea myself since Ajaria was the only waitress I'd met so far tonight.

I flashed Porsha a warning look not to tell Ajaria who I really was; she smirked and looked away. I knew she got what I was non-verbally telling her. I looked around and saw Richard sitting at a booth table with *no other than Mary*!

I quickly left Porsha's table as I squeezed and squirmed my way through the bottleneck crowd while holding an empty tray above my head as "I'm Not Gonna Let You" by Colonel Abrams played throughout here. I had to get a better look, but I knew I wasn't seeing things. I could definitely believe he was here, but I couldn't believe he was here with her.

Mary Landry.

I knew they were the same age, but she'd told me she would never come here again because of Deandra being last seen here. It was like she made a sacred vow to me over it. I felt she was only here with him because he was a wealthy DA who pretty much ran this city now, and he was definitely her quick ticket back into that lifestyle.

But what about her best friend?

I really needed to find out what the fuck was up with this.

I hurried to approach the table, but another waitress beat me to it! Shit.

But I knew this was her table since Ajaria told me they were assigned tables, and I knew since I really didn't work here that I wasn't assigned any tables, but no one had to know that. I stood back as I watched the waitress take their orders, and then walk away.

I quickly walked over to the booth right next to theirs since the people who had it reserved for them still hadn't gotten here yet. I pretend to be taking notes on my notepad, but if there was anyone who perfected the art of earhustling over some loud-ass music, it was me . . . .

"So, are you okay to be back here after so many years?" Richard asked Mary.

"Not really," she honestly replied. "It's just that I didn't think when you called me up and asked me if I wanted to go out on a date with you that you were gonna take me here. I have to admit that it's a great surprise like how you said it was gonna be, but it's far from a great one."

"Well, I'm sorry that you still feel a certain way about being back here after so many years—decades, in fact. I just don't want you to feel like you can't come back here."

"I didn't wanna come back here. There are a lot of other places we could've gone tonight—a lot of places that I've never been to since they were established when I lived in other cities for the past 30 years —so I can't lie to you, this was the last place I thought you were gonna take me to."

"Well, because this is the only place that's holding a date night that's exclusive to this club. I want this to be an unforgettable first date that we have."

"Well, just me being in here for the first time in 33 years because of Deandra last being seen here, I must say that this feels weird and I'm not too comfortable at all with it, I'll admit."

"Sorry to hear that. I guess I should've chosen someplace else to go."

"It's okay, we're here now."

They sat in silence for a few seconds.

"So, I have to bring this up since we are here," Richard said.

I listened very closely and made sure I had my phone on the loudest settings so I could catch what he was gonna say.

"What is it?" Mary asked.

"I saw your interview with the woman who runs the channel *I'm Their Speaker*. Who is she?"

I jumped up and was in front of them in seconds!

"Hello, I'm Lanisa. Would the two of you like a drink?"

They both stared at me as if they knew it was me. If there was any time I felt like I was so transparent, it was right now.

"*You're* our waitress now? Because the other one just took our orders, so if you don't mind, can you see where she is because I'm getting hungry for those delicious hot chicken wings they serve here for appetizers," Richard said.

"And I'm getting thirsty so I would love my drink," Mary said with a smile.

And I would hope you're only thirsty for your drink, I thought. "I'll see where your drinks and appetizers are at. Excuse me," I said, and left the table. I stepped a few feet from the table when their real waitress came from the left side of me with a tray of two drinks and a plate of hot chicken wings. I looked back and saw her walk right up to their table and put the drinks and plate down on it. I felt some kind of relief . . . but only for a few seconds. I got a tap on my shoulder. I looked around to a nice-looking elderly man with an elderly woman. "Yes?"

"Do you know where our son Rich is sitting with his date?" he asked.

I was almost floored by this for some reason. He just assumed that every waitress or staff member here knew who him and Richard were. And I couldn't say that I didn't know. "Yes, Mr. Elmhurst. Rich and his date are right over there. I'll take the two of you to him."

Richard's dad smiled at me. "Thank you . . . ?"

"Lanisa," I lied with a convincing smile. I actually felt like I was doing some real work as they followed me through this thick mess over to their son and Mary. "Here they are," I said with a smile as Richard and Mary looked up from eating as if they'd looked guilty that they didn't wait on them.

"Dad and Mom, nice to see you finally made it," Richard said.

They nodded at him with a smile.

"Thank you, Lanisa," Richard's dad said. He looked at Richard and Mary. "I see the two of you got started without us like I told you that you could do." Him and his wife sat down in the booth. I continued to stand as I waited to see if they needed anything. Richard's dad smiled at me. "My usual, dear."

"And mine as well," Richard's mom said to me.

"Coming right up," I replied with a smile. *Fuck,* I thought as I walked away. I caught their real waitress as I walked to one of the bars. "Um, Richard's parents are here and said they want their usual drinks."

"Okay, I know what they are. Thanks for letting me know," she said with a smile, and continued to another table with a tray of drinks on them.

Damn, that was easy, I thought. But my thoughts ran crazy about what they were all talking about. I glanced over at Porsha as she talked with Genesis. I scanned the area and it looked as if this was a great night to bring a date to, but I had to a hundred percent agree with Mary. This would've been the last place I would've wanted to come to if this was the last place I was at with my best friend decades ago, and she hadn't been seen or heard from since.

I walked towards the bathroom since I really did have to go. After I was finished, I opened the stall door to two young women standing at the bathroom sinks as they checked themselves out in the mirror. "I like your dress," I said to one of them, since I'd instantly recognized it as being a Poster Girl Carina dress made from aluminum in an ombre grayish-blue color that had lingerie-style straps and a slightly flared way-above-the-knee hemline.

"Thank you," she said with a smile.

"Isn't it gorgeous?!" her friend said to me.

"Yes, it is," I replied with a smile.

"My mom would've killed me if I bought a $635 dress just to wear for a first date with a boy I just met."

"Gotta make a great impression! Besides, you're way overexaggerating, Taylor."

I smiled at the two of them since this was how Porsha and I talked.

"No I'm not, Nayana. Come on, let's get back to our dates. It's not good to let them wait for a long time."

I stood in shock!

I practically ran out of the bathroom!

"Nayana!"

They both turned around.

"Yes?" she said.

"Can I talk to you alone for a minute?"

Nayana and Taylor looked at each other.

"Go on. I'll just tell them that you're still in the bathroom," Taylor said, as she stared at me in curiosity. And she had every right to wanna know why all of the sudden this "waitress" called her friend back to talk to her since I clearly said her name.

"Okay," Nayana said, and walked towards me. "Do I know you?"

"No, you don't know me, Nayana. Now look, I'm gonna feel very stupid asking you this but I just have to know since I don't hear names like yours that often."

"What is it you wanna know? You're not an undercover cop, are you?"

I gave her a confused look, but then again, it hit me . . . *hard*. "No, I'm not. I just wanna ask you what's your last name?"

"Capers," she replied as she still looked confused.

"Capers?" I repeated.

"Yes, why?"

Oh my god, I thought. "Is your mom's name Ashley?"

"Yes! Oh my god! You know my mom?!"

"Yes, I'm a patient of hers," I informed her, which I knew was true.

But I couldn't believe this. Here I was standing here talking to Ashley's daughter Nayana, and Deandra's granddaughter. A granddaughter she never met.

"Are you gonna tell my mom I'm in here? Because I'm only 17."

"No, Nayana, I'm not. But you know you shouldn't be in here since you have to be 25 and older to be in here. Is Taylor and your dates also 17 years old?"

"Yes," she said with her head lowered.

I sighed. "Look, like I said, you know you shouldn't be in here, and I mean it for more reasons than you just being underage. That's the start of it. You know your grandmother Deandra was last seen in here in 1990, right?"

"Something like that," she said, and then took a quick look around as if she was gonna be busted for being in here for being underage.

"Something like that?" I repeated. "She was last seen *here*, Nayana. She hasn't been seen since. This is no urban legend shit. This is real life. Your mom has missed out on a lifetime with your grandmother, and words cannot express how your great-grandmother Cloris feels about not knowing what happened to her daughter—your grand-mother. Have they talked to you about this?"

"Yes, but not that much. No one has brought it up that much until recently."

I might have something to do with that, I thought. I sighed. "Nayana, I don't think your great-grandmother and mom would want you to be here knowing the dark history it has concerning your grandmother and not only her, but other women, too. It's not a safe place for you to be especially since you're underage."

"There was nothing going on tonight for us teens. Besides, I'm tired of always coming here on the teen night; it's getting boring, and I feel I'm already getting too old for it."

"Your grandmother went to the very first teen night here back in 1990. So you have been here more than once. Does your mom know?"

"No, she doesn't. She said she never wants me to come here because of my grandmother last being seen here. She told me she's never been here because of it so she didn't want me to start going here, either. I just don't feel like I should miss out on things because what of happened here. Nothing bad has happened since."

"Maybe, maybe not, Nayana, but you have a personal, historical connection to this place, and it's not a good one."

"I know. Um . . . I need to get back to my date and my friends."

"By all means," I said.

She walked away, and then looked back at me. "You're not gonna tell my mom and great-grandma I was in here, are you? And about all of the other times I've been here for the real teen nights?"

"Not at all," I honestly replied.

"Thank you," she said with a slight smile, and walked away.

And I really meant that. It was none of my business to tell Ashley or Cloris that she was in here on a night she knew damn well she was not supposed to be here on, but as well as her being here on the nights for teens—it was her business to tell them. She was from a whole new generation and probably felt that 33 years ago was 333 years ago. I really believe she didn't know the half of what had happened to her grandmother, but I didn't believe for a second that she didn't care at all. She just lived in a different time, and I knew I had caught her by surprise. And she still didn't know who I really was, only that I was a patient of her mom's and for obvious reasons she thought I worked here. But I wanted to tell her so much more because I felt she had the right to know, but only her mom and her great-grandmother I felt were the ones who should tell her what I wanted her to know. But I admit even for myself that my work in Deandra's disappearances as well as others was far from over.

"Mackenzee!" I looked to my left and saw Porsha coming up to me.

"Porsha, what's wrong? You suddenly look upset."

"I am," she confirmed. "Genesis just told me that he's separated. Separated is not divorced. He told me he was single and had never been married. I told him I didn't wanna see him again because he already lied to me about something that big of a deal. He left me here so I was wondering if I could take your car home since he brought me here? I don't have a date anymore and I don't wanna stay here anyway. I hate this place."

"Sure, you can take my car home. I'm gonna stay until it closes to see if I can find out any more info for my investigation. Will you be okay to come back here and pick me up?"

"I should be. I just need to get out of here right now."

"I understand. You got my car keys on your key ring, right?"

She pulled her keyring out and showed it to me. "Got them."

We hugged.

"See you later," I said.

I walked into the main area once again as I worked my way through the bottleneck of the crowd. I caught a glimpse of Nayana and Taylor, as well as their dates. I saw them all get up and walk towards the front door. They were leaving.

I smiled in approval.

I looked out to the dance floor while everyone on it slow danced to Sade's "By Your Side" as Richard danced with Mary while staring me dead in my eyes.

CHAPTER TWENTY-SEVEN

I slipped on my shoes as I watched the last real waitress hurry out of the dressing room. I looked at the waitress uniform I wore one more time since I knew there was an excellent chance I was not gonna get that lucky again as I did in terms of how I was able to obtain the uniform to begin with, and as a result I was able to get in here with no problems because of it.

I headed towards the door.

Click.

I put my hand on the door handle.

It was locked!

"HEY!!!!" I screamed as I banged on the door. "I'M STILL IN HERE! LET ME OUT!!!"

The lights went out!

"3AM Eternal" by The KLF immediately began playing throughout the room when the lights went out as I still screamed and banged on the door. I had no idea what the hell was going on and instantly felt I was in a wide-awake nightmare. I felt whoever shut this place down either forgot I was in here . . . or if it was something far more nefarious going on.

"HEY!!!! LET ME OUT! LET ME OUT!" I continued to scream as I banged harder and harder on the door.

It wouldn't budge.

The door flew open!

"Come on."

It was Elron!

"Elron! It's me! It's me! Mackenzee!"

"Let's go," he said to me once again as he held on to my arm and led me down this dimly lit and smoky hall and outside. "Did you drive here?"

"Yes, but I let Porsha take my car home since she ended her date early. I had called her to come pick me up, but she didn't answer her phone."

"Thank goodness I was here," he said as he unlocked his car doors as I scanned my eyes all around here. "Get in."

I continued to scan the surroundings as I got into his car. "Are we the only ones here?"

"Yes," he said, as he drove off and out of the parking lot.

"What were you doing here?"

"I should be asking you that, Mackenzee, especially with you being in the waitresses dressing room."

"It was luck I was able to get that uniform from a man who worked at a dry-cleaning company. He was dropping it off while I was sitting in the parking lot trying to figure out how I was gonna get in since tonight was only for people who had dates. I lied to him and told him it was mine, but he obviously believed me since he handed it over to me; no questions asked."

He shook his head with a slight grin. "So you didn't have a date, I take it?"

"No, I didn't, otherwise I would not have needed to disguise myself as a waitress. I wanted to see if Richard would've wanted to go but I saw for myself that he went with—"

"Mary," he replied as he continued to concentrate on the road as it started to rain.

"Do you know why he asked her to be his date?"

He shrugged. "I have no idea, Mackenzee, you'll have to ask him."

"Or Mary," I said.

"Yeah, or her," he agreed. He glanced over at me. "Are you okay?"

"I think so," I said. "Did someone forget that I was in there or something? Because it just seemed that the last waitress in there rushed out pretty fast, and then when I tried to leave, the door was all of the sudden locked and the lights went off and a vintage club song started to play. And how coincidental that it's actually in the 3AM hour right now."

He sighed as he concentrated more on the road. He shook his head. "Look, Mackenzee. I'm just glad I was there and was leaving myself and had to walk past the waitresses dressing room to leave." He looked at me while we were at a stoplight as the rain continued to come down hard. "I don't think what happened to you was an accident."

The sound of thunder crashed hard in this stormy night sky!

"WHAT?!" I yelled.

"Should you be surprised?" He sighed. "I think someone knew who you really were tonight, Mackenzee."

"Yeah, well, that doesn't surprise me," I said, as I sat back in my seat. "I thought I disguised myself pretty well, but obviously not well enough."

"Like I said, I don't believe what happened to you was an accident. I told you that getting involved in what could've happened there all those years ago was dangerous. I believe someone was trying to send you a message."

"But who?!"

He shook his head. "I really don't know."

"I don't believe you," I said as I sat low in my seat as I glared at him.

"Mackenzee, *I don't know*. I'm telling you the truth. And there's something you need to know."

I sat up. "What?"

"First of all, before I tell you, I think you need to stop this investigation, *seriously*. You're getting into too much trouble and I don't wanna see you get hurt. I think you got lucky tonight; just as lucky as you got with getting that waitress's dry-cleaned uniform."

"Yeah, you're right, I did. But I can't stop now, Elron. I made a promise to Deandra's mom and her granddaughter Ashley to find out who did this. And I can't forget about Gazelle Ragland—"

"Or Tanisha Longfellow," he said, as he continued to stare straight ahead.

My mouth dropped. "Wait a minute! *Who?*"

He glanced at me. "Tanisha Longfellow."

"Your last name is Longfellow. Is she some relation to you?"

"She's my cousin. We were close since we were only two years apart in age. My dad and her mom are siblings."

I nodded as I continued to stare at him with my eyes as wide as I could get them. "I'm listening."

"And you better listen good, Mackenzee, because I don't wanna have to tell you any of this again."

"I'm listening," I said again.

He sighed. "Damn, what the hell am I doing? What am I doing?"

"You're ready to tell me about your cousin Tanisha, and it's clear you have something to say—and why do I have a feeling you've been holding this in for so long?"

"Too long," he confirmed. "Fuck! I gotta say this. Can't hold this in anymore."

"*I'm listening*," I stressed for the third time.

He sighed once again. "Tanisha was last seen at The Club in 2000. She hasn't been seen since."

I gasped! "Elron! How come you never said anything about this? *You know* I've been investigating this since we first met!"

"There's a reason."

"Well, what's the reason?"

"There's no proof."

"Well, I think it's been proof enough that you said that's the last place she was and she hasn't been seen or heard from since. But how do you know this? Did a friend or friends of hers who were with her that night tell you?"

"No, they weren't with her that night."

I gave him a perplexed look. "What?"

"I was."

I shrieked in shock! "NO!"

"Yes, I was, Mackenzee," he informed me. "And that's not all."

"Oh, shit! What is it?"

"There was someone else there."

"What the hell? Who?"

"Richard."

"NO WAY!" I shouted as my voice echoed over "Strike It Up" by Black Box.

"Yes."

"Wow. And I know you're telling me this for a reason." I looked at him. "So, let's hear it."

He sighed. "Richard and Tanisha were a couple in high school. She was two years older than him, so she broke up with him when she graduated from high school and went off to one of the state universities—but in a different state. He was devastated. I don't think he ever got over it."

"That's too bad. So, he was there that night for sure?"

"For sure," he reconfirmed to me. "We were there celebrating Tanisha's 29th birthday. I decided to treat her to a night there. He knew it was her birthday so I know that's why he showed up."

The Club: Summer 2000

"I felt like I spent a fortune on this fit—Bebe snakeskin-embossed headkerchief top and black flare-leg pants, not to mention these Chinese Laundry black shoes and Louis Vuitton Pochette," Tanisha said with a big smile as she bobbed her head to Destiny Child's "Jumpin', Jumpin'" as they walked around The Club. "Before I forget, thanks for taking me out tonight since my friends treated me to a fancy brunch for my birthday earlier."

"No problem, Tanisha, you know I said that I would," Elron said. "I got a table reserved for us."

"Cool! I was hoping I wouldn't have to stand up all night because it's crowded as hell in here as usual. It's been so long since I've been here; haven't been here for years and years, but it feels like I've never left here."

"Yeah, it's always been like this, there's no doubt about it," Elron said, as they sat down. They looked at the drinks and appetizers menu. "So, it's been a while since we've been able to go out like this alone, you know, just the two of us."

"Way too long," she said with a smile as she looked at the menu. "But we're here together now. I know it feels like I've been gone from this city forever, but I'm back . . . for now—but as you know, I just don't think I'll ever permanently move back here."

"And that's fine, Tanisha. This city isn't for everyone. You found that there was so much more out there in this world and I'm glad you did. I'm proud of what you've accomplished."

She smiled. "Thank you. But I just don't know if law school is really for me."

"Really?"

"Yeah, really. I haven't told my parents that because they want me to succeed at being a lawyer so bad since you know my mom is one, but I just don't know if it's really for me. We're two different people."

"You know Richard is a lawyer."

She cracked a slight smile. "I know."

"Maybe he can encourage you to keep at it."

She looked up. "I don't believe this."

"What?" Elron asked.

"You really talked this up, didn't you?"

"Talked what up, Tanisha?" he asked as his eyes scanned the crowd . . . .

And zoned directly in on Richard!

"He's looking right at me," Tanisha informed him, as Lucy Pearl's "Dance Tonight" now played.

"It's been a long time since he's seen you; since y'all have seen each other."

"Don't remind me," she replied with an eyeroll.

He grinned. "You two really haven't talked since you broke up with him to go to college out of state, huh?"

"Not one word," Tanisha confirmed. "And I'm really not interested in talking to him now."

"Oh, c'mon, Tanisha, be nice. It's your birthday today."

"And I don't want my birthday mood ruined. Did he tell you he was coming here today?"

"No, he didn't," he replied, as he watched Richard make his way over to their table.

"Hey, everybody!" Richard said with a big smile as he stared at Tanisha.

"Hey, man," Elron said, and slapped hands with him.

"Everybody? There's only two of us sitting here," Tanisha informed him.

"And how come I wasn't invited to your birthday party?" Richard asked.

Elron looked at her with a grin.

"Because it was Elron's idea to take me here since I haven't been here in years," she reminded him.

"I know," he said with a smile, and sat down next to her as he scooted more in the booth close to her. "Long time no talk . . . or see. You look beautiful."

"Thank you," Tanisha said.

Richard bobbed his head to the music as he took in the atmosphere.

"Get him out of here!" she mouthed to Elron.

Elron cracked a big grin and looked away. "Um, Tanisha was saying that she didn't think law school was for her after all."

"Elron!" she said.

"You don't?" Richard asked. "Your mom is a lawyer. Don't you wanna follow in her footsteps?"

"No," she said.

Richard and Elron laughed as the waitress came over to the table.

"Are you all ready to order?" she asked, as she sat another napkin down in front of Richard.

"It's on me," Richard informed them. "It's always on me as long as you're here, Tanisha."

The waitress smiled.

But Tanisha was not impressed. "Thanks," she replied with a mustered-up smile.

Elron told the waitress what he wanted to drink.

"Can you take that to the VIP section?" Richard asked the waitress.

"For what? Why?" Elron asked.

"Because Antonio is here with pictures of his newborn baby girl back there, my goddaughter. You're the only one who hasn't seen her yet," Richard reminded him.

"He is? Well, I might as well go back there and say hi to him and see pictures of his firstborn child, your goddaughter." He stood up and looked down at Tanisha. "Is that okay?"

"Yeah, I guess so," she replied as she stared at the people dancing out on the dance floor.

"Of course it's okay. Go on, Elron. I'll call him right now and tell him you're waiting for him." He got out his phone.

"That won't be necessary, man. I'll see you later, Tanisha."

"Of course. I'll let you know when I wanna go," she said, and then glared at Richard for a second as he checked out the atmosphere while looking in a different direction.

Richard continued to bob his head to the music as Elron left the table. "So, it's just us now."

"Yep, it's just us now," she said with a sigh.

"You seem upset."

She looked at him. "And I shouldn't be upset on my birthday. Elron paid for me to get in here since today is my birthday."

"And I'll be paying for everything else."

"Only because you want some pussy."

He laughed. "Yeah, I hope I get that lucky! And that will be nice for old times' sake."

She sighed as she once again rolled her eyes. "Look, Richard. I'm not trying to hurt you any more than I did when I broke up with you to go to college out of state. But you are forgetting that the past is the past, and I have no interest in rekindling anything with you. Our lives have gone in different directions, and you seem to still have a problem accepting that, considering that we've both been out of high school for years and years now."

"I just don't like the way we left things."

"I think we left things with a very clear understanding, and you know we did."

"Yeah, I know, but I wasn't any less hurt by it."

"I'm sorry," she said, as she continued to stare out into the crowd.

"Are you with someone now?"

"No, I'm not. Where's my drink?"

"How come you don't wanna know if I am?"

"Because it doesn't matter to me if you are or aren't, Richard. Look, I don't wanna talk about the past or anything related to it because all you can do is learn from it and move on from it."

"I was that bad of a boyfriend, huh?"

"Don't put words in my mouth, Richard. You know I never said that."

"But you were thinking it."

"Don't put thoughts into my head."

He sighed. "Look, why are we fighting like this? I just wanna get to know you again, Tanisha. The new you. We're both in our 20s now and I'm in my career as a lawyer. You know I can take care of you if you don't want to go to law school."

"I can take care of myself."

He sighed once again. "Listen, it's a little loud in here. Do you wanna go back to the private VIP lounge? I'm sure they'll let you in since you're with me and it's your birthday today. You can get free food and drinks because it's your birthday, and we can talk some more with it being more chill and quieter in there."

She looked at him. "Do I have to be with you to get in there?"

"You know you'll have a hard time getting back there if you're not, Tanisha. You haven't been here in years. You would've had to go with Elron to the back if you wanted. And besides, how come he didn't book a table in the private VIP lounge for your birthday?"

"Because he's not a showoff. And besides, he's my cousin—not boyfriend or husband."

"So, you're not married and don't even have a boyfriend?"

"Does it matter?"

"To me it does."

"Well, it shouldn't."

The waitress approached the table with the drinks.

"Take those to the private VIP lounge," Richard ordered.

"Richard!"

The waitress looked at Tanisha, and then looked at him, unsure what to do.

He got up. "Come on, you've never been in there before, have you?"

Tanisha sighed. "No, I haven't."

"And that's exactly why you should see it, especially on your birthday. You won't be disappointed. Come on."

Tanisha sighed once again and got up and walked with Richard to the private VIP lounge as the waitress followed with her tray of their drinks behind them.

"So, tell me about this private VIP lounge. I take it that it still exists?"

"Sure does. It looks better than ever now. It's totally renovated and completely away from the rest of the regular patrons at The Club. You pay for the private VIP experience."

"So I take it there are regulars who hang back there like you—"

"And Antonio . . . and yes, Richard. A lot of people who are important to this city, Mackenzee. It's even harder to get in there now than it was back then. I think they were a lot more lenient back then than they are now. They don't want it overcrowded at all."

"I understand that. So, what happened when Richard and Tanisha got to the private VIP lounge? And please don't tell me they never made it in there."

"They made it in there, all right."

The Club: Private VIP Lounge: Summer 2000

"This is nice, I'll admit that," Tanisha said, as she took in the atmosphere and sat down in a booth table as "Where I Wanna Be" by Donell Jones played throughout the lounge.

"Told you it would be. I feel it's just what you need to relax and chill on your birthday," Richard said with a smile as he sat right next to her, but a little too close for her comfort since they were almost strangers now.

"Could you scoot over more?" she asked.

"Sure," he said, and moved closer to her.

"You know that's not what I meant, Richard," she said, and scooted away from him and took a sip of her drink.

"C'mon, Tanisha. Don't be like that. I was just trying to be funny."

"You never really had a good sense of humor," she reminded him.

He shook his head. "Damn, you really don't wanna get to know Richard 2000, do you?"

"*Richard 2000*?! What kind of corny crap is that? Sounds like some cheesy video game."

He sighed. "I was just making in reference to my name and the year it is now, Tanisha. A lot of people do that."

"Not me," she said, and took another sip of her drink. "I'm not into that corny Y2K shit."

"Well, I am, and I've done great for myself since the last time we saw each other. I feel that I wanna have someone important to spend the rest of my life with, and if we're together like this again then I think it was meant to be."

"That's what *you* think, Richard, not me," she informed him. "And just to let you know, I don't live here anymore. I'm only here because it's my birthday and I decided to come back here and see my family and friends since it's been a long time since I've seen them. Elron decided to take me here to celebrate my birthday since I went out with old friends during the day today. I have a whole different life somewhere else far away from here, and tomorrow evening, I'm going back there."

"I understand. But are you really happy there? Because you don't seem happy at all, and from what it sounds like, you seem like you haven't been happy for a long time."

She scoffed. "What are you? A lawyer or a psychologist? Stay out of my damn business!" She got up from the table and started walking away.

He jumped up and went after her. "Hey, Tanisha. You know I didn't mean to upset you, okay? You don't have to leave. I wanted to be in here for a reason so I could talk to you even if we just remain friends." He looked over at Elron as he sat at the bar with his drink as he watched them very closely.

Elron continued to watch them as they walked out of the private VIP lounge.

"And? What happened?" I asked, as my eyes couldn't get any bigger. I was full of so much suspense I knew Elron had more to tell me. Much more to tell me.

He sighed. "I honestly don't know, Mackenzee. That's the biggest question, and you know the only one you can get to answer that question is Richard himself because I have not heard from or seen Tanisha since."

"Oh, I'm gonna ask him, all right! Now he can be connected to *two* disappearances? Deandra's and now Tanisha's. I don't believe this."

"Well, I don't know about Deandra's, but I believe he is hiding a lot about Tanisha's. He just acted as if she never existed all of these years after she disappeared."

"He's got a lot of explaining to do about that night, and I guess I already know the answer to what I'm about to ask you."

He sighed as he nodded. "Yeah, I know what you're about to ask, Mackenzee, and you're right. No one ever questioned him. I guess it had a lot to do with the fact that his dad was DA at the time and his dad being good friends with Police Chief Walter Nickerson—and they still are. Both of them were also good friends with the late Othello Pratt, a former mayor of this city."

"And I take it Orlando Pratt is his son since he's the current mayor —am I right?"

"Exactly right, Mackenzee. Orlando has been the mayor in this city since 1995. Longest in Saint Maran history."

"So Othello was mayor most importantly in 1990—the year Deandra went missing?"

"Sure was."

"And so when Gazelle and Tanisha went missing in 1995 and 2000, Orlando was mayor at the time and, of course, he still is. Just how does that man keep getting reelected when there were *two* disappearances at The Club under his watch as well as one disappearance under his dad's watch and no one has done a damn thing about it?"

"I know, Mackenzee. It's fucked up here, as you know. You also know how corrupt it is and how connected everything is. I may be friends with Richard, but I don't have a dad who's friends with anyone his dad is friends with. Besides, my dad moved away from here in the late 1990s; said he didn't like it here. He felt Richard had something to do with Tanisha's disappearance and has always believed it."

"And what do you believe?"

He sighed as he kept his eyes on the road as the rain still came down hard.

The Club: Private VIP Lounge: Summer 2000

Elron continued to sit at the bar watching TV and talking to others. He looked at his watch. Two hours had passed since Tanisha and Richard walked out of the private VIP lounge. He looked to his left and saw Richard walk back into the lounge alone as "I Wish" by Carl Thomas played. "Richard!"

Richard kept walking.

"Richard!" Elron said again as he went after him. He caught up with him. "What's up, man? Where's Tanisha?"

"I'm through with her, man," Richard informed him as he kept walking.

Elron stood in the same place as he watched Richard walk around a corner and completely disappear. He knew he didn't want to be bothered anymore. He went in the opposite direction and out of the main entrance and exit of the lounge where he came in as he went on his search for Tanisha. He made his way back into the main room where the party was winding down for the night. Tanisha was nowhere in sight. He got on his cell phone and called her since he knew she had one, too.

No answer.

"And I haven't had any answers from her . . . and especially from him, in 23 years."

"And that's exactly why I'm investigating this, and I won't dare stop until I get all of the answers. Richard just became the number one suspect in Deandra's disappearance, but especially Tanisha's."

He nodded as he continued to stare straight ahead. "Thank you, Mackenzee."

CHAPTER TWENTY-EIGHT

I stood at the front door of Richard's home. Luckily, I was able to convince the guard in the guardhouse at the front gates into this community that he was expecting me—and the guard believed me and let me in. I felt I had another wind of great luck. And I was determined. I was determined to find out once and for all if he was behind Deandra's disappearance, and now Tanisha's, but I knew one thing was for sure, he had a very strong connection to both.

I nervously rang the doorbell for the second time.

It opened to the beautiful young woman who was here the last time I was here.

"Hello," she said with a bright infectious smile, while wearing a black Dior oversized T-shirt with grey yoga pants and black UGG house slippers.

"Hi," I replied with a smile. "I'm Mackenzee. I'm a friend of Richard's. I wasn't over here for the very first time too long ago and noticed you were here when I was. Could I ask who you are to Richard?"

"I'm Christina, I'm his goddaughter."

It hit me.

"*You're* his goddaughter?! Who is your dad?"

"Antonio," she replied with a smile.

Oh my god, I thought. "What kind of car does he drive?"

"A black BMW 760-something. I'm not into cars so I don't know the exact model of it," she replied.

"With CLUB 88 license plates?"

"Yes," she confirmed to me.

I couldn't believe this. This beautiful young lady just told me who'd been following me in that BMW since I'd been investigating this case, and she didn't even realize it.

"Mackenzee." Richard came out of nowhere. He put his arm around his Christina. "What brings you here?"

"Um . . . I . . . just feel it's been a while since we've talked," I said, since I didn't want Christina knowing why I was really here.

He put on a huge grin, but I could see a lot of skepticism in him. "Come on in."

I walked in while Christina continued to smile at me.

"Thanks, baby," he said to Christina.

"You're welcome," she replied with a smile, and went back up the double wrought-iron staircase.

Richard continued to stare me down. "Let's go to my office."

I nodded with a smile. I didn't wanna say anything until we reached his office. He opened the double mahogany French doors to let me go in ahead of him, and this office pretty much looked better than his work office. With mahogany coffered ceilings and an enormous bookcase with pillars on each of them which covered both sides of his office and full of hundreds of books, I felt he actually did live as well as the living he earned, if that made any sense.

"Your office is absolutely beautiful."

"Thank you. Have a seat."

I sat down in one of the chairs in front of his desk while I checked out his amazing desk. I'd never seen one like it. "What a gorgeous desk."

He sat down behind his desk. "Thank you. It's a Francesco Molon. Cost a lot—more than the average imported luxury car—but I think it's worth it since I'm in here more than half the time when I'm home."

"I believe you," I said with a nervous smile.

He got his phone out. "Would you like a drink? Or should you be asking me that?"

My eyes got big as I stared in a frozen fear at him.

He cracked a wicked grin.

"What?!" I squeaked out in soft voice.

He let out a chuckle. "Are we gonna start playing games with each other already, Lanisa? Oh, I'm sorry, Mackenzee?"

I sighed as I stared at the floor. "How did you know?"

"Your perfume gave you away; never smelled anything like it on another woman. Plus, I recognized your voice. You may have tried to hide behind a wig and heavy makeup, Mackenzee, but I knew it was you."

"Are you gonna tell the people who own The Club that it was me?"

He grinned once again. "It depends."

"On what?"

"On why you were there pretending to be someone you weren't. How did you pull that off?"

"You probably wouldn't believe me if I told you."

"Try me."

I told him the story I told Elron as well as Porsha before I'd left to come over here.

"Wow, sounds like you got very lucky, huh? You must've considered it your lucky night."

"I did. And what where you doing there with Mary?"

"What business is it of yours?"

You don't have to be a fuckin' smartass, I thought. But he was right—what business really was it of mine? But he knew why I wanted to know. "Well, I was just surprised to see the two of you together, that's all. I didn't think someone like her was your type."

"She's not," he informed me.

"Then why were you with her?"

He sighed as he stared at me. "I just wanted to make sure she understood some things, that's all."

"What things?"

"Well, for one thing, that she understood that I had nothing to do with her best friend's disappearance from The Club 33 years ago, since there's been a lot of shit going around on that woman's little show on that video platform about my involvement in it."

I tried not to lose it. I felt in a lot of ways now that he knew it was me, I just couldn't prove it unless he just flat-out told me that he knew it was me. But then again, *he* couldn't prove it since he'd never seen me on there, and I did use a voice filter to make myself sound different than my natural voice to try and hide my identity even more. I took a deep breath. "Well, why did you feel it was so important to go out on a date with a woman who is not your type to try and prove to her that you had nothing to do with her friend's disappearance from 33 years ago if you in fact did have nothing to do with it? *And* you took her to the same exact place that her best friend was last seen at. Are you kidding me?"

"There was nothing wrong with me taking her there again, first of all, since she hadn't been there since Deandra disappeared from there. Yeah, she was uncomfortable at first, but then she started to slowly warm up to being there."

Yeah, I know, I got that part of y'alls conversation for that night on my phone, I thought. "You still haven't answered the first half of my question."

He gave me a sarcastic smile as he sat back in his gaudy chair and twiddled his BENU luxury pen. "And what's that?"

This guy is a fuckin' piece of work, I thought. "Why did you take a woman who is not your type out on a date just to prove to her that you had nothing to do with her best friend's disappearance 33 years ago?"

"I wasn't trying to prove anything, Mackenzee. I just don't want her to think I'm a bad person just because of the shit that's been said about me, about my dad when he was in office, about the present and past mayors, and the police department in this city. Someone is trying to bring this city down with shit they can't prove, that's why nothing has been done about these three disappearances."

I had to swallow my gasp! And it hurt my throat like hell to have to do it. He didn't even realize what he had said . . . .

Three disappearances.

I never even brought up Tanisha's.

Not once.

Not once since I've known him.

"There are *three* disappearances from The Club? Really?"

He continued to stare at me. He fucked up with me and he knew it. And he knew it that I knew it.

There was a knock on the door.

Christina entered. "Are we done?"

"*We're* done," Richard said, as he glared at me. He got up. "I have to continue with my session with my goddaughter since she wants to be a lawyer. You interrupted that, Mackenzee."

"I'm sorry," I replied with my head down. I got up as he got up as we walked towards the doors of his office and towards the front entrance as Christina stared at us from down the hall. He opened one of the front doors for me. I turned and looked at him. "I just—"

"Goodbye, Mackenzee."

CHAPTER TWENTY-NINE

"So, what are you gonna do now?" Porsha asked me, as she gave me a cup of hot tea, and sat on the couch with me in our family room.

"What do you mean what am I gonna do? It's clear to me that Richard knows he fucked up with me by mentioning that there were three disappearances when I've only talked to him about two of them. Tanisha's missing because he fuckin' killed her, I know it."

"But you can't prove it," she reminded me.

"Well, just because I can't prove it now doesn't mean I'll never be able to. I just need the time to find the proof. I felt like Elron had a thousand-pound weight lifted off of him when he told me the story from 2000 about the last time he saw Tanisha. Richard had everything to do with her disappearance. Elron said he came back into that private VIP lounge with a look that only a person who looked like they'd done something evil would look. He also said that Richard said he was through with her."

"Yeah, it sounds like he was definitely through with her for good, huh?"

"This isn't funny, Porsha."

"Am I laughing? Hell, I told you that I didn't want you getting involved with Richard because something about that man just doesn't sit well with me at all. He just seems to have an evil aura about him. Don't think just because he looks good that he's not evil, Mackenzee."

"Never said he wasn't, but yes, he's looking more and more suspect —that's a fact. And like I told you when I first got back here, he knows he fucked up with me and knows I'm gonna run with what he'd told me about him mentioning three disappearances, not only two of them. Little did he know, I already knew about the third one because Elron told me. Oh! And I almost forgot to tell you something else."

"What is it?"

"Antonio is the driver of the BMW with the CLUB 88 license plates! He's Christina's dad! She's actually over at Richard's house mostly because she's studying to be a lawyer."

"Yeah, I believe it. Only to probably end up being a corrupt one like her godfather."

"Well, I gotta prove he's corrupt. And just by what went on at The Club for all of these years and his dad didn't do anything about it—like not even wanting to be bothered with hearing about Deandra's disappearance and obviously not with Gazelle's, either—I think he got his corrupt ways from his dad because it's looking more and more likely that he's definitely involved in at least two of these disappearances, especially Tanisha's. And if Richard had something to do with Tanisha's disappearance—and it's definitely likely that he did—then you know his dad really didn't wanna hear about that one since Tanisha was Richard's ex-girlfriend. And like what Elron told me, she was a total bitch to him that night she disappeared, and Richard was the last one seen with her."

"This is just getting more and more fucked up and Richard is looking more and more like a suspect, especially when it comes to Tanisha's disappearance. These poor girls. I wish they will be found soon. It's just crazy to me that you've had all of these interactions with a man who could be responsible for at least two of them, and his goddaughter's dad is protecting him by policing your every move all over this city. And his own dad? Well, he's just as bad because you can tell he's really protecting him. I think his dad knows exactly what Richard has done."

"I think he does, too. Damn, I wish I had the proof. And speaking about proof, yes, he knew it was me who was the waitress last night. He said my perfume and voice gave me away."

"Thank goodness you use a voice filter on your show."

"And that's exactly the reason why I do."

The doorbell rang.

Porsha and I exchanged looks of curiosity and anxiety.

"Who is it? Are you expecting anyone?" she asked.

"I don't know, and no," I replied.

The doorbell rang again.

"Well? Aren't you gonna answer it?" she asked.

"Peek out of the peephole to see who it is first," I suggested to her.

"Why should I do it? I'm not the one investigating anything!"

She was right. I was the one investigating this, and if I wanted my investigation to continue and be able to solve it then I had to get used to unexpected visits that could or could not have something to do with what I was investigating.

I slowly crept to the door with Porsha closely behind me. We both jumped as the doorbell rang once again. I looked back at Porsha; she gave me a look of clear and pure fear in return. I looked out the peephole.

And opened the door.

"Hi, Mary. Come on in."

CHAPTER THIRTY

$\mathcal{M}$ary walked into the house as she took a cautious look around. "I'm sorry for stopping by here unannounced. I tried to call you to let you know that I wanted to come over, but you didn't answer your phone."

I checked my phone. She did call and text me while I was over Richard's house. "Oh, wow. Sorry about that. If I saw that it was you, you know I would've answered it." I knew I was over at Richard's house at that time and was so fixated on finding out if he would tell me more about Tanisha.

Mary smiled. 'That's okay. I'm just glad to be talking to you right now. But can I talk to you alone?"

I looked at Porsha.

"Sure, that's fine. I was just on my way out to go grocery shopping. I'll see you later, Mackenzee."

"Of course," I replied with a smile. I turned towards Mary. "Come on into the kitchen."

After making her some coffee and offering her leftover donuts from Dunkin' that I had bought for our weekly sweet treats, I really wanted to talk to her about her date with Richard.

"So, how well do you know Richard?" I asked. I wanted this

conversation to get going right away because I had a lot to say.

She took a sip of her coffee. "Not too well. I didn't know him back in 1990 when we were in high school since he went to East, and I went to West. I just thought it was weird that someone of his status would call me up out of nowhere and ask me did I want to go out on a date with him. He didn't even ask if I was single or not. Since I am, I told him that I would love to and that he could pick the place. But I couldn't hide my disappointment when he picked of all places in this city, The Club. He said it was because it was Date Night that night; I think he did it with ulterior motives."

"And what do you think the ulterior motive was?"

She sighed and took another sip of her coffee. "I think he was trying to find out information from me about Deandra's disappearance from there since I was best friends with her."

My eyes got wide with curiosity. "For real?"

"Yes, for real, Mackenzee. He also asked me who does the show *I'm Their Speaker*, since he saw me be interviewed me for it, but a waitress interrupted us to ask us what we wanted to drink. I don't think she realized she had the wrong table because our waitress had already asked us minutes before and took our orders."

If there was any time to come clean, it was now.

"Um, did Richard say anything about that second waitress who came to the table?"

"Yeah, he asked me did she look familiar to me."

"And what did you say?"

"That she didn't look familiar at all because I hadn't been there since 1990 so everything was new and looked new to me, but old and scary at the same time as well as surreal, because that's the last place Deandra was seen in."

I sighed. It was either now or never. "Mary. Before I go on, I just wanna say that I hope you don't see me any different."

"Different from what?"

"Different from how you saw me that night. I was that second waitress who came to you and Richard's table," I confessed.

"What?!" she said, as her eyes had widened with shock. "Are you serious, Mackenzee?!"

"Yes," I replied with my head slightly lowered in shame and guilt.

She laughed!

"Well! I think you disguised yourself very well! You really had me fooled! And it shows me just how serious you are about investigating these disappearances because I know you would not have gone there undercover as one of the waitresses if you weren't serious. Who did you get it approved from?"

"No one," I honestly replied.

"For real, Mackenzee?!"

"Yes, I'm for real. You're probably not gonna believe me when I tell you how this happened."

"Well, I'd love to hear it," she said with a smile.

I told her the story I'd told Richard, Elron, and Porsha about how I became a one-night undercover waitress.

"Wow, that was luck how you got that uniform and the woman who wore it having the night off. It was definitely your night."

"Yeah, it was," I replied with a smile.

"Does Richard know?"

"Yeah, he does. And he knew it was me from the start because he said my perfume and voice gave me away."

"That'll do it!" She sighed. "But I honestly think Richard was just using me."

I found this to be very interesting. "Why do you say that?"

"Because he just didn't seem all that interested in me. Look at me. I'm not exactly a city DA's type. Maybe if I was a lot slimmer again and had real long hair and was a few shades lighter that I would be more of his type—but I am who I am. And I don't appreciate being used just because he wants me to stay quiet about Deandra's disappearance."

"You honestly think that's why he asked you out on a date?"

"Mackenzee, I honestly think he was interested in me because I was on your show, and no, I did not tell him it was you, so you have nothing to worry about—and I wasn't going to. And he didn't ask me again. You clearly threw off his thoughts about it. Apparently, he has some kind of major connection to The Club because he took me in the back in the private VIP lounge for a while where I met a lot of people who are the big new wigs in this city and some of them have been for quite some time. I know big wigs is a very old term—older than me, actually—but that's what they are." She got out her phone. "Here's a picture that I took with all of them."

She gave me her phone so I could get a better look at the picture. The picture had her and Richard in it, as well as Richard's parents. It also featured Elron and Antonio, as well as some others that I didn't recognize along with their women. I kept looking at the picture as I all of the sudden recognized someone in the picture. And it instantly brought me some instant anxiety. "Who's this?" I asked, as I pointed to the small-framed man who came outside of The Club when I was in the back snooping around. The one who had the charges pressed against me for trespassing.

"That's Oliver Pratt. He's the grandson of the late Othello Pratt, who was mayor of this city for many years. His son, Orlando, is the current mayor, as you know."

"Yes, I know," I said, as I kept staring at the picture. "What is Oliver's connection to The Club?"

"He's the current owner."

"So that explains why he pressed charges against me for trespassing and was asking his cronies who I was."

She chuckled. "Yeah, that's probably or obviously why, Mackenzee."

"He probably doesn't care about what happened at the place he now owns, huh?"

"Probably not, Mackenzee. He is an arrogant asshole; I know that much. Just nodded to me when Richard introduced him to me while some whore hung all over him as they sat in one of those booths in a corner. Had me standing there looking like a goddamn fool with my hand out for those few seconds. I guess it's because he's a little half-pint punk with low self-esteem and can only get women because he owns that shit place."

I smiled. "I'm glad to see you still feel the same about it."

"Oh, there's no question that I do," she reconfirmed. "I felt as if everyone in that room knew what happened to Deandra right there in that club, and they just didn't give a fuck. Not the kind of people I want to be around. I think they only wanted me in that picture so it would look like I was on their side about everything."

"That's very interesting that you would say that because that's what I believe, too."

"I'm glad you believe it, Mackenzee. But you know? There's one thing I've always been good at and that is having a spirit of discernment. I know when something doesn't seem right, and all those guys are corrupt as hell, and their women just tolerate that bullshit because of the life they live with them. I just didn't have a great feeling at all when I was around any of them."

"Not even Richard?"

"Especially Richard."

"Really?"

"Yes, really."

"Wow," I said, and shook my head.

"I knew none of them were good people to be around, and it's like I knew I just flat-out didn't fit in with them and that Richard was definitely using me because he doesn't want me talking about Deandra anymore. I think he definitely has something to do with her disappearance because when I saw the interview you did with Trevor as he told the story about when he was last with Deandra, I believe very much now that it was Richard that Trevor walked past that night when Trevor and Deandra had parted ways because Richard was definitely headed Deandra's way from what Trevor had said in the interview."

"Did you ask Richard did he ever meet Deandra?"

"Yeah, I did, and he told me he never did. Now I believe he was full of shit."

"That's what I think, too. Well, I'm glad you find him to be a suspect in her disappearance."

"I find him to be the *only* suspect in her disappearance."

"What about Gazelle? Do you think your baby daddy Damian had something to do with her disappearance since you saw my interview with him?"

She sighed. "I honestly don't know. I just hope he was telling the truth about having nothing to do with it because I just don't know who he really is anymore."

"Sour grapes? Bad date? Feeling used and mentally abused? Baby mama-daddy drama?" Porsha asked, as we sat in the family room later on that night.

"All of the above, that's what I got out of it," I said with a grin, and ate some more of my freshly popped popcorn. "At least Mary was being honest. Richard just doesn't seem like he would be interested in her, and she had every right to feel used by him because I believe she was being used by him to find out if I'm the one who's investigating these disappearances. I also believe she is conflicted about Damian and just didn't wanna really tell me how she really feels about the fact that her child's father could've had something to do with Gazelle's disappearance. And I didn't even want to get into it about Tanisha Longfellow since she's Elron's cousin when it comes to Richard because I believe she would lose it, and I can't know for sure that she wouldn't go back and tell Richard that I'd told her about what Elron had told me."

"Yeah, I'm glad you don't a hundred percent trust anyone, Mackenzee, and you can't since you're investigating this."

"You know I can't. But I honestly can't get it off of my mind about how Richard mentioned there were *three* disappearances from The Club when I've only confirmed two of them. I gotta confront him about it."

"Mackenzee! Now you're talking crazy. I think you should think this over before you go talking about confronting him. If he had something to do with this *and* with Deandra's disappearance, then you already know what he's capable of. You saw the picture of Mary with all of those corrupt people in it who I think know a lot about what went on at The Club and just don't care as long as they keep their jobs and be able to live their lives the way they dreamed of."

"And I don't think that's fair at all. I'm tired of people claiming to care about others and not doing a damn thing to prove it or lying about nothing being reported about disappearances. All they care about is maintaining their power positions in this city." I pulled up the picture on my phone since I told Mary to send it to me. I shook my head. "They look like a bunch of gangsters except for Mary, of course, since I believe she was coerced into taking that picture with all of them."

"Well, if she said she was then I believed she was as well. But I wouldn't go that far in calling them that, Mackenzee. But I do believe a lot of them know a lot more than what they're telling about these disappearances, especially Richard."

"Exactly. And I also now know that Antonio— who happens to be one of Richard's best friends from high school—is the one who is following me around this city, so I firmly believe Richard knows that I've been on to him from the start."

"I hate to say this, but I think he has been on to *you* from the start, too. And since you know this, what are you gonna do?"

"Keep investigating until Richard admits to me what he's looking more and more guilty of." I looked at my phone. "Holy shit!"

"What?" Porsha asked, as her voice was piqued with curiosity.

"Oh my god! Is this person serious? I need to verify this."

"What? What do you need to verify, Mackenzee?"

"That this person is the reporter whose video I saw about Deandra. The one-and-only video I ever saw about her case. This was why I wanted to start my own investigation on her disappearance and found out that there are now two others. If it wasn't for this video, then I wouldn't know about these cases at all and would probably be casually going to The Club like the way we used to. She told me in this text that she would like to be interviewed by me on my show; says she has a lot to say including telling me what happened to the channel she worked for."

"Wow. Well, I can't wait to hear what she has to say as well."

"I'm texting her back right now to set it all up. I can't wait to hear all about it myself."

CHAPTER THIRTY-ONE

<u>I'M THEIR SPEAKER</u>
EXCLUSIVE INTERVIEW WITH VATRICE JOHNSON,
ORIGINAL REPORTER ON THE DISAPPEARANCE OF
DEANDRA WHITFIELD FROM THE CLUB IN 1990
WHAT SHE SAYS HAPPEN TO THE CHANNEL THAT
INSPIRED ME TO INVESTIGATE THIS CASE AS WELL AS
THE OTHERS ALL TIED TO THE CLUB

"Hello, everyone, and welcome to the show. Today I have a very special guest joining me from an undisclosed location for her safety since this is a sensitive topic, so please welcome, Vatrice Johnson, the reporter who inspired me to start this channel and investigate this cold case of Deandra Whitfield. And unfortunately since investigating this one, I found out that another woman disappeared from The Club five years later in 1995, but this all started with Deandra Whitfield's disappearance which I had no idea happened until I saw her video about it. So, Vatrice, tell me how you found out about Deandra's case."

"Thank you for having me on this show, first of all. And I definitely want to say that I'm glad your channel is still up since the one I worked for and managed along with the person who created it had been taken down after I reported on this story."

"And that's unfortunate because this is a case that needed to be told. But how did you find out about Deandra Whitfield?"

"I was just searching for cold cases from cities all across this country, well, in particular, stories about missing Black girls. I searched for pictures as well, and saw in a search a Missing Persons flyer for Deandra Whitfield, so I clicked it on. I saw on the flyer all the info that I needed to see, and I couldn't stop staring at how beautiful she was. It'd said she was last seen at The Club in the fall of 1990 and gave her age and stats like the way a flyer like that does. It also said she was the mother of a 2-year-old girl at the time. That poor little girl."

"Yes, it's very unfortunate. So you just went on that information and decided to report on it?"

"Yes, as well as me contacting the local Saint Maran Police Department and asking them could I speak to someone in regard to this cold case. They said I had to have legitimate credentials to be able to speak to someone there. I guess they're just not with the updated times of people being with independent news channels and everything, and I understand, some people just aren't. But I asked them did they have a cold case department or was anyone there at least working on any cold cases, and the person said they didn't know, so I just looked it up myself on their department website and social media pages and saw on their website that they had a number for information about cold cases so I just took down the information and relayed it to the viewers who saw the story. I guess someone did see the story and didn't like the fact that I reported on the case because the channel was shut down the next day."

"Wow. Unbelievable. So, you called the number that was given about information about the cold cases?"

"Yes, I called it because I wanted to see if it was legit, but no one ever answered the phone."

Just like when I called them, I thought. "Well, that doesn't surprise me. It's clear someone or some people didn't want you reporting on this case. How were you able to do the report right outside of The Club?"

"My crew and I got there very early, like in the early morning hours. We didn't want anyone chasing us off the property, and that's what us independent news stations who just broadcast on video platforms have to do. They don't consider us legit at all, and that's unfortunate because some of us usually have the best stories that no one had ever heard of, and you're proof of it."

"I am definitely proof of it, Vatrice. I was shocked to see this story because I'd never heard of it and it happened 33 years ago. And then when I saw your channel had been removed, I didn't even know what I was actually getting into because of it."

"But I'm glad you did because you're finding out more than I probably ever would've. It's just that I feel something is very corrupt in Saint Maran with the people in power and every-thing because I believe it was definitely someone or some people in power who got the channel shut down. And the man who ran the channel—not gonna say his name for privacy purposes, plus, I don't want him suing me—just told me the next day when I tried to get on it and saw that it was shut down that they wouldn't even tell him why they shut it down. He said he didn't want any trouble and just wished me luck at finding new work."

"Wait, what?! That's it? That's all he had to say about it?"

"Yeah, that's all he had to say about it, but I think he knows exactly why they shut it down, and since he owned the channel, he didn't even try to appeal it. It's like he just didn't wanna go through all of what he knew he would have to go through to get it up and running once again."

"Wow. Well, something definitely sounds fishy about all of that. The channel gets taken down without any reasonable explanation for it and your partner didn't even wanna fight it?"

"Not one single bit. I tried not to think too much about it, but I knew something definitely wasn't right because we've reported on several other cold case stories from all over the country and nothing happened to the channel at all, but as soon as I reported on the Deandra Whitfield disappearance story, it was shut down the next day, the very next day. Something *definitely* isn't right about all of this, and if I got shut down from finding out then I'm glad someone like you picked it up and started your own channel about investigating something that has been long overdue. There's obviously a reason why your channel is still up and the one I worked for was shut down. I hope you find out why and get all the answers you need about what's going on in that city. I feel like you're working for both of us now."

"And I'm doing all I can, Vatrice. Believe me. I'll keep you updated on my progress."

"So, she essentially skated around what really happened to the channel?" Porsha asked me later on that night.

"Yeah, I feel that she did, but I didn't wanna pressure her. I think she was just trying to protect herself and there was nothing wrong with doing that since she told me that she does work a 9-to-5 job now while looking for independent news work on someone else's channel that's more stable."

"Why don't you hire her?"

"You know why. I can't afford to pay her."

"Perfectly understandable. But what do you think she really wanted to tell you that she just couldn't tell you during the interview?"

I sighed. "I think she feels that the man who created the channel —Joe—and yeah, that's his real name but of course by her request I withheld it while interviewing her. But I think Joe was probably paid off by someone in this city to shut his channel down since Vatrice did the story about Deandra. I know someone here was involved in getting it shut down; I just wish I knew who it was and can prove it."

"Aren't you afraid they're gonna shut you down?"

"No, actually I'm not," I honestly replied.

"And why not? This is why you made up the channel because of the story you saw Vatrice do. The channel she works for gets shut down but yours is still up and running and that's all you've talked about is these disappearances. Can you explain it?"

"Actually, I can. I think someone knows it's me but they can't prove it, and they know they need the proof that it is me so they can shut me down."

"Or do a lot worse," she said, as she gave me a look of concern. "I'm scared for you, Mackenzee, I really am. I always have been since you started investigating this. I think Richard knows it's you, but like you said, he can't prove that it is. And you owe Mary more than you'll ever know for her not telling him it's you that's doing your show."

"Yes, I know I do. But I made her sign a disclaimer before I interviewed her that she was not allowed under any conditions and/or circumstances to reveal who I am to anyone, and she obviously remembered signing it. I just don't think she would've told him anyway. I'm just glad she sees Richard for who he really is."

"And who he really *is* is the number one suspect in at least two out of the three disappearances from The Club."

I nodded as I stared passively at the TV. "And I can't wait to prove it." I got on my phone.

"Who are you calling?"

I put it on speaker.

"Hello?"

"Hey, Elron. It's Mackenzee," I said in an upbeat voice.

"Hey, Mackenzee, how are you doing?"

"Just fine. I was wondering if you caught my latest show with my interview with Vatrice Johnson?"

"Yeah, as a matter of fact, I did. And I'm glad you called me because that's what I need to talk to you about. I think doing that interview was a big mistake."

"What?! Why do you say that?"

"Look, I think you're treading in some dangerous waters, and I need to talk to you about it in person. People are starting to ask me a lot of questions about you."

"Like who?"

Porsha kept staring at me. Her concern for me once again showed all over her face.

He sighed. "Just meet me at my house tomorrow. Don't worry, no one will be here. I live by myself. I just need to tell you some things."

"About Tanisha? About Richard?"

"About some things, Mackenzee, okay? Look, just make sure you're safe tonight, okay?"

"What?! You're scaring me, Elron."

"Me too," Porsha mouthed.

"I don't think anyone knows where you live, but then again you can't be too sure so I just want you double check your locks and security system. You do have one, right?"

"Of course. I'll do that."

"Okay, I'll call or text you tomorrow morning. I gotta get going to the grocery store to buy some food for a special meal I'm making tomorrow. Bye now."

"Bye," I said. I got up and looked outside the window.

"I'm staying at my parents' house tonight," Porsha said.

"You can't, Porsha. This is your home. Don't worry. We have a great security system. Let's just double check to make sure all the doors and windows are locked."

"I told you we should also have a Cane Corso or Rottweiler for security as well."

"Or both. But we can't afford any dogs right now, I told you that," I said, as we went around the house making sure everything was locked up. I checked the alarm to make sure it was on, something I'd done every night. If I didn't do it, Porsha did it.

"Maybe we should sleep out here on the couches tonight," she suggested.

"Good idea since we know we will be together in the same room. There's a TV in here," I said with a smile.

But I had to admit that what Elron had told me had me scared, and not only did it have me scared, but it also had Porsha terrified. I had no intentions on bringing her all into this, but I felt that this investigation was important, but I didn't want any threats and fear to compromise our safety and security. I honestly knew that someone was trying to scare me, and as a result it was having an effect on Porsha as well. I knew this was all a part of getting to the truth about something, and if they had me scared, then I was closer to the truth than I'd ever realized it.

CHAPTER THIRTY-TWO

"Can't wait to eat the food Elron made for me; made for us. I know I'm only going over his house with you because we got this buddy system in place now where we have to go everywhere together since you're investigating this case. But damn, knowing how Elron can cook some food, I already feel spoiled!" Porsha said, as she drove us to Elron's house.

I smiled. "He is a great cook so I can see how you can feel spoiled. I just need to hear what he has to say, that's all. I think he's ready to confess to me."

"About what?"

"About how Richard definitely had something to do with Tanisha's disappearance as well as Deandra's. And I need the proof of it because I wanna be able to tell Cloris and Ashley about it and have Elron come with me to the cops if need be. I mean, that night he let me out of that locked waitress dressing room and told me the story about the last time he saw Tanisha, he just had a different demeanor about him, like he's been holding in something for so long and he finally told me—but I think he has more to tell me; *I know* he has more to tell me. I think Richard told him exactly what happened to both Tanisha and to

Deandra, and he knows if he goes to the cops with it that they're not gonna do a damn thing about it, and probably hurt Elron on top of it. I think I'm gonna have two of these disappearances solved tonight, Porsha."

She nodded as she concentrated on the road. "Let's hope so." She made a right turn at the corner at a stoplight and went into the backway of a gas station. "Sorry, I'm almost out of gas. We have time to stop, right? Since Elron's not expecting us for another 20 minutes?"

"Yeah . . . oh my god!"

"Holy shit!" she said in response to what we both saw.

And we were both reacting to pulling up right behind the black BMW 760i!

And the CLUB 88 license plates confirmed that it was Antonio's car!

No one was at the pumps.

"He must be inside," I said, and put my hand on the door handle.

She grabbed my arm! "Mackenzee! NO! If he's inside I don't want you confronting him about anything, okay? Just let me get this gas and we can get the hell out of here and off to Elron's!"

"What if he follows us to Elron's?"

"I'll hurry up as fast as I can," she said, and got out of the car.

I jumped out of the car and walked fast towards the front door of the station!

"MACKENZEE!"

I walked in as unassuming as I could while I searched each of the aisles for Antonio . . .

And there he was!

Wearing a $6,000 Louis Vuitton Varsity black and white blouson jacket depicting a musical theme with playful graphics along with a white tee, jeans, and sneakers. He had Louis Vuitton sunglasses over his eyes as he checked out the selection of energy drinks. *Yeah, The Club must pay you good for following me all around this city,* I thought.

I pretended to check out the selection of drinks that were right in front of me when I knew just by looking at them that I'd never had any of them and probably never would. I couldn't believe I was standing just several feet away from the man that'd chased me all over this city, starting with the night I met Richard. I could not let him get away from me without asking him a few questions of my own but without making him suspicious as to why I was.

I slowly walked up to him.

"Um . . . excuse me?"

He turned and looked at me as he sized me up. I could see his eyes through the sunglasses he was wearing as he more eye-fucked me than anything. "Yes?"

"Are you Antonio?"

"Yes, I am." He turned his attention back to the selection of drinks. He picked two out and shut the door. "Nice to finally meet you, Mackenzee."

For some strange, unexplained reason, I was shocked that he knew my name.

"How did you know my name?" I stupidly asked, and I knew I only wanted to know this just to see what he would say.

"Richard told me," he replied as he stared down at me. "But all the big, important people in this city know who you are, Mackenzee. You've made quite a name for yourself."

This guy knows, I thought. "Well, I don't see how that is because I haven't done anything significant for people to know about me in this city. And Richard and I are not dating."

"I know the two of you aren't. I'm his best friend. We've been best friends since high school."

"Yes, I know about the two of you being friends for that long. But how well did you know his girlfriend from high school, Tanisha?"

"Excuse me, I gotta be somewhere," he replied, and turned his back on me and walked away.

I followed him to the checkout register. "You're not gonna answer my question?"

"I have nothing to say about it," he said with an obvious fake smile, as he put the two drinks up on the counter.

"Is that your black BMW out there?" I asked.

"Yes," he replied, and paid for his drinks using a debit card. "Why?"

"Do you work at The Club?"

"I'm part-owner," he informed me, and left the counter with his drinks.

Since I had nothing to pay for, I followed him out the door as we walked towards the cars. I saw Porsha staring at me as she sat in her car while she shook her head. She knew I'd went in there to talk to him.

"Is Richard part-owner?"

He grinned. "You ask a lot of questions, Mackenzee."

"I'm just a concerned citizen."

"Yeah? Concerned about what?"

Don't play dumb with me, I thought. "About what has gone on in this city."

He looked at me as he knocked on the window. "There's nothing that has gone on in this city, Mackenzee, past or present. Best city in this country to live in."

Now I know you're full of shit, I thought.

The window rolled down to Christina!

"Hi, Christina!" I said in an upbeat tone.

She looked at her dad.

"Do you know this woman, baby?" he asked.

I stared at Christina. I knew it was her and she knew it was me.

"No," she replied, and took her drink from him and rolled up her window.

Lying-ass heffa! I thought. I stared with full-blown embarrassment all around my surroundings and right into Antonio's eyes through his sunglasses as he stared back at me, and then into Porsha's eyes.

"Let's go!" she mouthed from her car.

"Excuse me," I said.

"By all means," Antonio said, as he went to the gas pump and took the pump off the holder.

I got into the car as I watched him pump gas as he stared at me as he was now on his phone. "Come on, I don't wanna be late getting to Elron's. Now I really have a lot to talk about with him."

"And I don't want that dude following us," Porsha said, and drove out of the parking lot. I looked back as Antonio stared at me as he continued to talk on his phone while he filled his car up with gas, and until we were out of each other's sight.

CHAPTER THIRTY-THREE

"I can't even tell you the last time I had fried chicken this good. Everyone thinks they're the best at making it, but only one person was and still is—my mom . . . and now you," I said to Elron as we ate at his kitchen table as Porsha ate downstairs in his basement so we could talk which was a whole other very nice living space.

"Thank you, Mackenzee. It's one of my favorites, too. And I actually learned the recipe from my mom who is still around, so we have that in common," he said with a smile, and ate some more of his rice.

"So I see where you got your great cooking skills from. Thanks for making this for the two of us. We were craving some fried chicken—homecooked fried chicken—for so long. So tired of eating fast food all of the time."

He smiled. "No problem at all. You deserve a great homecooked meal for the work you've been doing." He sighed. "And unfortunately, I just don't have any great things to say about these disappearances."

I took a sip of my soda as I stared at him. "Well, I'm right here and all ears."

He nodded, and then got up. "Excuse me."

I nodded as I chewed my mac and cheese. I watched him as he left the kitchen. He came back less than a minute later.

"Just double checking the security surveillance. Usually, I'll do it from my phone but since I have two ladies here with me, I want to make sure we're safe."

"And you're scaring me just by saying that, Elron."

"Nothing to be afraid of, Mackenzee. You're safe here and this is a safe neighborhood for the most part. We may not have the biggest houses in this community, but everyone is quiet and friendly."

"That's good to hear," I said with a smile. "So, you told me you had more to say about Richard."

"A lot more to say."

I wiped my mouth with my napkin. "I'm listening."

"Now of course you can't tell anyone anything that I'm telling you, Mackenzee. I think you know that by now."

"Yes, I know," I said, as I stared at him in suspense. I could imagine the way I was looking at him.

He sighed. "This is about Deandra's disappearance."

"Okay. I'm listening."

"Because what I told you before about how Richard didn't mention anything to me when him, Antonio, and me were at the mall that day about how things went between him and Deandra at The Club the night before? Well, it didn't end there."

"It didn't? What else happened?"

Richard's House: Fall 1990

Elron walked into Richard's bedroom. His parents weren't home. "What's up, man? What did you have to tell me about what happened with you and Deandra, man?" he asked, and sat at Richard's desk as Richard sat on his bed.

Richard bobbed his head as "The Boomin' System" by LL Cool J blasted throughout his room.

Elron turned the radio off. "What's going on, man?"

Richard got up and sat on the side of his bed. "Look, man. You know how Trevor moved away and everything, and Deandra is missing."

"He had everything to do with it, man. No one moves away that fast and didn't have any involvement in her disappearance. She's been missing for almost two weeks now and hasn't been found and he was the last one to see her at The Club?"

"He wasn't the last one to see her at The Club," Richard informed him.

Elron stared at him in shock. "What?! What are you talking about, man? I thought you didn't tell me anything about being with her that night because nothing happened."

"Nothing did happen."

Elron shook his head. "Okay, now you're confusing me, man. I thought something happened between the two of you since you followed her to the back of the place that night. Remember, I had to leave early so I was hoping you and Antonio would tell me what I missed. Now you're talking in circles telling me that nothing did happen?"

"That's what I'm telling you. Nothing happened between me and Deandra, that's because nothing had time to happen. While we were walking towards the back where the private VIP lounge is since I wanted to show that to her, someone else showed up."

"Who, man?"

"Orlando."

"Orlando? Orlando Pratt? Doesn't he own The Club?"

"Yeah, he does. I was telling him that I wanted to show Deandra the private VIP lounge before her friend Mary got back there to pick her up, and he said he would show it to her and that I should probably be getting home since I'm only 17 and it was getting late. I was no match to him since his dad, Othello, is the mayor of this city. Deandra told me it was okay that he showed it to her instead of me, so I just let her go with him."

"Holy shit, man! You *have* to go to the cops with this! Or at least tell your dad about it!"

"My dad told my mom and me that Deandra's mom and her best friend Mary came to his office to talk to him, but they didn't have an appointment so they were turned away. They asked could they make one before they left, and my dad's secretary took their information down but never got back to them since he had a very full schedule and still does. He just doesn't have any proof of anything about her disappearance from there or anywhere, and the cops haven't given him anything about Deandra's case since it is an active Missing Persons case."

"And isn't your dad good friends with Orlando? And with Othello? *And* with Police Chief Nickerson?"

"Yeah, our families are very good friends with their families. But there's no proof Orlando did anything to Deandra. He's way too old for her."

"You know damn well that doesn't mean a damn thing, Richard."

"Yeah, I know, but the bottom line is, *I* didn't have anything to do with her disappearance, and *I* was not the last one seen with her, and I will always maintain my innocence in it."

"Do you believe him?" I asked, as I stared with my eyes bucked out at him. I could only imagine how I looked to him.

"Maybe in this case I do. He just didn't sound like he was lying back then. And that Orlando, I heard, was very conniving. The man is in his 70's now and is the current mayor of this city, but he owned The Club back then. Came from some wealth from his dad Othello's side of the family he who inherited a ton of money—and who, as you know, was the mayor of this city at the time Deandra went missing. He gave some of his inheritance to Orlando so that's how he was able to open The Club in 1988."

"So Orlando Pratt is the original owner of The Club?"

"Yes."

"So no one other than him has owned it?"

"Well, he was owner up until 1995 when he decided to run for mayor of this city since his dad decided not to re-run for office. Everyone pretty much knew he was gonna win it; his opponent didn't even have chance. The Pratts definitely know how to keep powerful positions within their family in this city."

"That's obvious," I said, and ate some more of my rice. "So, who was the owner of The Club starting in 1995?"

"Oliver Pratt, Orlando's son and Othello's grandson."

"For real? His dad gave him ownership of a popular nightclub back then? Wasn't he, like, only 20 at the time?"

"22 years old to be exact. Same age as me, Richard, and Antonio. Imagine owning a nightclub that was already in the making of being an iconic place in this city and you're only 22 years old. He took over ownership at 22 since, like I said, his dad decided to run for mayor and won, of course. He wanted Oliver to have something he'd built for him. Just the typical passing down of generational wealth. But Oliver didn't know how to run anything, especially at that age. He went to that all-boys school, St. Benedict Military Academy—the brother high school of the all-girls high school, St. Cecilia. Both schools are right outside of this city."

"I know. That's where Ashley told me she had gone to high school, as well as Kamiah told me her sister, Gazelle Ragland, went there as well."

He nodded. "Oliver didn't know anything about business especially since he dropped out of business school just a few months before because he said it wasn't for him after all—funny, huh?"

"Yeah, that's interesting, all right."

"Since he dropped out, he pretty much had to have everyone else run things for him. But being the boss of a club like that in this city got to his ego a lot, and I mean *a lot*."

"Yeah, I believe it. That fucker had me arrested for trespassing on his precious property, and Mary said he was an asshole; wouldn't shake her hand when she met him that night she went out on that date with Richard."

"That's Oliver for you. Personally, I don't like the man; never have."

"Well, he just doesn't seem like a likeable person. He showed no mercy for me at all that day he had me thrown in jail. I know in a lot of ways I can't blame him because I was doing what I was doing—trespassing on private property—but damn, I didn't hurt anyone. It was my very first time doing it, I had no criminal record prior to the incident so he could've just let me go with a fine—and I would've found some way to pay it—but he wanted the book thrown at me. Luckily, Richard bailed me out and had all of the charges dropped against me, now I'm questioning why he did that to begin with."

"Richard likes you, Mackenzee, so I really wouldn't think so hard into it. Just be thankful that he did."

"I am," I honestly replied. "But it's more sounding like it was Oliver's dad Orlando—who is mayor of this city—that had something to do with Deandra's disappearance more than it sounds like it could've been Richard or even Trevor."

"That's what I think, too, Mackenzee." He sighed. "But I can't be sure if I feel that Richard is completely innocent of Tanisha's disappearance despite him always telling me he is."

"Well, judging by what you'd told me, Elron, I can't exclude him, either. I know this is definitely more personal since she is your cousin, so I know you really have to be careful about what you say about it."

"Yeah, I absolutely do. And it's been so hard not saying anything about it for so many years. When I told you about Tanisha's disappearance, I felt that thousand-pound weight finally get lifted off of me, but there was a weight that was still heavy on me, and that was not getting myself to fully believe that Richard had nothing to do with her disappearance. Like I said, he told me numerous time he didn't have anything to do with it, but I honestly don't know what to believe."

"Well, I can't blame you for that. But does Richard own The Club along with Oliver?"

"No, he doesn't. Oliver actually asked him did he want part ownership in it well over 20 years ago, but Richard said he didn't. Oliver has even asked him more than once in these past years and he keeps telling him he wants nothing to do with part ownership of it. He said he will continue to support it, though."

"Even if he did have something to do with Tanisha's disaprance?"

"Yeah, I believe that; never try to figure out someone's thoughts, Mackenzee."

"You're damn right about that."

"But I also believe more and more now that he's declining part ownership because he knows Oliver's dad could've had something to do with Deandra's disappearance."

"Sounds like Oliver's dad could've had something to do with Gazelle's, too, and that's probably why he suddenly ran for mayor in 1995. You mean to tell me that Chief Nickerson never had his cops question Orlando about these disappearances?"

"Not once."

"This city sucks."

"Yeah, it's fucked up, Mackenzee. No one had ever really talked about these disappearances when they first happened like the way you would've thought they would, and then they were just forgotten about. I mean, I would've even thought they would've talked about Tanisha's more at least, but they never did."

"Well, that's why I am talking about them. But before I go on, how did Antonio become part owner?"

"Because Oliver wanted him to. Antonio was one who grew up on the poor working side of this city. He was the type who had parents that didn't care how late he stayed out, even on school nights. But because he had Richard and me as his best friends back then, he was influenced by our lives and was able to build a successful sneaker business in this city when he was in his late 20's and opened his store online as well. When Oliver saw that, he asked did he wanna be part owner—as well as investor—of The Club. He jumped at the chance of it since like Richard and me, Antonio had loved going there since he was a teen."

"Yeah, and he apparently loves following me around the city because he thinks I'm trying to ruin what he's part owner of as well as what he's an investor in, when all I'm doing is trying to get at the truth of where these girls are. We have three missing women in 5-year intervals that have gone missing from The Club from 1990-2000 and no one in this city has done a damn thing about them. Now we both have reason to believe that the mayor of this city could've had something to do with one of these disappearances?"

"Or two of them. I just don't think he had anything to do with Tanisha's."

"Yeah, I don't think he did, either, because he wasn't owner anymore, but you never can tell. I think Richard is still the number one suspect in Tanisha's disappearance."

Elron sighed. "I hate to say it, but I think he is, too. I also think he's hired me as his personal chef and has always been so good and appreciative of me because he's hiding something from me about Tanisha. I just don't wanna believe that one of my best friends could've done this to my favorite cousin."

I stared at him where I could see all of the pain in his eyes. "I hope not, either, Elron. But you might have to accept the fact that he did if I can get some solid proof of it."

"I know, and that's what I definitely need. Proof of it."

"Also, I almost forgot to tell you that I saw Antonio at the gas station before Porsha and I got here."

"Oh, boy."

I grinned. "Yeah, Porsha just happened to pull into the gas station and right up to a pump that was right behind his car. She didn't want me talking to him, but I just couldn't miss the opportunity to introduce myself and ask him a few questions."

He sighed, and then cracked a grin. "And what did you ask him, Mackenzee?"

"I just asked him if he was Antonio, and he confirmed to me that he was. I also asked him was that his BMW out at the pumps and he told me that it was, so I knew right there that he was the one who has been following me all around the city. I also asked him how well did he know Tanisha, and he wouldn't answer that for me."

"He didn't know her that well. She was Richard's girlfriend, not his," he answered for me.

"Oh, okay. Because I thought maybe he was fooling around with her, too."

"Nah, Tanisha wasn't like that. Besides, I think she would've told me if she was but of course would've told me not to tell Richard and I would've kept it a secret. What else did you ask him?"

"Did he work at The Club, and he told me what you just told me—that he's part owner so he wasn't lying about that. He went on to say that I asked a lot of questions, and I just told him I was a concerned citizen. He asked me what was I so concerned about, and I told him I was concerned about what went on in this city. He then went on to say that there was nothing bad going on this city and that this was the safest city in the country. We both know he was full of shit."

"For real," Elron said with a nod, and took a sip of his drink.

"And his daughter, Christina? Said she didn't know me when I said hi to her when she rolled down her window so Antonio could give her the drink he bought for her! I clearly said her name and it was like he was surprised that I knew who she was. I met her over at Richard's house—*twice*! Lyin' little bitch!"

"She probably thought she would get in trouble with him if she said she knew you. You've been talked about a lot, Mackenzee, so a lot of people in this city know who you are, even though they can't prove that you're the one who hosts your show."

"I'm not trying to make enemies in this city. I'm just trying to investigate these disappearances from an iconic establishment that people all over the world have been to, and that Oliver and his dad and now everyone who's someone big in this city is trying to hide. I think there are a lot of people who are in a lot of power, but their positions are just as useless as they are because they don't take advantage of it in the way they should, not in the way they shouldn't. They have resources they haven't used for decades to solve these disappearances and it's like they wanna act like these disappearances never happened. Just about almost every city in this world has had at least one disappearance or murder in it since its existence; this city is no different. Saint Maran needs to stop acting like they do no wrong, and it all starts with finding out what happened to Deandra, Gazelle, and Tanisha, because I have a strong feeling that all three of them never left this city."

He stared at me as he took a sip of his drink. He put his glass down and let out a deep sigh. "I have a strong feeling you're right."

CHAPTER THIRTY-FOUR

"So it sounds to me like Elron could still believe Richard had something to do with Tanisha's disappearance, huh?" Porsha asked us, as she drove us home in the pouring-down rain.

"Yeah, I think he does. And if he feels like he does, how the hell could he still stay best friends with him for so long? If someone was last seen with a loved one of mine and I haven't seen or heard from my loved one since? I would *not* be talking to that person to this day until they told me the truth about what happened to my loved one."

"Maybe that's why Elron is staying close to Richard because he wants to see if he finally confesses to him about having something to do with Tanisha's disappearance after all, even though he has told him several times over the years that he had nothing to do with it. The fact of the matter is, Richard was the last one seen with her, and she hasn't been seen since? And Elron witnessed him come back into that private VIP lounge without her that night and said he told him was through with her?"

"Yeah, that's what he told me," I replied as I stared out the window.

Porsha shook her head. "Damn. It's like Richard told on himself back then and Elron is just in some serious denial."

I sighed. "Yeah, he just might be, like, seriously. I just wish I had some proof that it is Richard, but you know now that he's at least been pretty much excluded from Deandra's disappearance. I do have a lot of reason to believe that Orlando Pratt had something to do with hers judging by the conversation Elron told me him and Richard had two weeks after Deandra went missing."

"Yeah, doesn't sound like Elron is lying about any of this. I really feel sorry for him since Tanisha was his favorite cousin. Sounds like they were really close."

"Yeah, they were." I looked at the front of our house as we approached it . . . and someone was standing at it. "Who is that standing at our front door?"

"I have no idea, especially since they have an umbrella over them," Porsha said. "Are you expecting anyone?"

"Not at all. Are you?"

"No, I'm not."

Porsha slowly turned into our driveway which didn't have an attached garage where we could walk directly into our home. I noticed how the person standing at our front door turned in our direction.

Minutes later, we got out of the car as the woman continued to stand at the front door.

"Hi. Can I help you?" I asked, as Porsha stood slightly behind me as we both had our umbrellas over our heads since it was still storming pretty hard.

"Yes. I'm here to see Mackenzee Lawson," she informed me.

I could see Porsha looking at me. "I'm Mackenzee Lawson. Can I ask who you are?"

"I'm Mrs. Yolanda Cozine. I'm personal secretary to Saint Maran Police Chief Warrick Hatcher. You do know who he is, right?"

"Yes, I know." I looked at Porsha. She nodded. "We know. Nice to meet you, Mrs. Cozine. But since this was an unexpected visit, is it possible that you can show me some kind of credentials?"

"Sure. I knew you would ask," she said, and dug in her purse and pulled out her work lanyard that clearly showed she was in fact the personal secretary to this city's current police chief.

"Please, come on in, Mrs. Cozine," I said, as I unlocked the door. "This is my best friend, Porsha. She lives here, too."

"Nice to meet you, Porsha."

"Nice to meet you, too," she replied with a smile as they shook hands.

"Sorry the house is not how it should look. We haven't had time to clean it. Please, have a seat in the kitchen since it looks a little better. Could I put on some coffee for you?" I asked.

"That would be great," she said with a smile as she took off her raincoat and sat down.

I started to slightly panic because I didn't know if we had any coffee after all.

"I'll get it started," Porsha said, as she pulled out a new bag of fresh ground coffee.

"Thank you, Porsha," I said with relief as she grinned back at me with a nod. "So, how did you know about me and where I live?"

"The Saint Maran Police Department has everyone on file who has a driver's license so it's easy to find them in the system when they get pulled over or just having to show ID for whatever the case may be. We found out about you through DA Richard Elmhurst III, and I shouldn't be saying this, but you sparked Chief Hatcher's interest because you've been asking a lot of questions about some supposed disappearances of women from The Club from 1990-2000 and could even be the woman who has that online show called *I'm Their Speaker*. You've been talking a lot, Mackenzee, about things that you are claiming happened in this city that you can't prove."

I was about to tell this woman to get the fuck out of my house. I looked at Porsha. She stared in suspense at me because she knew I was about to go off about all of this. It was clear she was sent here to get me to stop talking about these disappearances and thought I was just being completely ignorant in that fact.

"But before you say a word, Mackenzee, there is something I need to tell you about myself," she informed me.

"What is it, Mrs. Cozine?"

"You can call me Yolanda since I'm not at work," she informed me.

"Okay, Yolanda. What is it?"

She sighed. "What I need to tell you is that before I became the personal secretary to Chief Hatcher, I had numerous jobs. All of them are irrelevant now except for one."

"And which one is that?"

"That I used to work as a waitress at The Club in 1995."

"Shut up!" I shouted. "Sorry."

She laughed. "It's okay. I could tell I genuinely caught you by surprise when I told you that."

Porsha brought two mugs of coffee over for Yolanda and me. "I'll be in my room. Nice meeting you, Yolanda."

"Nice meeting you, too, Porsha," she replied with a smile.

"Oh my god!" Porsha mouthed behind Yolanda's back before she went into her bedroom since I was facing her. I knew she wanted me to tell her all about it, and she knew I would.

"So, you worked as a waitress at The Club in 1995? That was the only year?"

"Actually, I worked there from 1994-1997, and never heard anyone mention anything about what'd happened in 1990 with Deandra Whitfield disappearing during the very first teen night there. But no one really talked much about Gazelle Ragland, either. It was something most just forgot happened or never believed that it happened to begin with. But the very few who talked about it were saying all sorts of stuff."

"Like what?"

"Like she went off with Damian Wesson, who was the popular professional football player and a native of this city, and he killed her and had his friends dump her body in a place where it would never be found, stuff like that."

"Do you believe that?"

"Well, I honestly just don't know what to believe. It's been so long since her disappearance, but I can remember that night clearly since it was rare that Damian showed up there since he didn't live here anymore, and he was a professional athlete. But what I do remember while I was working there that night was that Damian is definitely telling the truth when he said he was not the last person seen with Gazelle."

I gasped! "Really?! How do you know this?"

"Because I was working in the private VIP lounge that night, and Gazelle did not walk in there with Damian Wesson."

"Who did she walk in there with?"

"She walked in there *and* out of there with . . . with Oliver Pratt."

"NO!" I shouted. I shouted so loud it echoed off the walls.

"Yes, Mackenzee. I remember it like it was yesterday. Everyone knew who Damian was, and everyone knew who Oliver was, and everyone to this day still do. I served Oliver and Gazelle at their table, and they were talking about how they hadn't seen each other since they saw each other at some dance their junior year in high school that was held at his school since he went to Saint Benedict and she went to Saint Cecilia—they're brother and sister schools."

"Yes, I know. Oh my god. I don't believe this. It's clear Oliver had everything to do with Gazelle's disappearance, I don't see any doubt about it now. Damian was telling the absolute truth. I just didn't know what to believe."

"Yeah, Oliver was celebrating just becoming owner of The Club and wanted Gazelle to celebrate with him. He was buying drinks for everyone in that private lounge, even though there weren't that many people in there. After staying in there for over an hour, her and Oliver left. And it's clear from what Damian had said in his interview with you that he waited for Gazelle to come back to him, and she never did because it was clear he didn't wait for an hour, and she'd forgot all about obviously ditching him when she saw Oliver. While I was at the bar waiting for the bartender to make the drinks for a couple at the other table I was assigned to for that night, *I saw Oliver and Gazelle leave together.*"

"This is crazy. I can't believe I'm hearing this, and I believe you a hundred percent. No one else was really known to be the last one seen with her except for Damian. Oliver was never even brought up once. I know Damian didn't know who he was because he would've said if he did. He saw the guy from behind that Gazelle said she knew and wanted to talk to, but she never said to Damian who Oliver was and it's clear Damian wasn't lying when he only saw him from behind. And I thought his dad Orlando had something to do with this and that's why he ran for mayor so he wouldn't be questioned about it."

"I think Orlando has something to do with hiding this from everyone, most definitely. He would do anything to protect that asshole son of his. I talked to Chief Hatcher about it recently and he even said without proof there's not much I could really do—but he wanted me to come here and talk to you about what you know before he legally acts on anything. Throughout the years, I have just forgotten about this and even thought Gazelle was faking her disappearance. But when I saw that interview you did with her sister Kamiah, then I saw just how real this really was and how long it'd been that no one really cared that these girls had come up missing after being at The Club, a place I worked at for three long years. And one girl disappeared while I worked there and I actually saw her walk out of that private VIP lounge with the new owner, and she hasn't been seen or heard from since."

"Damn, there's got to be a way to prove all of this," I said as I shook my head.

"DNA is the best way," she informed me. "We don't have Oliver's DNA in a database since he has no criminal record, and we don't have a body, either, so it's gonna be pretty hard to prove all of this—but not impossible. I just want you to keep doing what you're doing and even though I know it's you now doing the show, I'm still keeping your identity a secret. I think what you're doing is great and it's been way too long that no one has done anything. I think we're one step away from solving at least one of these disappearances, so keep it up and be very careful, Mackenzee. You know how it is in this city."

"Well, I know now that someone who has a big connection to someone in a position of power in this city does actually care, and now I got even more confidence to keep going on with my investigation. But can you answer me one more question?"

"What is it?"

"How come no one ever answered the line for the cold cases task force when I called it? And Vatrice Johnson said no one answered it when she called it, too?"

"That's because it was still in negotiations about whether or not it should've been formed to begin with."

"What? That doesn't make any sense."

"Not at all, Mackenzee, but that's Saint Maran for you. Chief Hatcher took it upon himself to form a cold cases task force, but Mayor Pratt didn't want to have the city fund it because he told Chief Hatcher that there weren't that many cold cases in this city to have a special task force. I guess he forgot about the disappearances at The Club, one that now we both believe his son is directly linked to."

"Yeah, that's probably why he didn't want the task force formed, much less people calling a special line with info about cases he'd rather forget about."

"Exactly, Mackenzee." She looked at her watch. "I better get going since it's getting late and my husband is probably wondering where I am. I'm glad to have met you and talked to you about this. Now I see that you're for real then I will definitely be speaking to Chief Hatcher about you. He may even want to meet you so don't be surprised."

"I'm willing to meet him and talk to him about this," I said with a smile.

I walked her to the door.

"Chief Hatcher doesn't encourage independent investigations, but in this case I'm sure he will make an exception because you have brought something to light that has been hidden for way too long in this city, and he's not originally from here so he had no idea about any of these cases from back then."

"I'll talk to him anytime," I stated once more.

Yolanda nodded with a smile. "I'll be in touch."

CHAPTER THIRTY-FIVE

"Right now, I only want the two of you to know this. I'm not even broadcasting this on my show yet because I need some solid proof of it, but from what Yolanda told me last night, I believe her a hundred percent and I couldn't wait to tell the two of you this."

I had Mary and Kamiah's undivided attention as they sat at my kitchen table. I just couldn't wait to tell them this since I felt this was a major break in the disappearance of Gazelle Ragland, and even though this had more to do with Kamiah, I felt Mary needed to be here to hear what I had to say as well since this case particularly involved her baby daddy Damian.

"What is it, Mackenzee?" Kamiah asked, as she stared at me with wide-eyed suspense.

"Does it have to do with Damian?" Mary asked.

"Yes, since he was a suspect in Gazelle's disappearance and was known to be the last person seen with her. Look, I'm not gonna beat around the bush here because it's been long enough since Gazelle has been seen and heard from. Yolanda Cozine was a waitress in 1995, and she worked the private VIP lounge the night Gazelle went missing." I sighed as I stared at Kamiah. "And she saw Gazelle walk in and out of the lounge with Oliver Pratt, *not* Damian."

"WHAT?!" they both yelled out.

"Yes, that's what Yolanda told me. Just remember, this was 1995. There was no social media, no livestreaming, no constant IG picture taking, no FaceTime stuff. I believe everything she told me. And she's serious about getting these disappearances solved just as much as we are because she was there that night and actually served Oliver and Gazelle."

"So Damian just made up the story?" Mary asked.

"No, he told the absolute truth. He wasn't the last one with her, Yolanda confirmed to me that Oliver was. Remember, Damian had no idea who Oliver was since he didn't go to either Saint Maran East or West schools."

"I knew who he was," Kamiah said as her head was lowered.

Mary and I looked at her.

"Did they date in high school?" I asked.

"No, but she wanted to. Gazelle was always attracted to those guys who had money, and she would bring up Oliver at times, but she said he was one of those puny guys and wasn't cute at all, so she wasn't attracted to him in that aspect, only to his wealth. Plus, he always had that asshole aura about him as well. He knew he was some ugly half-pint punk who could only get girls because his dad owned The Club at the time and his grandfather was mayor of this city."

"The more things change the more they stay the same," Mary said.

"Wow, you weren't lying, Mary. Sounds like this guy hasn't changed a bit," I said.

"Sure hasn't," Mary replied. "When he wouldn't shake my hand that night Richard introduced me to him, I knew he was no damn good. But I'm not gonna lie, I didn't think that he could quite possibly be directly involved in the disappearance of one of the girls at The Club, but then again it's all believable since he took over ownership of it that year."

"And that's what Yolanda told me him and Gazelle were in there celebrating. She said they stayed in the lounge for an hour, and then left. She never saw Gazelle again after that night."

"He had everything to do with it; I now believe that," Kamiah said. She looked at me. "But we need to prove it. It's been way too long that nothing has been done. This is the closest I feel that I've ever been to getting her disappearance solved. They need to bring him in for questioning."

I nodded. "And that's very close to happening. Since Yolanda is the personal secretary of Police Chief Hatcher, she said he is interested in these disappearances, so I feel we finally have someone on our side."

"And it's about fuckin' time," Mary and Kamiah said.

"Yolanda does sound credible . . . very credible, in fact," Elron said, as I sat over at his house as he prepared a special meal for a couple's 10th wedding anniversary.

"She really is. I thought she came over my house to try and talk me out of doing this investigation since she's Chief Hatcher's personal secretary because I know how corrupt almost everyone who is in some powerful position in this city could be and still is. But when she said she was a waitress at The Club in 1995 when Gazelle disappeared and that she was last seen with Oliver and that she was their waitress while they were in that private VIP lounge? I knew she was telling the truth. She just didn't sound like she was making everything up as she went along, you know?"

"Yeah, I know, Mackenzee." He checked the oven and then came over to the kitchen table and sat with me. "Look, this is kind of hard for me to process because you telling me what she told you is the first time I'm hearing this. Yeah, I have to admit that Oliver should've never been ruled out when it came to Gazelle. They knew each other in high school, that's what he's told us over the years since her disappearance."

"So he has mentioned her?"

"Yeah, but not that much. I guess he just didn't wanna draw that much attention to himself. Besides, everyone obviously thought Damian Wesson had something to do with it."

"I've ruled him completely out now, and I let Mary know that since that's her baby daddy. Oliver has a lot of explaining to do, and he needs to give a DNA sample if he wants to be cleared of a pending charge. This has gone on for way too long, and we still don't know about Deandra and your cousin Tanisha."

He sighed. "Yeah, I wish I knew, Mackenzee. But I agree that Oliver does need to provide a sample even though there hasn't been any body found in Gazelle's case. If he has nothing to hide then he should have no problem providing it. Has there been a warrant out for him yet?"

"Not that I know of. I haven't heard back from Yolanda yet. She said she would call or text me if anything develops in Gazelle's disappearance. But she told me that she told Chief Hatcher about her interaction with Oliver and Gazelle that night at The Club when she went missing, and she asked him could she talk to me about it since I'm independently investigating it and have my show about it. Yes, I confessed to her that it is me and she promised she wouldn't tell anyone except Chief Hatcher."

"Yeah, I think it's okay that she knows as well as Chief Hatcher. In this case, it's important that they do know it's you."

"It is. Well, he told her she could talk to me about these disappearances, that's how she ended up at my house after I'd just came back home from being over here. Wow, it just seems like things are unraveling so fast now."

"It does seem that way, Mackenzee, but I think it's been long enough that things have been at a standstill. Damn, I wish there was some way to get his DNA."

"You can try," I suggested.

"Mackenzee . . . ."

"What, Elron? What? *We* need to do this. *You* need to do this. It's clear that you're friends with him, and you hang out at The Club often —do you not?"

"Yes, I do," he admitted. "But that's going a little too far, I have to admit. I just don't wanna get caught. I'm not a cop."

"And neither am I. We don't have to be. You know damn well that I can't ask Richard for obvious reasons."

He laughed. "Yeah, you're right about that!"

"So *please*, Elron. I'm begging you. *Please* help me in getting Oliver's DNA. Just take something of his like a can of soda or a tissue or his drink when he's done with it. This does not have to be hard. This *has* to be done."

He sighed as he stared at me. "I agree, Mackenzee. But I'm probably not the right person to do it."

"At this point, I think you're the only person who should do it."

He sighed once again. "I'll see what I can do."

CHAPTER THIRTY-SIX

Oliver worked on his computer in his private office at The Club as Keith Sweat's "Something Just Ain't Right" played throughout it when he got a knock on the door. "Come in!" He looked up from what he was working on. "Dad! What's up? What brings you here?"

Orlando slowly walked over to one of the chairs in front of Oliver's desk and sat down. "Where do I begin?" he asked. "Turn that music off."

Oliver picked up his phone and pressed a few buttons, and his office fell silent. "So, what's going on?"

"I was hoping you would be able to tell me that, son," he replied with a serious glare in his eyes.

Oliver shrugged. "Well, you're here. I didn't come to your office. It's clear you wanna see me about something and you didn't even call me to let me know. I could've been in a meeting, Dad."

"And you would've had to cancel it because what I need to talk to you about is really important."

"Oh, shit! What is it now?" he asked, as he sat back in his chair.

Orlando gazed around his former office. "My, have times changed. But then again it feels like it was yesterday when I had this office. I actually thought I would be here forever owning this place, but I knew I always wanted to be mayor of this city like my dad—like your grand-father—but I wanted to build something and then pass it down to you, and then you could pass it down to your kids, but it looks like this is where the generational wealth stopped since you never gave your mom and I a grandchild."

Oliver sighed. "Oh, come on, Dad. Are we gonna start on that again? I told you and Mom a long time ago—decades ago—that getting married and having kids just wasn't for me. I'm 50 years old now, so you see by now that I meant every word of it."

"Yeah, you meant it all right," he replied. He shook his head. "Look, son, enough of this beating around the bush, okay? I'm here on a serious matter. In fact, it's so serious that it could quite possibly put all of what I'd built for you and what you have built on to this place in jeopardy."

Oliver stared is dad down. "What are you talking about, Dad?"

"Don't look at me like that. We got some trouble, and it has every-thing to do with this place."

"What? What are you talking about? What kind of trouble?"

Orlando sighed and shook his head. "Look, son. I have been mayor of this city for 28 years straight, and that was all possible because the people of this wonderful city love our family and trusted me to run it. Before me, it was your late grandfather who lasted for 12 wonderful years. I thank God every day that I have been able to serve all seven of these four-year terms and there's absolutely no limit to how many I can serve since we're blessed to live in a city that has this kind of law in place. I wanna make it to 30 years as mayor—I will be the longest-serving mayor ever in this city's history, especially for a Black man. It will be historic. But we got some problems now, some big problems. Trouble; some big trouble."

"Dad, will you stop talking about all of the problems and big trouble you're saying that we have now and tell me what they are? You've been sitting here for a few minutes and it's like you're talking in circles—"

"I got a call from Chief Hatcher today," he blurted out.

Oliver stared at him. "And? So? What did he want?"

"You know he's an outsider since he wasn't born or raised here, so you know he has no idea how things are really run in this city."

"But he should by now since he's been the chief of this city for years now."

"Not necessarily, son." Orlando sighed as he shook his head. "Look, I thought all of this went away for good."

"What went away for good?"

"Don't start talking in circles, son."

"I'm not talking in circles, Dad! You're the one who came here talking about how we got some big problems and big trouble, but you refuse to tell me what they are."

"I was hoping that *you* would tell me," Orlando said, as he sat back in his seat.

"What?! What are you talking about? I have nothing to tell you."

"Stop lying. Stop lying right now. This place is in trouble and has been for some time, and I'm not talking about financial-wise. Now I gave you this place because I wanted you to have something even though you dropped out of business school, and most importantly, I thought you would make it better."

"I've made it more than better, Dad. I've made it iconic," Oliver reminded him.

"But it's not gonna mean shit if those girls disappeared from here!"

Oliver stared at him. "Dad, just where is all of this coming from? What girls? What disappearances? If girls disappeared from here then I never heard about it because nothing has been reported about any girls disappearing from here. They've been saying that shit for decades now."

"You just lied to me."

Oliver stared up at the ceiling, then stared back at his dad. "Look, I don't know anything about any disappearances, okay? I don't know where all of this shit is coming from. I run a clean business here. We don't do anything illegal here. We uphold the same business practices and ethics and standards that we always have ever since you opened this establishment back in 1988. Now whoever's starting this shit is just trying to bring us down. They do this all of the time, Dad, you know that. They even tried to ruin your campaigns several times. Just haters, that's all. If they can't be us, then they hate on us."

"Stop with all of that hater bullshit, Oliver. Although I know some of it is very true because we've all experienced it as a family, but this is even more serious. Chief Hatcher called me today asking me did I know about any disappearances that happened here in the years 1990, 1995, and 2000."

"You didn't own it anymore starting in 1995."

"I know, that's why I'm asking you because you did and still do."

Oliver shook his head. "Nothing happened here in those years, Dad. Nothing at all. None of those years. If something did, it would've been all over this city and on the news and everything, you know that."

"I know that a lot of things were kept out of the media, too."

Oliver stared down at his desk.

"Son, look at me."

He slowly lifted his head as he stared him right in the eyes.

"You know I'll do anything to protect you; to protect this place. To protect any and everything that's ours. But I can't protect you if you're not honest with me. My memory is not what it used to be, so I can't recall anyone ever briefing me about these disappearances that happened starting in 1990 and ending in 2000. The other one happened in 1995, and it better be a damn coincidence that I just happened to sign over ownership to you that year so I could run for mayor. Don't make me look like I made the biggest mistake of my life by giving you this establishment."

"You didn't. *I* made this place iconic," Oliver stated once again. "And I'll do whatever I can to keep it this way."

"And so will I. But my memory isn't wiped out of everything. I remember when I had that very first night for teens here in 1990. That was the night that people are claiming that first girl went missing."

"I don't remember."

"Well, I do."

The Club: Teen Night: Fall 1990

Deandra stared back at Richard as he stood in the same spot while he stared right back at her with full concern as she walked with Orlando to the private VIP lounge and disappeared around the corner.

"How long have you known Richard?" Orlando asked.

"I just met him," she replied with a nervous tone to her voice.

"You mean you just met him tonight?"

"Yes. I just met him while I was talking on the phone. He was talking on a phone right next to me."

He nodded with a smile. "He's a nice young man. Wants to be a lawyer like his dad who's this city's DA in case you didn't know."

"No, I didn't know that. What's a DA?"

He laughed. "District Attorney. He's a big influential man in this city, just like my dad Othello who is mayor and has been for quite some time. So, you're in a position to be in some of these influential circles in the future if you settle down with the right man here in this city. The younger a beautiful young lady like you hears and practices it, the better."

She blushed. "Thank you."

They approached the private VIP lounge.

"Here we are. Come on in," he said with a smile.

She walked alongside him in this dark and practically empty lounge as Bell Biv Devoe's "When Will I See You Smile Again?" played throughout the room. "Wow. This is really beautiful. How come it was so crowded out there where I was earlier but there's no one in here?"

"Because we don't have this room available for the teen crowd tonight. Not sure if I'm gonna have it in the future since I do own this place."

"That will be nice if you do. My friends and I will find some way to be able to pay for this experience."

"And it will cost extra for the experience," he informed her with a smile. "I want you to meet somebody."

"Um, I think my friend might be here to come pick me up."

"The front door will page me to let me know if she lets them know," he replied with a smile as he approached a booth table in a corner. "Oliver?"

Oliver looked up from his drink of Pepsi at his dad and then at Deandra, and smiled big. "Yes, Dad?"

"This is Deandra . . . ?"

"Whitfield," Deandra replied with a smile.

"Whitfield," Orlando said with a smile. "Sorry, I didn't get your last name before we got in here. Deandra Whitfield, this is my son, Oliver Pratt."

Oliver continued to smile big as he shook Deandra's hand. "Very nice to meet you, Deandra."

"Nice to meet you, too, Oliver," Deandra said.

"Please, have a seat," Oliver said.

"Okay, but I can't stay for long. My friend is coming here to pick me up soon."

"My dad will let me know when she gets here."

"I sure will. You two have a great time getting to know one another," Orlando said, and walked away and out of the lounge.

"So, what school do you go to?" Oliver asked.

"Saint Maran West. You must go to East since I've never seen you at my school."

"I go to Saint Benedict Military Academy. The all-boys school that's outside of this city. I'm a senior."

"Oh, that expensive school. I know about it as well as the all-girls one, Saint Cecilia. But I'm a senior at Saint Maran West, the public school."

He nodded as he kept staring at her. "Wow, my dad definitely made this night better for me. Didn't have that great of a night tonight since I hung out mostly in here with my friends since I'm the only one who has access to it since my dad owns this place. But this night just got better since he knew just who to bring in here to me to make me feel good. But I have a feeling you didn't have a great night here tonight."

She blushed. "Thank you, Oliver. And you're right, I didn't. Long story. But I'm probably gonna have to get going soon. Maybe we can see each other some other time?"

"Hell yeah, we can!"

She laughed. "Sounds good."

"But I can't let you leave here without showing you something. I think I have just the right thing to cheer you up from whatever it is that has you so down." He got up. "Come with me. I think you're gonna love this."

She got up. "Well, okay. But after you show me what you wanna show me then I really need to see if my friend is here. She should actually be here by now."

"I'll walk you to the front when she gets here."

She smiled. "Thank you."

"You never paged me, Dad," Oliver said.
"You know you didn't need a page from me, Oliver. What the hell happened to that girl that night?"

CHAPTER THIRTY-SEVEN

"Thank you for meeting with me, Mackenzee. And on behalf of this city, I would like to say that I'm sorry—personally and professionally—for how this city had handled these disappearances for over 30 years now. And for someone who wasn't even born yet back when these first started and has taken an initiative that no one else wanted to do and began to independently investigate them is very thoughtful and courageous," Chief Hatcher said.

"Thank you, Chief Hatcher. I just wanted someone to hear these stories. Too many young Black women go missing and it's like no one cares. But when they start to go missing from the same place and there's witnesses as to where they were last and it all goes back to the same place? Then that's a problem. I just couldn't believe that no one had done anything in this city for over 30 years when it came to the first disappearance in 1990, and then two more after that in 5-year intervals. It was as if these girls were just written off to being runaways and no one should care about them."

"That's definitely not how I see them, and that's definitely not how Yolanda sees them. And it's definitely not how you see them or their families. I'm glad she brought these disappearances to light for me, and I'm glad you have revealed yourself to us be the woman who has the *I'm Their Speaker* show. If it wasn't for that, I don't think anyone would've ever gave any thought to these disappearances."

"I never forgot about them; they were always in the back of my mind since I found myself to be a direct witness link to one of them," Yolanda said.

"And I'm so glad you came to my house to talk to me about it. I don't think I would've ever found you on my own. So many people in this city have been so quiet about this, and I just don't think it's right." I looked at Chief Hatcher. "And I hope I've told you enough where you can at least bring Oliver Pratt in for questioning and have him submit a DNA sample."

"Well, I called his dad, Orlando, when Yolanda told me about the conversation she had with you, and he told me he would talk to Oliver about these disappearances—not sure if he has or not. But I feel there's definitely enough evidence and not hearsay about what could've happened those nights in that club that led to at least Deandra and Gazelle's disappearances, and we haven't ruled out Tanisha's, either. So I'm waiting for Judge Milton Bridgeton to get back from vacation so he can sign off on a search warrant for The Club."

"Damn, of all times he's on vacation," I said as I shook my head. "Well, the families have waited for this long so I guess it will be worth it to wait for a search warrant since that place has never been searched before. What about Oliver's DNA?"

"We'll get it from him when we bring him in for questioning," Chief Hatcher informed me. He looked around his office. "And since you provided enough information about Tanisha's disappearance from The Club, we're going to bring DA Richard Elmhurst III in for questioning and we'll also be collecting his DNA. Are you okay with that?"

"Yeah, I'm okay with it," Elron said!

"Like I knew you would be," I nodded with a smile.

I need to see you. Meet me at my house ASAP. Don't disappoint me.

Richard.

I stared at the text not knowing what to do. But what I knew I was about to do was try to get some sleep for tonight. I felt good in the fact that there was going to be an official search of The Club if Judge Bridgeton signed off on the warrant, and I was hoping that there wouldn't be any problems with him doing so because I just never knew who he knew in this city.

But now that I knew Richard was being brought in for questioning regarding Tanisha's disappearance, I didn't know if it was a good idea that I'd talked to him, much less see him right now. But I had to know why he wanted me to meet him at his house and why he needed to see me and why it was so urgent.

I got dressed and looked in on Porsha. She was sound asleep. I crept out of the house and headed to Richard's.

Twenty minutes later, I crept through the front door of Richard's home. He told me he'd left the door open for me as if I was his girl-friend, and he really did.

"Richard?" I said, as it was dimly it and "Separated" by Avant played throughout this foyer.

"I'm upstairs in my bedroom," he said over the speakers.

It was clear he was watching me.

But I didn't know if I wanted to go up to his bedroom. Now I knew what he definitely had in mind. "I don't know where it is."

"Come upstairs, Mackenzee. *Now.*"

I turned around and looked at the front doors . . . and heard them lock!

Fuck.

I felt I was now trapped.

I took a deep breath and began to slowly walk up the left side of this beautiful wrought-iron double staircase.

"Come to the end of the hall and make a right," he said, as it was obvious to me that he was watching me and was still talking over the speakers. "It's the first door on the left."

I walked through the door since it was wide open and into a room that was completely dark. "Richard?"

He appeared out from nowhere in the room with a small drink in his hands, and I could smell the hard liquor from where I was standing. The lights slowly got a little brighter as he stared at me as he took another sip of his drink, and it was clear he had this "Separated" by Avant song on repeat. It was clear we were standing in some kind of suite area of his master bedroom.

"What did you wanna see me for?" I asked, as he slowly walked towards me.

He stood in front of me as if he was gonna eye-fuck my clothes right off of me. "Have a seat."

I sat on the couch facing his 90-inch TV mounted on the wall as it showed an episode of *Forensic Files*. "What did you wanna see me for?" I asked again, as he stood over me.

He sat right next to me. "This was the song that was playing the last time I saw Tanisha," he informed me.

"At The Club in 2000?"

He took a sip of his drink. "Yes, at The Club." He shook his head. "I guess it was a perfect fit because I said I was through with her after all of her disrespect of me that whole night. But nothing was more disrespectful than what she finally did. Sealed the deal that I was officially through with her."

I continued to stare at him in total suspense. "What did she do?"

He smirked and let out a wicked laugh. "Yeah, I knew you would like to know, especially since you got Chief Hatcher all involved in this."

"A direct witness in the 1995 disappearance of Gazelle Ragland got Chief Hatcher involved in this, not me. Before then, I thought he was like all of you other corrupt assholes in this city who didn't and still don't give a shit about what happened to three young women who disappeared from y'alls little precious iconic establishment in these past 33 years."

"It's not my establishment. I don't own any part of it."

"And why don't you have any part in it, Richard? There's obviously a reason."

"Yeah, there's always a reason. But before I get to that, how did you know Tanisha went missing in 2000? I never brought up what year it was the last time I saw her."

He fuckin' got me.

I just broke my promise to Elron about not saying anything about Tanisha's disappearance to Richard since there was no proof that he was in fact responsible for it. But now I started to believe he had me over here because he wanted to tell me that he was the only person responsible for it, and quite possibly wanted to silence me for good because of it.

I needed to get the fuck out of here.

"I gotta go."

"So soon?"

"Yes, so soon."

"You just got here. And you don't have to go anywhere, Mackenzee, so stop lying."

"I'm starting to feel uncomfortable."

"About what? I'm not doing anything to you but talking to you."

"I don't feel comfortable talking about what we're talking about."

He laughed, and took another sip of his drink. "*Now* you don't feel comfortable talking about what we've been talking about. Wow, that's very interesting that you say that now, Mackenzee, especially since you're all alone with me. You were comfortable talking about it to Chief Hatcher, as well as to others, including interviewing family of the missing women and witnesses. And you're definitely comfortable talking about it on your *I'm Their Speaker* show."

"You can't prove that's me."

"I already did."

I looked at him. "How?"

"Because you never said it wasn't you."

I sighed. "You still can't prove it." I inched away from him. "Look, I think I better go."

"Why? You still haven't thanked me for that nice dinner Elron made for us."

"I thanked you and him that same day for it, Richard."

"You haven't thanked me in the way I want to be thanked for bailing you out of jail?"

"You want pussy from me that bad, huh? Is that it? I mean, I don't understand why you just can't let me go home. You talked me into coming over here because I thought it was about something important. You tricked me."

"I never tricked you, Mackenzee. That's a lie."

"Well, the last thing you should be concerned about is getting some pussy from me."

"I have nothing to be concerned about."

I looked at him. "And why is that?"

"Because I haven't done anything wrong."

"Then why don't you just talk to Chief Hatcher about it?"

"How do you know that I haven't?"

"You have?!" I said, very interested in if he did or not, because that could make the difference of whether or not he really had something to hide.

He inched back over to me as he slowly pulled me closer to him. "You sure are beautiful, Mackenzee. If you weren't so into this independent investigation of yours, we could quite possibly have a potentially serious relationship."

"I want these girls found. Their families deserve to know what happened to them. It's been way too long that nothing has been done, and you know that. You have a direct link to one of them, and it was said she was last seen with you."

"Who said she was last seen with me?"

I didn't want to say it was Elron. I just couldn't. I'd already broken my promise to him and he didn't even know it, so I didn't want to be in deeper shit with him. I felt I was on my own with trying to explain how I knew all of this, and that I could've been sitting right next to the person who was responsible for why Tanisha hadn't been seen and heard from in 23 years.

He continued to stare at me. "I'll tell you the whole truth and nothing but the absolute truth . . . if and only if I could get some of this pussy tonight," he said as he slid his hand slowly in between my legs. "Come on, now. It won't take that long."

CHAPTER THIRTY-EIGHT

"Good morning."

I looked up to Richard staring down at me with a smile.

I couldn't believe that I went against everything I morally stood for last night just to get him to tell me the truth. I could've slept with the person who was responsible for Tanisha Longfellow's disappearance, considering the fact that after he got what he wanted from me, he fell into a deep sleep . . . and so did I.

I cleared my throat. "I gave you what you wanted last night, and you didn't tell me what you said you were gonna tell me."

"After breakfast," he said with a smile. "I need something good to eat after that night we had last night."

"HEY, RICH MAN, THE FOOD IS READY!"

I dove under the covers!

It was Elron!

"Thanks for letting me know, man," Richard said, as I heard Elron walk into the room.

"I gotta get going. Talk to you later," Elron said.

"Okay, man."

I heard them slap hands as I stayed as still as I could until he was gone for good.

Several minutes later, I heard someone come back into the room. The covers were lifted off of me.

"He's gone, so you can stop hiding now," Richard said with a huge grin.

I sighed as I got out of bed. "Did you tell him I was here?"

"No, because it was none of his business."

"Are you gonna tell him?"

"What for?"

"Just wanted to know." I put my clothes on. "And I wanna know what it is you were gonna tell me last night that you didn't tell me."

"Come on down and have breakfast with me and I'll tell you."

Minutes later, I walked down to the kitchen with him to Milli Vanilli's "I'm Gonna Miss You" playing on the speakers. I was wondering why he wanted such a sad song playing while we were supposed to be eating breakfast, but I knew that this song had every-thing to do with Tanisha. It was too obvious. But the table was nicely set with a traditionally delicious-smelling breakfast spread of pancakes, bacon, eggs, and sausage along with coffee, milk, and orange juice. I noticed how there were two plates at the table.

"He obviously knew someone was here otherwise he would not have put two plates out."

"Yeah, he knew, but he didn't have to know it was you. Am I right?"

"Yes, you're right. Did he ask you if it was me?"

"No, he didn't. He's been one of my best friends for over 30 years. He knows I will tell him who it is if I wanted him to know, otherwise, he knows it's not important to know who it is—in other words, it's none of his business."

I sighed as I put my napkin in my lap. "I just don't want him to ever know it was me."

"Why? Are you secretly seeing him, too?"

I gave him an offended look. "No, I'm not seeing him. And I wasn't aware that we were."

"We're not," he confirmed to me with a grin, and took a sip of his coffee.

I sighed as I shook my head. I tried very hard not to let him get to me since it was so early in the morning. "Are you gonna tell me now what you were supposed to tell me last night? I'm sure you have a busy day today and so do I."

"Busy day doing what? Interviewing more witnesses for your investigation? Editing your *I'm Their Speaker* show?"

I put my napkin on the table and got up. "I think I should go."

"Sit down and eat. Elron didn't make all of this food for nothing."

I sat back down. "Could you *please* tell me what happened between you and Tanisha that night she disappeared?"

"I don't wanna talk about her right now, I'm eating," he said, as he looked at his phone and shoved some of his pancakes in his mouth. At this point I was hoping he would choke on them.

I shook my head as I put my napkin back in my lap as I tried to eat some of this food since after all, Elron made it. I honestly didn't know how he could stay best friends with someone like Richard for so long, especially when he could've had everything to do with the disappearance of his favorite cousin. And the more I sat here and tried to get it out of him, the more and more he looked guilty as I thought of him to be all along.

He looked at his phone, and got up. "I gotta go."

"What?"

"You heard me. I gotta go. Do you wanna take your food and the rest of it here with you?"

I sighed. "Yeah, I guess."

"Great. I'll have Maritza, my maid, wrap it up for you."

"Where are you going?" I asked, because I felt that this was my business especially after what I reluctantly gave him last night, only for him not to tell me a damn thing this morning.

He looked at me as if he was trying not to break out into laughter. "To talk to Chief Hatcher."

"That son of a bitch! How could he lie to you like that?!" Porsha asked, as she gobbled down the breakfast I'd taken with me from Richard's house as we sat at the kitchen table.

"Because he's a manipulative motherfucker," I said as I shook my head. "And I fell right into the trap of his manipulation. He told me he was gonna tell me the absolute truth when it came to what happened to Tanisha that last night she was seen if I gave him some pussy—excuse me, I know you're eating."

She laughed. "It's nothing I haven't heard of before. Doesn't bother me, you know that. But I just think it's wrong for him to say he was gonna tell you something and made you believe it and then he tells you that he's talking to him *today*?"

"I don't even know if he's doing that. I just think he has a lot to hide when it comes to Tanisha's whereabouts. I think he knows exactly what happened to her because he had everything to do with it. I've pretty much ruled him out of Deandra and Gazelle's disappearances. But Tanisha's is definitely more personal because she was Elron's cousin and he's best friends with him, and Tanisha was Richard's girlfriend, a girlfriend he never got over when she broke up with him to go to college out of state. I don't see how Elron can stay best friends with someone like Richard for as long as he has knowing he saw for himself that Richard was the last one seen with Tanisha. But Richard has a lot of explaining to do to me, but especially to Elron."

"He does. But tell me, what was it like to have sex with a man who is 50?"

"Like how it is to have sex with a man in his 20s or whatever age he is. Trust me, Porsha, men are men. No difference between them, especially when it comes to them wanting some damn pussy. You know that. Every woman whose ever had sex should know that."

She laughed. "You're right about that!"

"I'm glad you had time to see me today, Ashley. I just couldn't wait anymore to tell the two of you this," I said, as I sat in Ashley's dental office where she had beautiful pictures of her mother Deandra—some of them with her by herself and some of them with her in them. I stared at one in particular, and it was one of her with Deandra when she was just a few months old.

"No problem at all, Mackenzee. My grandmother and I very much appreciate what you're doing for my mom and for the other two young women. I just don't know how much more time would've had to pass before someone actually did something," Ashley said, as she sat at her desk.

"You got that right, baby," Cloris said with a smile. "And just to think I thought that Chief Hatcher was just like all the police chiefs before him. I'm glad someone has finally taken the time and listened to someone about these disappearances, and that someone is you, Miss Mackenzee. You're definitely a people person."

"Thank you, Cloris. I was shocked when Yolanda Cozine came to my house that day and told me what she'd told me. And that Chief Hatcher didn't know about these disappearances until she'd mentioned them to him after seeing my show about them. He had enough reason to believe that these disappearances from The Club in 5-year intervals were very real, and therefore wants the place searched. He's just waiting for Judge Bridgeton to get back from vacation to sign off on the search warrant."

"I can't believe this is finally gonna happen. It's been so long," Cloris said with a weary smile.

"It has, Cloris, and now I feel we are finally getting somewhere with all of this. And I want to tell you that the main suspect in at least two of these disappearances, including Deandra's, is Oliver Pratt."

"Oliver Pratt?!" they both said.

"Yes," I reconfirmed.

"The current owner of The Club is the main suspect in my baby's disappearance?" Cloris said.

Ashley looked at me.

"Yes, he is. I didn't wanna put a lot of this on my show until I can have some solid proof of it, but for both Deandra's and Gazelle's disappearances, witnesses are saying they were last seen with him. When I personally spoke to Chief Hatcher with Yolanda present since she is his personal secretary and was a waitress at The Club in 1995 when Gazelle disappeared, I was able to lay out a good case for why he should have the place searched and to bring Oliver in for questioning and for a DNA sample . . . and it was clear that I did because he's had a warrant written up to search The Club and is gonna have Oliver brought in for questioning at the same time if he's there. He just called me personally before I came over here to tell me that they've been trying to get Oliver in for questioning, but they haven't been able to get a hold of him."

"Yeah, all of the sudden he disappears," Ashley said.

"Don't worry, Ashley. Wherever he is, he can't hide forever. He lives for that damn club. But little does he know, for the first time ever, it's gonna be searched."

"And that search warrant can't be done fast enough," Cloris said.

I looked at my phone. "And you just got your wish, Cloris. Chief Hatcher just texted me back personally. Judge Bridgeton has just signed the search warrant so it's all set."

"For when?" Cloris asked.

Ashley stared at me in suspense.

I smiled. "Tonight."

CHAPTER THIRTY-NINE

"Where are you going tonight?" Ashley asked Nayana as she stood in the door of her bedroom.

"To the movies with Taylor," Nayana replied as she put the finishing touches on her makeup.

"Is that the only place?"

"Yeah, probably. But we'll also probably just hang out at Starbucks after, but I'm not sure. We'll probably just go back to her house or come back here. Is that okay?"

"Sure, that's fine, honey. Is she coming here to pick you up?"

"No, I'm going to her house," she said.

"Okay, call or text me when you get there."

"You know I will, Mom," she said with a smile. She watched her mom leave her bedroom and got out her phone. She stared at the text:

It's that time of the month once again!
Teen Night @TheCLUB
Exclusive Private Access to the Private VIP Lounge only for those who
receive this text. Just present this text at the private back door and a
night in The Club's Private VIP Lounge is all yours!
See you there!

．．．

Ashley got on her phone.

"Who are you calling?" her husband Norman asked, as they sat in their family room watching a movie.

"Nayana. She was supposed to call me when she got to Taylor's; she should've been there by now."

"That's where she said she was going tonight?" Cloris asked, since she over their house for their monthly movie night.

"Yes, to the movies with Taylor. I would've rather had them both stay here and watch a movie with all of us since we only have our movie night once a month, but she's only 17-years-old so I understand she wanted to go to the movies with her friend. They said they were probably going to hang out at Starbucks or come back here or go back to Taylor's. She said she wasn't sure, but I know for sure she should've called me by now. I know it doesn't take her this long to get to Taylor's," Ashley said. She hung up.

"Not answering?" Norman asked.

"No," Ashley said, as she held the phone in her hands.

He got out his phone. "Let me try." He called his only daughter as he waited for her to answer. He hung up less than a minute later. "She probably has her phone off and she knows we told her to never leave it off when she's away from us. Let's just wait a few minutes."

"Now she knows she better answer her great-grandmother," Cloris said, and called her. She was met with the same non-response.

"She knows the way I get when she doesn't answer her phone when she knows her or her dad is waiting to hear from her," Ashley said. She got back on her phone.

"Trying her again?" Norman asked as Cloris stared at her.

"I'm calling Taylor," Ashley informed them while she had it on speaker.

"Hello, Mrs. Capers," Taylor said.

"Hi, Taylor. I just wanted to know if Nayana made it to your house yet?"

"She said she was coming to my house tonight?"

They all instantly exchanged looks of concern.

"Yes, Taylor. She told me the two of you were going to the movies."

"She never told me that. I'm still at home waiting for a male friend to come pick me up for a date tonight. She told me at school she had no plans for tonight."

"What?!" Ashley said.

"Yes, Mrs. Capers, that's what she told me," Taylor informed her.

"If you hear from her, Taylor, tell her to call me immediately, okay?" Ashley said.

"Yes, Mrs. Capers," Taylor said.

Nayana arrived at The Club to the usual very large crowds and milelong line with eager teens from Saint Maran and outside cities waiting for their chance to get in. But she knew she didn't have to stand in any line tonight. She parked her car and got out with confidence and walked up to where she was instructed to go—to the back door for private access to the VIP lounge.

"Good evening," one of the men said who was guarding the door.

"Hi," she said with a smile, and showed him her phone of the text that was sent to her.

He nodded with a smile. "Follow that gentleman right inside the door. He'll take you where you need to go."

"Thank you."

She followed the man to the private VIP lounge.

He opened the door for her. "Here you are. Enjoy the night."

"Thank you," she said again, as she stepped inside . . . to an empty lounge. She looked around as there was no one behind the bar and no waitresses around. She knew this was teen night, so they weren't serving any alcohol. But she thought there would be at least a bartender serving drinks like they did in the main room. She went over to one of the booth tables and sat down. "I guess I'm very early. I'm the first one here." She got on her phone and looked at the text once again, and waited to see who else got the same text as her as "17" by Rick James played throughout the lounge. "They play really old music in this lounge for a teen night," she mumbled as she still looked at her phone.

The doors to the lounge opened once again, and a man walked in . . . and came straight to her table. "Hi. Are you Nayana Capers?"

"Yes! How did you know my name?"

"I know a lot of people's names, baby. I'm Oliver Pratt. I'm this club's owner."

Ashley jumped at the ringing of her phone. "Nayana?!"

"No, Ashley, it's Mackenzee."

"Mackenzee, I can't get in touch with Nayana. She told me she was going to Taylor's and then to the movies, but Taylor told me she told her at school that she had no plans for tonight."

"Shit! Um, I think I might know where she's at."

"You do?! Where?!"

"The same place where the search warrant is gonna happen in about an hour and now I really want you and your grandmother and husband to be there when it goes down—Chief Hatcher said it was okay that you all are there and you'll be there outside under police protection while the search is being conducted. It's Teen Night tonight at The Club."

"We're on our way," Ashley informed me.

CHAPTER FORTY

$\mathcal{A}$ bouncer came busting through the private VIP lounge along with several other men!

"Boss, we got trouble! We're being searched by the cops!" he informed him.

Oliver quickly turned on the surveillance TV and saw a raid of police hurrying the horrified, unsuspecting teens out the door so the place could be thoroughly searched.

"What's going on?" Nayana said.

"Come on!" Oliver said, and grabbed her hand so she wouldn't get away from him. "Don't let those motherfuckers come back here where I am!" he told the bouncers.

"What's going on?!" Nayana said again in a frightened voice as everything looked like a blur as Oliver had a tight grip on her arm as his men protected them as they all ran all the way to his office. "Get back out there and tell those cops to get the fuck out of here! They have no reason to be here!"

"Right away, Boss!" one of the men said.

Oliver locked the doors to his office and put chairs up against the door, and then turned on his surveillance TV as police searched all over the place while still hurrying the hordes of clubgoing teens out the door. He got on his phone. "If they want a fuckin' war then they got one! They're not taking my place down! They're the enemy now! FUCK CHIEF HATCHER!!"

"WHAT THE HELL IS GOING ON?!" Nayana screamed!

"SHUT THE FUCK UP!" Oliver yelled back at her as screaming and crashing sounds of things being thrown around and even blasting sounds of doors being blown off of their hinges shaking the ground. He grabbed Nayana and threw her into his office bathroom and put another chair up against it.

She cried as she sat on the floor as she couldn't believe what was going on. She knew now that something wasn't right about the text she'd received. She shook as she got out her phone.

"NAYANA! WHERE ARE YOU?! WE'RE RIGHT OUTSIDE OF THE CLUB!" Ashley screamed as she and Cloris and Norman were under police protection as they stood back and watched the teens being evacuated from The Club since it was officially being searched, and the search was led by Chief Hatcher.

"I'm inside The Club, Mom! I'm in a man's office named Oliver!" Nayana cried.

"MY BABY IS INSIDE THERE! SHE SAID SHE'S IN OLIVER PRATT'S OFFICE!" Ashley screamed to any cop who would listen.

"Oh my god!" I said, as I stood back with the rest of them. I looked to my left and saw Kamiah, Gazelle's sister and some of her family members I'd never met, as well as family of Tanisha Longfellow come running on to the scene as well that I'd never met. It was clear to me that Elron told them what was going on. Mary and her son Demetrius arrived minutes later. I briefed them all on what was going on from what Chief Hatcher had told me.

"We just notified Chief Hatcher," a cop informed Ashley.

"Thank you!" Ashley said, as Norman held her as he did with Cloris.

I looked around where there were now hundreds of people out here, including all of the teens who were here for a night of fun but had it interrupted, and they had no idea why. I even heard some of them yelling to the cops about having their night ruined by this "stupid raid" of this club. They didn't understand, but hopefully before this night ended that they would.

I watched as more cops as well as the SWAT team arrived as they jumped out of cars and armored trucks with their guns drawn and pointed as they went to the back of The Club where the back deck was where they had private parties during the warmer months. I was glad they were doing a thorough search of this place.

"MACKENZEE LAWSON?" a cop yelled to the crowd I was in.

"Yes? I'm Mackenzee Lawson," I replied.

"Chief Hatcher wants to see you. Follow me," he said. He lifted up the tape to let me through and escorted me to where Chief Hatcher was.

As I walked through the parking lot, I looked back at the families of Deandra, Gazelle, and Tanisha. I knew they were eagerly waiting to hear what was going on.

The cop brought me right up to where Chief Hatcher was as he stood in his back of The Club with his gun drawn by his side. "Mackenzee. Glad you're here."

"I was not gonna miss this. What's going on?"

He sighed. "My men just informed me that they found something."

CHAPTER FORTY-ONE

I took a deep breath as I followed Chief Hatcher towards whatever it was that he had to show me. I started to get weak in the knees. I couldn't believe that this was happening. If his men said they found something, then it was obviously a very serious finding.

One of the cops lifted up another set of crime tape as Chief Hatcher and I walked under it and right to a black brick building that matched The Club, but it was very small in size comparison. I looked at Chief Hatcher.

"What is this?"

"A storage shed. A place where The Club obviously stores stuff." He sighed. "They've informed me that they have found three separate human remains."

I now felt faint. I couldn't believe how real this was. "They have?" I asked anyway, knowing what he'd just told me, but it wasn't quite hitting me. It was like I felt as if I was watching a horror mystery movie on TV.

"Yes, Mackenzee," he replied as he stared down at me. He could see it all in my eyes that what I'd investigated was finally being confirmed.

Three separate human remains.

"I don't want you going in there, okay? That's what the coroner is on his way here for," he informed me.

"It's them," I said, as tears welled up in my eyes. "It's them."

"We'll know officially after proper identification," he told me. "My men are in The Club right outside of Oliver's office trying to talk him into coming out of there. It's clear he's barricaded himself in there. We also know he has a teen girl in there, who you all now say is Nayana Capers, daughter of Dr. Ashley Whitfield-Capers and granddaughter of the pending victim, Deandra Whitfield."

"Yes," I replied. "It's them," I said again. I felt like I couldn't stop saying it. I looked up to the night sky as tears welled up in my eyes. "How am I gonna tell them this, Chief Hatcher? They're all standing in this parking lot waiting for answers, answers that they have been waiting for for decades."

"That's not your job, Mackenzee, it's ours. If it wasn't for you, I don't think these bodies would've ever been found. Your investigation is what led us here. I can't thank you enough for taking these disappearances seriously since no one else in this city hadn't for 33 years. All we have to do now is officially identify all three of them."

"We need more good cops like you, Chief Hatcher."

He smiled. "And we need more good concerned citizens like you, Mackenzee."

"CHIEF HATCHER! THEY WANT YOU INSIDE THE CLUB! OLIVER IS THREATENING TO HURT THE GIRL!" a cop yelled out to him.

"No!" I shrieked!

"You stay right here with these cops, okay? They'll take care of you."

"Okay," I said, as tears streamed down my eyes as I watched him run with a bunch of other cops back inside The Club.

Twenty minutes later, Chief Hatcher was still trying to talk Oliver out of hurting Nayana.

"Oliver, look. There's no one inside this club right now. Everyone has been evacuated. I don't want anyone hurt, okay? You need to give yourself up. We found what we wanted to find and we want to question you about it. You haven't been charged with anything, okay? Just let us all end this peacefully, okay?"

"GET THE FUCK OUT OF HERE!" Oliver yelled through the door as he now held Nayana by gunpoint behind his desk. "I HATE WOMEN!"

"Oliver, please. We need for you to surrender peacefully. We don't want any trouble," Chief Hatcher said.

"THEN YOU SHOULD'VE NEVER CAME HERE! YOU HAD NO BUSINESS COMING HERE!" Oliver continued to yell.

And he continued to yell more insults and profanities at the cops and about his hatred for women and for the world.

"Enough of this shit," Chief Hatcher said. "That girl is going home with her family if I have to go in there and get her myself so you better—"

A gunshot blast shook the floors!

Several minutes later, Chief Hatcher and his officers got through the barricaded door. And found Nayana sitting in a corner by a safe crying as she covered her head. Oliver was found with a self-inflicted gunshot wound to his head.

Chief Hatcher got Nayana up on her feet and embraced her. "It's okay, honey. You're safe. Your family is outside. You're safe now." He looked at the safe as he still held Nayana. "Get someone in here to get this safe opened," he instructed one of the officers. "I'll take you to your family."

"Okay," Nayana sobbed as she would not let go of Chief Hatcher as they walked out of Oliver's office amidst all of the chaos where she was reunited with her family.

CHAPTER FORTY-TWO

*C*hief Hatcher stood at the podium in front of media from all over the country as he got ready to speak. "Good morning, everyone. Thank you for attending this last of many press conferences regarding the disappearances of Deandra Whitfield, Gazelle Ragland, and Tanisha Longfellow from The Club in the years 1990, 1995, and 2000. The suspect was Oliver Pratt, 50, of Saint Maran and owner of The Club starting in the year 1995. It is now confirmed through DNA that he is the only suspect in their disappearances, and there was DNA of his found on the victims who have all been positively identified by family and through DNA as Deandra Whitfield, 17, who went missing in 1990; Gazelle Ragland, 22, who went missing in 1995; and Tanisha Longfellow, 29, who went missing in 2000. All three of their remains were found in a storage shed behind The Club weeks ago, as you were all notified of.

"We also found a lot of items belonging to all three victims in a safe in Oliver's office, a safe that was out in plain sight. We found purses, IDs—driver's licenses as well as Deandra's high school ID and her driver's license—makeup, and jewelry. I was also given a lipstick by Mackenzee Lawson, the independent investigator on these disappearances, that belonged to Deandra Whitfield so it can be used for

DNA testing. Deandra happened to have an identical tube of this lipstick in her purse, so we were able to collect DNA from the lipstick Mackenzee gave to me as well as the one found in her purse in Oliver's safe. All of the items found in this safe belonged to all three victims, and no one else.

"Oliver also left a suicide note. I'm not going to read the whole note to you all, but he did confess to killing all three women by strangling them and putting their bodies into the storage shed during The Club's closed hours. The note went on to say that all three women were lured out of the private VIP lounge and outside to an area that was a spacious deck for private parties. When all three rejected his advances, he strangled them to death that same night. He knew Gazelle when they were in high school—but they didn't go to the same high school—and had a genuine interest in her, but claimed she changed and not for the better. He didn't go into too much detail about Tanisha, only that he hadn't seen her in years prior to seeing her that night he murdered her, and he'd just met Deandra through his dad that night he murdered her. Deandra's granddaughter, Nayana Capers, was sent a text by Oliver from The Club that night he took her hostage when we searched the place. According to interviews conducted with The Club staff members, she was the only who received this text, so it was clear he was setting her up to hurt her just like he did with her grandmother 33 years ago. He even made inappropriate statements in his suicide note about what he wanted to with Nayana, statements that I will not reveal at this press conference out of respect for Deandra Whitfield's family. This suicide note was written a day before we searched The Club.

"I can't end this press conference today without thanking Mackenzee Lawson for the millionth time for bringing this case to light, and Vatrice Johnson who reported on it to begin with which inspired Mackenzee's investigation. And my personal secretary Yolanda Cozine for telling what she witnessed in Gazelle Ragland's case. You ladies deserve more credit than you will ever know, and the city of Saint Maran will work on being the kind of city that will never tolerate silence or corruption when it comes to any missing person—female or male, young or old. Ladies, please stand up."

The media clapped as Vatrice, Yolanda, and I stood up to be acknowledged by Chief Hatcher. I smiled at the families of Deandra, Gazelle, and Tanisha as they wiped tears from their eyes and clapped along with everyone else. I looked right at Elron as he smiled big at me and gave me the thumbs up. I knew everything I'd went through to get to this point was well worth it.

CHAPTER FORTY-THREE

ix Months Later

"I'd like to welcome you all to a very special day today, and it is the unveiling of the official memorial site in memory of Deandra Whitfield, Gazelle Ragland, and Tanisha Longfellow, who tragically lost their lives at The Club in 1990, 1995, and 2000. Here stands in the place of where this former iconic place once was, is now a site forever memorializing three beautiful women who wanted to come here for a night of fun. Their nights didn't have to end the way it did, but now since there is no more The Club in the city of Saint Maran, we want people to always remember why it isn't here anymore, and as the new mayor of this city, I will make sure that nothing like this ever happens again for as long as I'm in charge of the beautiful city of Saint Maran," Ross Welch said, who was an outsider elected mayor after Orlando Pratt abandoned his responsibilities as mayor of this city after the suicide of his son who was proven to be the murderer of three beautiful women who, like Mayor Welch said, only wanted to come here for a night of fun. Orlando Pratt and his family hadn't been seen or heard from since.

I smiled at the beautiful black marble headstones with pictures of Deandra, Gazelle, and Tanisha on them, along with their names engraved in them in a beautiful white script and the year they were born and the year they tragically had their lives taken from them. There were also quotes given for each of them from a family member, and many beautiful colorful flowers. I was also very proud to see how many people were here, and it numbered at well over a hundred. I smiled at Chief Hatcher as he smiled back at me. He was a great man and so was Mayor Welch, who approved of the memorial site and to have The Club officially torn down and the memorial site in its place. It honestly looked like a whole different place that's because I knew it was as well as everyone else who was here today.

"There's one more thing we have to present today," Mayor Welch informed the crowd. "For the first time ever, we are giving out our very first Saint Maran Concerned Citizen of the Year Award. And this award goes to Miss Mackenzee Lawson!"

For some reason, I was so surprised at this. I shrieked in shock as I smiled big as everyone stood and clapped for me. I looked out in the audience at my parents who smiled and waved to me, at Porsha who did the same thing, and the hugs and congrats I'd gotten from the families of Deandra, Gazelle, and Tanisha.

"You know you deserve this award, Mackenzee. Congratulations," Elron said with a big smile.

"Thank you," I replied as we hugged. I stood with a big smile as Mayor Ross put a beautiful genuine 24K gold medal around my neck, as well as gave me a beautiful inscripted plaque. I was not expecting all of this! "Wow," I said, as tears welled up in my eyes. "I was only doing what I thought was right; doing what should've been done for these women decades ago, and I will do it all over again, there is no doubt about that. I am their speaker, and I will be any missing person's speaker, any murder victim's speaker, because they need a voice. Nothing gets done when everyone stays silent. Nothing gets done when everyone stays corrupt. I'm glad to see that Saint Maran is going in the right direction with new people in power who really care about this city and the people in it, something that has been needed for a very long time. This is a great start to this. We can always rebuild anything to make it a better place, because a city is only as good as the people in it. This feels like a new Saint Maran and that's because it is, and I'm glad to be a part of it because no matter where in the world I am, this will always be my home, and now I'm proud to say that it is once again. Thank you all."

Everyone clapped as I shook the hand of Mayor Welch and other people in power, as well as hugged Chief Hatcher. Several minutes later, I talked to Cloris and Ashley, as well as Ashley's husband, Norman.

"Nayana is excited about going to college next year," Ashley said with a smile. "She says she'll never forget what you did for her, Mackenzee."

"She's a beautiful young woman, Ashley. The two of you raised her well," I replied with a smile. "Wish her luck for me when she goes off to school."

"We will," they replied with a smile.

"If you're wondering why I haven't asked for Deandra's diary back, it's because I want you to officially have it," Cloris said with a smile.

I hugged her. "Thank you, Cloris."

"I agree. I know my mom would want you to have it," Ashley said with a smile.

"I think so, too," Norman said as well with a smile.

"Ashley?"

We all turned around . . . . to *Trevor McPherson*! Ashley's dad!

"Trevor?" I said.

"It's me, Mackenzee," Trevor said with a smile. "Nice to meet you in person."

"Nice to meet you, too," I replied with a smile.

He turned to Ashley. "Hi, baby."

"Dad," Ashley said, as tears welled up in her eyes. She broke down and cried in his arms.

Tears welled up in my eyes as well as Cloris.

"I'm so sorry, baby. I never meant to leave you for 33 years. Never. I hope it's not too late for us to catch up. I know your mom would've wanted it this way," he said as he still held her.

"I know she would," Ashley said as she sobbed.

"I know she would, too," Cloris said as she patted her eyes with a tissue.

"I love you," Trevor said to Ashley.

"I love you, too, Dad," Ashley sobbed as they still held each other.

Tears streamed down my eyes as they talked to each other as he was introduced to Norman, his son-in-law, and told all about Nayana who was at a job interview. I looked at my surroundings and saw another unexpected reunion—Mary was introducing her son Demetrius to his dad, Damian! I smiled as I let them have their privacy. They all walked over to Deandra's headstone and talked in front of it while looking at it. There was no better feeling than to see so many people brought back to together after so many years. And I knew Deandra, Gazelle, and Tanisha were very much loved and would never be forgotten.

As people cleared from the site as they walked around and socialized with others, I saw Richard standing by his car as he stared back at me. I excused myself from extended members of Tanisha's family.

I approached him as he stood by his car. "Hi."

"Hi. Long time no talk or see." He smiled as he looked at my medal and plaque. "Congratulations."

"Thank you. I'm shocked that I won something so prestigious from this city."

"You deserve it, Mackenzee. At least I thought so since I was one of the many who voted in favor of you receiving it."

I gasped in shock! "You did?! Richard, wow! Thank you!"

"No problem, Mackenzee. Like I said, you deserve it. Do you wanna go grab some lunch to celebrate?"

I side-eyed him. "As long as that's all we do."

He grinned and opened his door on his passenger's side. "Get in."

I texted Porsha to let her know I was going to lunch with Richard and that I would talk to her later. She gave me that grinning emoji in return.

"So, The Club is no more," he replied with a smile as he concentrated on the road.

"Are you mad they tore it down?"

"Not at all. It had way too much stigma to it. It was never gonna be looked at as the same again. Oliver offed himself like I knew he was more than likely gonna do; his dad abandoned his job as mayor of this city since he knew he was not gonna get reelected. So much for those trying to get to 30 years, huh?"

"Yeah, and all of those years he knew his son more than likely killed all three of them and did nothing about it."

"And he wasn't going to until you came along, Mackenzee. Wow, you really made this city a better place again already. I never thought The Club was gonna get shut down and get completely demolished at that."

"It didn't need to be there anymore. Oliver was just a fuckin' coward. He was so fucked up in more ways than one."

"Yeah, he always had been. That's why I didn't want to have anything to do with ownership of The Club because I knew he probably had something to do with all three disappearances, not just two of them."

I sighed. "Richard . . ."

He smiled at me. "Apology accepted." He put his hand on mine. "I mean it."

"And I mean it, too. I'm really sorry I thought you had something to do with Deandra's and especially Tanisha's."

"Well, it did appear that I could've had something to with their disappearances and now murders. But no, I couldn't go that far. I will always feel something for Tanisha even though she felt nothing for me. I was never fully able to let go of her. But Oliver was the one who won her over that night, but I knew she really wasn't interested in him, only interested in him because he owned The Club. Besides, she said she was never moving back here. I believe she only wanted to get with him that night just to make me jealous. I'm convinced of it. But then it was clear when he wanted some from her she refused his advances. Oliver could never get pussy like the way me and my friends could. But I knew I had to be through with her for good after that night."

"I'm sorry, Richard."

"It's okay now. Everything is okay now."

"Yeah, I think it is, too.

"So, what's up with Antonio? I haven't seen him following me all around the city?"

"He's still around. He has no ownership or investment in The Club anymore since it's no more, so he's pursuing other business ventures. I'm still privately teaching Christina about the law since she still wants to go to law school."

"Lyin' little heffa," I said as I stared out the window.

"What? What did you call her that for?"

"Because she said she didn't know me when I saw her dad at the gas station and she was sitting in the car and he asked her did she know me because I said hi to her."

He laughed. "He told me about that."

"Is there anything else you want to tell me before I officially move on from these cases?"

"There is something," he informed me.

"What is it?"

"I'm the one who paid for Ashley Whitfield-Capers high school tuition, as well as college and dental school. I also paid for her and her husband to have that nice dental office."

"You?!"

"Yes, it was me, Mackenzee. You wanna see receipts?"

"If you have them," I said with a grin.

"I do," he said with a smile. He sighed. "I just felt so bad that this poor girl lost her mom, and at the time I did suspect it could've been Oliver who had everything to do with it—but I couldn't prove it. I felt I had to do something for her. I'll appreciate it if you don't tell her, though. She doesn't need to know. It's just my secret philanthropy. I'm blessed to be able to come from a wealthy family myself and have made a nice life for myself. She's done very well for herself. I'm sure her mother is looking down on her and is very proud."

"I'm sure she is," I said with a smile. I looked up at the beautiful blue sky just as Ella Fitzgerald's "Blue Skies" began playing on his radio. "Beautiful song."

"It is," he said with a smile. "It's blue skies in the beautiful new Saint Maran, as you said at the memorial site."

"It's a new Saint Maran, all right, and as long as I'm here, it's gonna stay this way."

"I'm sure it will."

We smiled at each other as I felt I was getting to know Richard all over again, just as I wanted people to get to know this city in the way it was meant to be known for all along, and I was committed to making sure that will happen from now on and forever.

ABOUT THE AUTHOR

Sheila Murdock is a combination of her birth name and her late grandmother's maiden name on her mother's side. When she's not writing, she enjoys watching movies and TV shows—old and new—on YouTube, Netflix, and Amazon Prime Video, but always loves a surprising show she can find on cable TV. She also enjoys reading all kinds of non-fiction, but has a particular interest in African-American historical and contemporary non-fiction, but will read an occasional fiction book. She enjoys listening to old-school/throwback rap, hip-hop, and R&B, and jazz music from any era.